Dreams

The Arie Chronicles

Volume 2

by Dani Hart

DREAMS
Copyright © 2014 DANI HART
Copy Edit by Paige Smith
Cover Artwork by Desi's Art Designs
Formatting by C.J. Pinard

ISBN-13: 978-0991601257
ISBN-10: 0991601254

dreams

/drēm/
plural noun

A series of thoughts, images, and sensations occurring in a person's mind during sleep.

Prologue

Staying strong when my heart ached was the single hardest thing I had ever done. I tried to pretend. I tried for Amary. She was still lost and confused in this new place and cried nightly for her mom. I would rock her to sleep, snuggling next to her until her breathing became level and settled. And then at night, just like after my mom died, I was left alone with my thoughts and memories. My dreams took me to unfamiliar places that I couldn't remember when I woke up. Sometimes I felt peaceful, and other times I felt helpless. There were nights I woke up scared and choking on my tears. Tonight would be no different.

I had finally left Amary's room. She kept waking up every time I tried to leave, so it was a longer than usual night for both of us. I was exhausted, and my source of inner strength was almost completely depleted. That's when the anger started to infiltrate. I was sitting on my bed, clutching my knees tightly to my chest and digging my nails deeply into my skin, hoping that would hold it at bay, but I was failing miserably. Was the darkness hidden within all of us finally inching its way through because I wasn't strong enough?

Maybe they were all wrong about me?

Maybe I was wrong about myself?

I dug deeper, clenching my eyes shut until the strain shot shards of pain to my temples. Tears drizzled past the tight barrier I had created and drenched my face as the whimpers escaped. I tried to suffer quietly, hiding my breakdowns from everyone, but tonight was too strong. Tonight the pull to break free of the façade was taking control.

It started with a methodical pounding of my forehead on

my knees and then escalated to a violent cry that had been building since the night Ashe died. I took a fistful of sheets in my hands and tried to rock myself to comfort.

Back and forth.

Back and forth.

Why wasn't it working? Why did it work for Amary and not me? Why was I abandoned with no one to comfort me?

Back and forth.

Back and forth.

My nails dug into the sheets, shredding them effortlessly as I continued to sway. It wasn't enough. My anger wasn't satisfied. It needed more. I stopped the rocking, feeling the heat layer my body as I searched the room frantically. I was losing control. Someone would hear.

I couldn't let go.

I had to conceal.

I couldn't. I dug my face into my mother's blanket, clutching it hard and screaming into it as loud as my lungs would allow, and then I flung it off the bed and threw it across the room. I manically made a split-second decision to run, so I launched myself through my open window, my feet bursting under the energy of the pressure it released from the earth. Shockwaves traveled over my ankles and dissipated as they reached my hips.

I ran across the yard, not even pausing at the riverbed. I continued over the sharp pebbles into the water, letting the pain feed my anger more. The water electrocuted my skin the deeper I got, but I didn't care. When I reached the center, I felt safe enough to let go. I threw my hands to the side and let out an earth-shattering scream. The moon responded with a pulsing blue light, each wave finding my center, causing convulsions and calming the rage that overwhelmed me.

The fight was diminishing, and my body was relaxing, but the ache would never truly go away, no matter how much nature tried to heal me.

My heart was irreparable.

Chapter One

The more days that passed the harder it was to decipher between reality and dreams. Everything was so vivid in both. In my dreams, no one was gone, and we all lived together in peaceful serenity. Not that reality wasn't pleasant here, but it was harsh when I thought back to all the people I had lost to get here. It would weigh heavily on my conscience for eternity. I missed girl time with Starling, the comforting touch by River, and the passion Ashe ignited within my soul.

I missed my mom.

As I stared out over the valley, it felt like it had been years since I had last seen my old reality, but in actuality, it had only been a few weeks. Time moved so slowly here that it was almost torturous. I wanted to acclimate into the community, but I wasn't ready. I had even been absent from Amaryllis on numerous occasions. She had really taken to Sage, thank goodness. Sage was my Starling here. I just hadn't found it in me to give anything back. I spent every day from sunrise to sunset here in this spot, gazing at the world. My mind was blank for the most part, which was comforting. At times, memories would slither their way through the cracks in the walls I had been working at building around them, trapping them until I was ready to deal with them again. When they managed to leak out, it hurt. The pain was immediate, hitting my chest hard and filling my body with insurmountable aches. This place was both magical and infectious, which made me wonder when it would infect me with the peacefulness everyone else seemed to carry with them like a halo over an angel.

It was sunrise, and the valley was buzzing with morning life. Dragonflies whizzed by my nose as they dove down the cliff to the river below. Behind me, birds perched on branches growing out of the stone cliff sang their lovely songs to each other. The waterfall was soothing as it descended and crashed into a foam of magnificent splendor below. I focused on nature to meditate away the truth that surrounded my new reality, my new dream, or maybe, my new nightmare.

My body tingled, warning me that someone outside of my bloodline was entering the sanctuary. When intruders entered, it was a tingle that sent my heart racing, unlike the calming effect when it was Amary or Tivon. It was a subtle difference, but effective.

"Hi," Sage said behind me. "Would you mind if I sat with you?"

"No," I mumbled. She sat next to me and stared quietly at the morning business that nature was attending to. Everyone here had their own unique beauty except for the signature amber eyes. Her strawberry blonde hair was cut in a short bob. It was perfect how it framed her high cheekbones, thin lips, and narrow eyes. She was my height, which was nice to have a friend as vertically challenged as me. Her skin was pale, and a light brushing of freckles dotted her nose and lessened as they fanned out over her cheeks. She was thin like me, too.

"Thank you for taking care of Amary. I just need some time," I said as I looked away.

"I know. Kids are more resilient to change than adults," she responded, trying to make me feel less like a jerk.

"Is that what we are? I thought being an adult was supposed to be easier," I replied sarcastically.

"No, honey. It's much harder. We carry the burden of truth for the younger ones. There's nothing easy about that."

Her words were always sincere and comforting. It

reminded me of how River made me feel. "I miss them." A tear escaped down my cheek. I wiped it away, quickly trying to conceal any physical evidence of my own private misery.

"I know you've heard this before, but it will get easier. And they aren't gone; they're just absent for now."

She put her arm around me and pulled me in so I could rest my head on her shoulder. "I want to see them again, but at the same time, I don't. If I let them go, then maybe time will heal. For all of us."

"Don't do that to yourself. If you want to see them, then do it. Did you know they can feel when you're watching?"

I looked at her questioningly. "I didn't know that."

"Your mom had visions when Tivon was watching her. They know. I think it would help all of you. I'll be by your side, if that helps."

"Okay." I stood up, and we walked behind the waterfall. The cool mist felt nice on my warm cheeks. Sage stood next to me and held my hand. I closed my eyes and let my heart guide me. It penetrated my body and traveled up my spine to my brain and set off synapses firing in every direction. Images of River's crystal blue eyes and Starling's sweet smile flashed through me. Only a light squeeze of my hand could pry me away from them. I opened my eyes and reflected in the stream of water were those eyes and the smile of a broken friend. They faded, and it was replaced by an image of Star walking up to the door of her boutique. I was saddened to see my bookstore with the blinds pulled down and a *Closed* sign in the window. I never had a chance to find someone to take over in my absence. That bookstore meant so much to my mom and me, so to see it abandoned made my new life that much more real. The image faded and manifested into my meadow. River was lying down in the butterfly circle staring at the sky. His expression was hollow.

He was waiting for me.

His eyes suddenly registered recognition. *Could he feel me watching him?* As I reached out my hand to the image, he reached his hand to the sky. A beautiful purple and blue butterfly landed on his finger. Sage leaned into me.

"That is your butterfly, Arie. It carries your essence. It feels the draw to River."

"That's amazing, Sage." A teary smile invaded my face, knowing that River could feel I was with him and that he wasn't alone. He mouthed the words *I love you*. The butterfly flew off his hand, and the image disappeared. "Thank you, Sage." I squeezed her hand.

"Soon you will be ready to visit them."

"Sometimes I wonder if that's fair to them. You know, popping in and out of their lives, never giving them a chance to move on." I sighed sullenly.

"It's not about moving on. It's about acceptance. They have accepted that they only get you in small doses now. Just like you, they will take what they can get, and it will be enough."

I turned to her and gave her a hug. "I don't know what I would do if I didn't have you. Thank you for not forgetting about me." She hugged me back tightly. I stiffened as a vision paralyzed me.

Sage was locked in an intimate embrace with Pyrrhus. I could feel the heat between them radiating off their skin.

I pulled away from her quickly.

"What's wrong? Are you okay?" she asked.

I didn't know what to think, but I did know the trust I had been putting into Sage had just been shattered. *Why wouldn't she have told me about her and Pyrrhus?* She was keeping secrets, and now so would I. "Nothing. I just thought I heard something. Sorry, we should get back to the village."

"I'm sure Amary's looking for me...us," Sage corrected herself.

That stung a little. Amary had built an affectionate attachment to Sage in the weeks following River's departure and my abandonment of, well, everything, but that needed to change. The vision could have been innocent enough, but I wasn't willing to take the risk, not if it put Amaryllis in danger. "Let's go." We walked out of my private sanctuary that wasn't so private anymore. I told Sage about it soon after River left, but now I was regretting that decision.

As we walked through the forest, I felt small surges of energy pulse through me with the slightest touch of a flower or tree branch. The funny thing about this place was it responded to my emotions. When my walls were up and I felt numb and distant, the less it fed me, and the less it protected me. When I was vulnerable, it fed me like a four-year-old with a chocolate addiction. I had made the mistake of closing off my emotions when I first came here, which put me in danger and almost got River killed. I promised myself I wouldn't make that mistake again, so I never completely shut off my emotions, but I kept them restrained. I didn't want to feel the pain from the responsibility of so many lost lives, including Amary's mom, Misty, and Ashe. It was just easier to pave cement around my heart, only leaving a small hole for it to breathe.

Sage led the way back to the village. Amary was running around with some of the village kids, but when she spotted us, she broke free and ran to us and latched onto my legs tightly.

"Arie, are you going to play today?" She looked up to me expectantly.

"I would love to, buggie."

Sage patted her head. "I need to be going. See you guys later, okay?"

I contrived a small smile. "Sure." I watched as she headed to our house. She worked for Tivon as a personal assistant, I guess. I never really asked specifics, but she ran around for him a lot, which kind of concerned me now after that vision. I hated thinking the worst, but after everything that had happened, it was hard not to focus on the negative. I debated whether to tell Tivon since he worked so closely with her. I probably should, but I also didn't want to stir up trouble if it

7

was nothing. I was conflicted.

"Will you come to the river with me and watch the butterflies?"

"I would love to." She grabbed my hand and led me to our new home. It was Tivon's, but he had welcomed us with open arms and even had our rooms from our other life replicated, so we could have a piece of it with us here. It was a thoughtful gesture.

The familiar buzz tickled my skin as we entered the front door. It was our own organic alarm that protected us both inside this house and at the waterfall. It never failed to make Amary giggle. It was pure sweetness that filled the air with innocence. I inhaled it deeply, wishing it were that easy to recapture my own innocence from the past.

As we passed through the house to the back, I spotted Tivon and Sage in the office off to the right. Tivon was sitting at his desk, and Sage was standing next to him. He looked up and smiled as we passed by. Amary tugged my arm, and we were in the backyard in no time. As soon as our bare feet hit the grass, she was off running to the river. I walked slowly, letting my strands of hair lightly brush my neck as the breeze surrounded me. I closed my eyes and remembered the way the breeze made me feel in my other life, electric and alive. It had a similar effect here, as well, but knowing what the feeling was now took away some of the magic I felt when it was a mystery. Now I knew it was nature feeding me life. *Essence*. It was building me up for something, but what, no one knew. I was the first of my kind, and Amary would be the second once she ascended. My dad, Tivon, had created us by stealing my essence when I died before nature could consume it, and he split it between my mom and Amary's mom, hoping it would give me a second chance at life somewhere else and restore the balance of nature disrupted by my murder. It did, but he never imagined it would create an evolved nature spirit. The people here were both intrigued and scared by me at the same time. Even if they didn't show their trepidation, I could feel it when they were near. It ensured that I would always feel like an outsider, no matter how close I got to any of them. Those moments were when I missed my past life the most. While things were emotionally dark for me there, I knew how unconditionally loved I was by River and Star. I never knew how much that confidence would be missed. I thought I had found that with Sage, but today had changed that security.

"Arie, come on!" yelled Amary excitedly.

That kid always made me smile. I joined her and climbed upon the rock that I had last shared with River the day he went back to the other reality. I softly touched the spot where he sat. My hand absorbed the residual essence that River left behind. I could feel it travel through my fingertips, dance around my wrist, and tease its way up my arm as it warmed its path straight to my heart. It caught my breath in my chest. This place never ceased to amaze my imagination. It felt as if River were still sitting next to me on this rock, looking out into the sparkling water of the river as the sun's rays bounced off the soft ripples. Amary climbed up and sat on the other side of me and rested her head on my arm.

"Do you miss him?" she whispered.

"Very much."

"I can feel him. Can you?"

"I can." I leaned my head over onto hers and wrapped her up in my embrace.

"I miss my mom."

Those words would always knot up my stomach. Tivon had told her that her mom was at her other home, so the secret of her death would be our burden to carry. She was too young to have her innocence taken away. It had already been bruised by the kidnapping, so we wanted to protect her youth for as long as we could.

"Will I ever get to see her again?"

"I don't know, buggie. I don't know." I squeezed her tighter.

"Are you back? I mean, will you be around more now? I

like Sage, but I love you."

Aw, man, this kid was going to make me cry. "I love you, too." I kissed her head and closed my eyes to take a moment to regroup.

"Arie, look. It's back."

I opened my eyes and saw the orange and red butterfly fluttering back and forth in front of us. I reached out my hand as an invitation for it to land, which it obeyed.

"He's so pretty."

"What makes you think it's a boy?" I giggled.

"I don't know. I just think it is."

"*He* is pretty. I wonder why he keeps coming back." I moved my hand around to inspect him closer.

"He must like you. We should keep him," she said elatedly.

"Oh, buggie. Creatures shouldn't be trapped. They need to be able to live freely. If he likes me so much, he won't go very far." I remembered when my mom told me that exact thing. The last time the butterfly visited us was the day River left when Amary and I were at the waterfall. He had circled us so quickly that his colors blurred into an image of flames engulfing us. The magnificence was indescribable.

He suddenly flew off and left us. Amary slid down the rock and laughed as she chased it around the yard. I loved watching her play with her beautiful, long, soft-brown curls trailing behind her as she hopped around the grass. I envied her, and that envy would make me protect her with my life. I wouldn't let her meet the same fate as her mom or Ashe. Ever!

Chapter Two

I had been avoiding the circle of my ascension. The path to it was just as tainted with awful memories as the circle itself. I needed closure, though. I needed to face my demons. It was time to move on and accept my new reality. As I walked past the last house in the village, I paused at the path that led to the death of so many. The dirt was dry, and the delicate bushes bordering it gracefully hung over displaying their purple blooms. I looked ahead into the forest and was still amazed at how tall and enchanting the trees and glossy foliage were. A very talented artist created this place. I imagined it was my mom and smiled to myself.

My first step onto the dirt sent tingles through my toes. I could feel nature's excitement at my return. *I wished I could say the same thing.* I was nervous, but I knew I needed to do this. I took another step and waited until the tingles settled in my bones before I started my slow pace on the short walk. As I walked through the forest, the vines of the bushes almost seemed to intertwine themselves around my fingers when I grazed by them, each touch feeding me a little of its essence. My skin felt like a charged lightning bolt ready to strike at something, at anything.

I stopped abruptly at the unnaturally manmade clearing from the battle that horrible night. The trees that were sacrificed lay sadly on the ground. Some on top of each other. Their leaves were already browning and littering the ground in crumbles as if the trees had wept them off. It was a despondent sight in such a picturesque place.

I sat down on one of the fallen trunks and stared at the spot where Ashe had saved my life. Those mysteriously beautiful butterfly flowers that graced my mother's gravestone at home had sprouted up in that one sacred and defiled piece of earth. Only a few would know why it was blessed with such magnificence. A tear dropped for the hope of a lost future. I would never know the truth about Ashe. I would only have the residual aftertaste of his life that still coursed through my body, but was fading quickly now that he was gone.

"I see you're trying to move on," Tivon spoke behind me.

I put my head down and watched the grass as the wind forced it to prickle my feet.

"That's a good sign," he added.

"I'm trying, but it's not easy," I mumbled out with broken words.

"Destiny never is." He put his hand upon my shoulder awkwardly.

Tivon was still learning how to be a father, so his gestures were hesitant and never quite smooth or assertive. I loved him for the effort, though. "Why do I feel like Ashe is still alive?"

"Essence transforms and reunites with the universe in another form. No one is ever truly gone."

"I don't feel my mom anymore." That was hard for me to admit aloud.

"She wasn't from here, so that makes sense. But her essence will always be with you." He pointed to the ring on my finger.

I caressed the opal as I asked, "How long has Sage been working for you?"

"Ever since you left. Why, my child?"

"I had a vision of her and Pyrrhus."

"Oh, and so you think something isn't right with her?"

"Yes...I don't know. It was just weird. I could tell she loved him."

"She did. They had a relationship after you were killed. She didn't know he was the one who killed you. No one did. You should really talk to her about this."

"Yeah, I probably should." I stared back at Ashe's spot. "Why do those flowers tend to sprout up at gravesites?"

"Well, you know they are butterfly flowers, right?" I nodded. "They are the sacred way someone's essence is reborn into a butterfly, so they adorn the places of the lost. Wherever you see a patch of them, you know where a soul was lost and reborn."

I thought back to the first time I experienced the energy of the forest and how happy the flowers had made me when the blooms came alive and flew away as beautiful butterflies. Their significance changed the way I viewed that beauty. They were there because someone had died there. Goose bumps rose on my arms. "It's sad that something so beautiful came out of something so tragic."

"But it's a beautiful way to remember their life. Don't you think?"

He was always so positive. I wondered how he got to be so strong.

"I wouldn't call it 'strong,' Arie. Hardened would be a better word for it."

I looked at him a little shocked. "I thought you could only read my thoughts at home and at the waterfall?"

"I guess I was wrong. Sorry," he muttered guiltily.

"It's okay. Still going to take some getting used to, though."

"I'll let you finish your journey on your own."

He stood up and disappeared down the path back toward the village. I sighed sadly. Alone again. It was a feeling I was going to have to get used to if I were going to get stronger. I didn't know if I wanted to be hardened. Not yet, at least. A glimmering light in the middle of the butterfly patch caught my attention. I jumped off the tree trunk and walked over to it. When I pushed the flowers out of the way, the butterfly blooms came alive and scattered around me. Stuck in the ground was the dagger of life and death. I was more than shocked to see it since I thought Pyrrhus had taken it that night. *What was it doing here?* It was dangerously beautiful with a scroll design embossed on the antique silver handle. I knew it was silly, but I was afraid to touch it. As soon as I reached my hand to it, my ring began to glow brightly. Something it hadn't done since my ascension. Was it warning me to stay away? In the past, it had only reacted to things related closely to me. This dagger was not mine, and it had never glowed for Ashe, so why was it glowing now? To test my theory, I pulled away my hand, and the light ceased. I reached for the dagger again, and it lit up once again. This time I touched it. My ring pulsed slowly as I followed the design down to the blade. It was smooth and felt warm on my fingertips. As I reached the sharp blade at the base, I wrapped my hand around it and pulled it out of the ground. It slid out easily and without any residual dirt. In fact, the metal blade shined brightly in the sun, showing no signs of use. *How was that possible?* I turned it over carefully in my hand, inspecting it for even just the smallest scratch or divot. There was nothing, as if it had just been created. Holding the cause of my lost love in the palm of my hand elicited in me feelings of hate, resentment, and power. What exactly did it mean to be the dagger of life and death? I understood the death part, but how could it represent life if its purpose in life was to kill?

I had the sudden urge to cut myself. What would happen if the blade penetrated my skin? After all, I was invincible here, right? I was curious. I turned my wrist over and touched the point lightly to it. The tip burned my skin like a searing iron ready for branding. I pulled away the blade, and the little burn mark disappeared immediately. This gave me the courage to try again. I took the blade and swiped it hard against my wrist. It sank easily into my skin as it burned its way down to the bone. Blood spilled out as I dropped the dagger. I felt nothing.

How odd to see the damage I inflicted, but to feel no pain. The rushing river of blood slowed down to a trickle. I watched in amazement as the skin from the inside out sealed up like a needle and thread stitching together a piece of fabric. But this time, a raised scar marked the area. I ran my finger over it just to confirm what happened was real.

My ring continued to glow in the proximity of the dagger. I didn't know what to do with it. It had been proven to be lethal, and it didn't belong in this reality where only peace was supposed to exist. I was afraid to leave it for someone else to find. I needed to find something to wrap around the blade to keep it from cutting me. I foraged around the area and settled on a piece of bark that was split halfway down that the dagger could easily fit into like a holster. I picked it up and slid it into the bark and shoved it into the back of my jeans. The bark was scratchy against my skin, but better that than the blade.

I continued my journey to the circle of my ascension. I could feel the forest watching me as I passed by. Creatures were scurrying around everywhere, crunching dead leaves in the process, the sound echoing in my ears. My senses were at their maximum decibels in the forest away from everyone, and it came alive as much as I did when we were alone together. We fed off each other. I let the tingles enter me freely as I reached my destination. The glossy green foliage that served as the door to the circle was chopped apart. My heart sank as I ran through it. The circle had been defiled. The grass had turned brown, and the flowers on the perimeter were wilted. I didn't remember this happening during my ascension, but why would someone do this? This is where I spent my last moments with my mom. It was sacred, and to see it like this was gut-wrenching. I felt like my mom's gravesite had been robbed.

My back was heating up where the blade rested, so I pulled it out. It was burning its way through the bark. The blade was glowing, as was my ring. *What the hell was going on?* I had an idea. I walked to the center of the circle and held the dagger high above my head as I prepared to sacrifice the ground. I took a deep, promising breath, and with all my strength, I plunged the blade into the ground. A burst of energy propelled me across the field. The force with which I hit the ground knocked the wind out of me, and I struggled for a moment to catch my breath. Suddenly, the grass beneath my fingers transformed from stale brown and dead to bright green and alive. I interlaced my fingers through the blades. *They were real.* I looked up and watched as life fanned out from the dagger, and all the grass in the circle returned to its former splendor. The wilted flowers were now blooming with vitality, and the large foliage that shielded the sanctuary mended back together as if never shredded. A swarm of butterflies circled around in the sky above me. I stood up and walked over to the dagger. The glow faded out as the last drop of life filled the area. What I witnessed was truly amazing. The dagger of life and death. It could take a life, but also restore life. A feeling of shock flowed through me. *What if it could bring back Ashe?* That's crazy talk, right? As if on cue, the butterflies spiraled down and circled the dagger and me. I could feel their energy penetrate my skin and reach my center. As the butterflies fluttered in sync, a light surrounded me, and a vision filled my head.

I was back at the battle that killed so many, including Ashe. I watched the scene replay. I was charging at Pyrrhus. I could feel the anger that enraged my heart. I wanted to kill him, and then I saw the gleaming of the blade, but it was too late to stop. Ashe jumped in front of me, taking the blade and saving my life. I felt my heart break all over again as the light faded from his eyes. He fell into my arms as Pyrrhus pulled the dagger out of his brother's back. That's when I noticed in his moment of rage he plunged the dagger into the ground rather than taking it with him.

The light around me burned out, and the vision ended. The butterflies scattered haphazardly around the circle and then flew out. I fell to the ground, feeling physically exhausted for the first time since I had been here. I wasn't sure what the purpose of the vision was except to confirm my suspicion about Pyrrhus leaving the dagger behind. There had to be more to it, though, but I just didn't know what. What I did know now was that the dagger belonged where Ashe had taken his last breath. I pulled it out of the ground and stood up. I spun around, slowly taking in the renewed beauty of the circle and remembering how it felt to be in my mom's arms again even for just a moment. This was truly my time to let her go. I raised my eyes to the sky and felt a steady flow of tears stream down my cheeks. "Goodbye, Mom." The sun's rays comforted me now that there was no one else left to hold me. I let the moments pass quietly and then retrieved the bark holster from the ground and shoved the blade inside and put it back into my jeans. I walked to the opening serving as both the entrance and exit. Before stepping over the threshold back into the forest, I stole a quick glance back. I could swear I saw a faint outline of my mom in the center, but it faded away too quickly to be certain.

Finished with the objective of my visit out here, I headed back to Ashe's resting spot. I kneeled down in front of the blooms of flowers, hoping for a small reminder of how it felt when he touched me or the familiar scent that flooded my senses when he was near. I had so many unanswered questions, and my heart didn't get the closure it needed.

I plucked a bloom and inhaled deeply. The fragrance was Ashe, masculine and sweet. I couldn't hold back the tears. Even though he lied to me, my heart still missed him. The moment consumed me, and rather than fight it, I let my heart bleed one last time. As the last tear hit the ground, I pulled the dagger out of my jeans and forced it deep into the center of the patch. It penetrated easily as the earth opened up to swallow it, leaving only the tip of the handle visible. It would be safe here. It belonged here.

Chapter Three

With the encouragement of Tivon, I thought it would be best to talk to Sage about my vision before I let my mind turn it into something bigger than it probably was. As I reached the edge of the village, Amary split from the group of girls with whom she was making friendship bracelets and ran to me. She always greeted me with a huge smile and admiration. I hoped I could live up to her expectations. She slammed into me with a giant hug.

"Hey, buggie, are you having a good time?"

"Yep, I made you something."

She handed me a purple and pink friendship bracelet made out of soft plastic strips. I remembered making these with my mom because I didn't really have any girlfriends growing up. It was always just River and me. "Thanks, buggie. I love it." I bent down and gave her a kiss on the head.

"Can you put it on?"

"Of course," I said as I slipped it around my wrist. "I'll never take it off." Her smile could have lit up a street. She was so happy here, but I knew the time would come when she would ask about seeing her mom, and the façade we had created would crumble.

"I made one for my mom, too."

"That's great, buggie. She'll love it as much as I love mine."

"Can you save it for me?" she asked as she handed a

rainbow one to me.

"Absolutely. Let's keep it with the other things that you have for her."

She let out a little giggle and ran back to her friends. Her beautiful, long curls always bounced so freely when she ran.

I headed back to the house to find Sage. I peeked into the office, but neither Tivon nor she was in there. The house was pretty quiet, so I retreated to my room. I lay down on my mom's blanket and stared at the ceiling. It was amazing how a material object like this blanket could bring me so much comfort. I didn't know what to do here. At home, I had the bookstore to run and the house and meadow to maintain. Here, I had nothing. I turned over on my stomach toward the window and watched the sun start its daily descent. No sunset anywhere in the world in the other reality could even compare to the ones here. They were magnificent. Magical was a better word. They displayed a multitude of colors in every hue, and their rays sparkled with life as they stretched out to the earth. Touching them felt like a bolt of electricity. Sunrise and sunset held the most power, so much so that I had to limit my exposure for fear of sensory overload. I knew that wouldn't happen, but it made me feel light-headed and somewhat lucid, like I drank a bottle of cough syrup. Once was enough. There was a light knock on the door, so I called out, "Come in."

"Hi," Sage said as she popped her head inside. "Your dad...I mean, Tivon, said I should come talk to you. Is everything all right?"

I sat up. *This was going to be an awkward conversation.* "Oh, um, yeah. Come inside and sit down." She sat in the chair in the corner. River was the last person to sit there. It made me kind of melancholy, because with every second that passed while Sage sat in it, her scent would replace his.

"Is it okay that I'm sitting here?" she asked, looking concerned.

Apparently, I didn't have much of a poker face. "No, it's

fine. It's just that River was the last one to sit there, so I was just remembering. That's all."

"Are you sure because I can sit somewhere else?"

She started to stand up. "No, really, it's fine. That would be ridiculous. It's meant for sitting, and it's not like no one is ever going to sit in it again."

She cinched herself back into it. "So, what's up, Arie?"

She looked uncomfortable.

"Well, you know I see visions sometimes." She nodded her head. "It seems random, but I know there's a purpose for the timing now." I was starting to get nervous. I fidgeted with the blanket to avoid eye contact. "At the waterfall, when I hugged you, I had a vision." I looked up to gauge her reaction. She remained emotionless.

"Okay?" she muttered quietly.

"I'm sorry. This really isn't any of my business, but—"

"It's all right, Arie, really. We're friends. Just tell me," she cut me off, encouraging me to continue.

I sighed and blurted out, "It was of you and Pyrrhus." My cheeks warmed as a blush formed on them. Her cheeks reddened to match mine.

"Oh." She looked down to her lap, appearing ashamed.

"I'm sorry. I shouldn't be in your head like that, but I don't know how to control what I see and when I see it." I felt horrible, but the intent of this conversation was so I could find out why she kept it a secret from me.

"No, it's fine. I know you can't. It's just not my favorite thing to talk about, but you have a right to know."

"It was just upsetting to see you with *him*. He killed me."

She shot up her now panic-filled eyes. "You have to believe me that I didn't know that when I was with him. I swear, Arie. I had no idea."

She was whimpering now, and tears were flowing freely down her red cheeks. I slid off the bed and squeezed in the chair with her to try to ease her pain. She snuggled into me. "I believe you, Sage," I whispered as I hugged her tightly.

After she calmed down a bit, I broke the silence. "Do you want to talk about it?"

"No, yes. Oh gawd, I don't know."

Her confliction confirmed how deeply she fell for Pyrrhus. "I promise I won't judge." I got up and sat on the bed across from her to give her space.

"Before you died and before he professed his love to you, I thought he loved me."

That broke my heart for her. I stayed silent to give her time to confess.

"I was so stupid. I had no idea. I was totally blindsided. I saw you guys when he told you. I was proud of you for rejecting him, but I was so upset that I ran off. Had I stayed just a minute longer, I might have been able to prevent your murder or at least been a witness."

I was in shock. She was there the day he killed me. Was she telling the truth about how much she saw? Nothing inside me made me feel like she was lying, and my gut had never steered me wrong in the past. "But the vision was after my death?" I questioned her.

"Yes," she said as she looked back down in shame. "After you died, I was vulnerable and lonely. You were my best friend. Pyrrhus took advantage of my vulnerability. He came to me a few days later and begged for forgiveness after I told him I knew he was in love with you. I was weak, so I took him back. I really believed him when he told me you were just a silly infatuation. I was so stupid," she said as she buried her face in her hands and started to cry again.

I didn't know what to say that could help her. All I could do was listen and be there for her. I could tell the wound was still raw.

"Then one day he just disappeared until you came back."

The devastation shook her body. She held on to hope that he still loved her and would return. Instead, she learned the truth about him, and I could tell it broke something in her. "I'm so sorry, Sage. I didn't mean to make you relive that. I just didn't know what to think."

"I know, Arie. We're all on edge now. Tivon thinks this is only the beginning of a nightmare."

"Why does he think that?" I asked, getting a little alarmed.

"The shadow stalkers that reside here in our reality are made from the darkness in their soul, but they are usually tracked. There were far more the night of your ascension than there should have been. He thinks they have found a way to jump realities permanently."

The thought sent a shudder throughout my body. "What do you mean 'permanently'?"

"Well, as you know, we can only be in different realities other than our origination for a short period of time. We can only do it so many times in our lifetime, and not everyone can jump realities. When I say 'permanently,' I mean they can come and go freely with no limitations."

"Is that possible? I don't know much about all of this, but how would they be able to do that?"

"No one knows. That's what they've been working on since that night."

"Who are *they* exactly?" Tivon had briefly mentioned some sort of council, but he never elaborated on it.

"There's a group of elders who watches over things. They only came together after your murder. Before then, there wasn't much need for them. That was when we thought we were invincible to the reality that holds the darkness."

I looked at her, perplexed.

"I know this is a lot for you. You're still getting reacquainted with the normal here."

"No, it's okay. I'm glad I'm in the loop. Better than being in the dark. No pun intended."

She giggled. It was nice to see her smile after her meltdown.

"What have they found out?" I started biting the skin around my nails, a nervous habit I picked up right after my eighteenth birthday.

"That's the thing. They haven't. They have no idea what's going on or how they're doing it. To be honest, it's all speculation right now. They can't confirm any of their theories. They just know things aren't right."

"So, my ascension didn't really restore balance? It was all for nothing?" The thought ripped me to my core.

All the deaths were for nothing.

Leaving River was for nothing.

I was trying my hardest to contain the nausea in the pit of my stomach.

"Arie, I wouldn't say that. You're here for a reason. The universe always has a reason. You're the most powerful nature spirit we have ever seen. That can't be a coincidence. Please, don't think it was for nothing."

She went down on her knees in front of me and clasped my hands that were now shaking.

"I need to be a part of all of this, Sage. I need to know what's going on. I can't be kept in the dark like the ascension. I can't do that again. It made me crazy." She stood up, holding on to one of my hands tightly.

"Then let's go talk to Tivon."

I didn't know why I was so nervous walking to Tivon's office. Maybe because I was afraid he would say no. I didn't really know him yet, so I wasn't sure what to expect. As we rounded the corner, I could see Tivon pacing, looking visibly upset. I whispered to Sage, "Maybe we should come back later."

"No need to whisper, my child." He stopped moving and looked at us thoughtfully. "Is there something you wanted to discuss?"

"This is for you to talk over." Sage squeezed my hand and walked outside to join the families congregating around the pictorial river.

I inched forward slowly. "If you're busy, it can wait."

"I will never be too busy for you. We have already lost so much time together. Come in and tell me what's on your mind," he said as he waved me into the room.

"You could just read it."

He let out his signature chuckle that filled my heart with warmth. "Yes, I could, but you have asked me not to. Remember?" He took a seat behind his desk.

His office was simple and pleasant like the rest of the house. Only the necessities were present. There were a desk, his office chair, and a couple of plush couch chairs for visitors. In the corner was a desk for Sage. The office was located on the corner of the house, so two walls were blanketed with windows boasting the beauty of the outdoors. Sage's desk was situated in the coveted corner adorning the windows. What I found strange was that there weren't the usual items on the desk associated with a work environment. No papers, pencil holder, stapler, or file organizer. There wasn't even a phone.

"Is there something wrong?" he asked.

"Oh, no. I just expected...I don't know."

"A messy office?" he replied smartly.

"Well, something at least. There's nothing here." I was baffled.

"Have a seat. There's a lot you don't remember about our ways."

I obeyed and sat in one of the richly colored brown chairs. My body melted into it. It was the most comfortable chair I had ever sat in. The fabric seemed to mold to my skin and lull me to sleep. My eyes were feeling heavy, and my muscles relaxed. "Why am I so tired all of a sudden?" I could hear Tivon's infectious chuckle in the distance. I started to giggle with him. "I don't know why I'm laughing, but I can't stop." It was like the time my mom took me to the dentist, and they gave me the laughing gas anesthetic to pull a tooth.

My giggles turned into a foggy vision.

I was running through the dark forest in the purple shimmering dress from my ascension. My ring was lighting the path in front of me, blinking quickly to the beats of my heart. My insides were searing with anticipation as I raced forward. I halted and closed my eyes to listen to the sounds around me. The crickets were chirping, the frogs were croaking, and the bats were screeching. I concentrated on the burn inside my core, trying to find the source to relieve its fire. The forest went silent as I took a few more steps to my destination. My heart was finally home. I was at Ashe's resting place.

"I'm sorry, Arie. It's been so long since I've had visitors that I almost forgot about the magic within the chairs. They are meant to calm the spirit to allow for pleasantries."

Within a second, my head cleared, the vision disappeared, and I refocused on Tivon. I was no longer sleepy, and, to be honest, I felt a little silly for letting myself lose control. "Okay, that was weird. That was a lot more than just soothing."

"Really? How so?" he asked.

I wasn't sure if I wanted to tell him. I knew Ashe earned his respect in his final moments, but I was still reluctant to share that part of me with anyone. "Tivon, I'm curious about something."

"Yes?"

"I know you can hear my thoughts, but can you see my visions, too?"

"That's a good question. As of now, I've not seen them. Why? Did you just have one?"

I prepared myself for the lie with a silent breath. "Maybe, but it was hazy, so I'm not sure what it was. I thought if you saw it too, you could tell me what it was." I looked down to my lap in regret. How could I lie to him? He had been nothing short of amazing to me.

"What's on your mind, Daughter?"

"I really want to be a part of what's going on with you

and the elders. After all, it has something to do with me and whatever I have become. I just can't face this blindly, like the ascension." I was practically begging now. I didn't realize how much I wanted something to do until now. I needed something to keep my mind busy. Time heals, but I was hoping it would help me forget, too. This would help me move forward.

"Of course, Arie. We were actually just discussing your involvement when you walked in."

I looked around, slightly confused. "What do you mean?"

He chuckled. "Yes, about that. Elders are able to communicate telepathically. It's what makes us unique."

"Oh, that would explain the absence of a phone. How does one become an elder if you don't age here?"

"We do age. The universe ages us physically as it sees fit, which is why you see a variety of generations here, much like the other reality. Elders are decided by abilities, bloodline, and the years of existence their essence has."

"How do you decide all of this?" I was intrigued.

"We don't. The universe decides. We are nature spirits and solely guided by nature. To go against it is unnatural and what creates darkness within us. We accept and are honored by our purpose."

"What is that exactly?"

"To protect nature, the universe, and the essence that it's made of."

It was fascinating to hear I was a part of something larger than just my simple life in my other world. It made me a little uneasy, though, thinking about the responsibility that came with it. Would I live up to the universe's expectations for me?

"I have faith that you will," he said with a smile. "I think that's enough for now. We can talk more later."

I stood up, feeling like that was what I was supposed to do. Was that my instinct or the universe telling me? All right, now I was overthinking everything.

"We'll talk more later about your involvement."

"Okay. Thank you," I said as I shuffled out of the office. I sneaked a peek back and caught Tivon pacing again. I wondered what was happening. He seemed nervous. I just had to trust he would tell me when the time was right. Out of nowhere, Amary tackle hugged me, knocking us both to the ground and causing us to burst into laughter.

"Well, hello there, little buggie," I said as I tickled her. She giggled uncontrollably.

"Stop," she said between breaths.

My tickles turned into little spider fingers that caused her to laugh even harder. When I felt she had enough, I placed her onto my lap. "What do you want to do today?"

"Can you take me to the waterfall and show me my mom?" she asked pleadingly.

Oh gawd! What do I do? What could I possibly say to that? "Sure, but I'm uncertain if it'll work."

"I know, but can you please try?"

Her brown eyes penetrated my heart. "Of course, sweetie." I hugged her tightly and kissed her head, hoping this didn't bite me in the ass. "Let's go."

Chapter Four

As we passed Tivon's office, he stopped us.

"Where are you girls off to?"

"Amary would like to see her mom," I said, silently pleading *please understand my subliminal tones or just read the panic pounding in my head.*

"Oh, I see."

He returned a knowing glance, thank goodness.

"Well, just remember, the waterfall will show you what's in your heart." He winked at me.

What the hell did that mean? All my heart was filled with was the pain of watching Misty die and Amary being left motherless, like me.

"Come on, Arie," Amary said while tugging my hand.

Certifiably petrified, I looked at Tivon.

"It'll be okay. Trust in yourself and what's meant to be."

Really?! More decrypting crap! So not helpful right now. All right, it takes about ten minutes to get to the waterfall. I have to think. I needed a plan. I needed to be prepared for the worst.

"Arie, you're going too slow," Amary complained animatedly.

"All right, all right, buggie. I'll try to keep up."

The familiar buzz of the organic protection shield zapped our skin as we crossed the threshold of the front door. Amary was making it impossible to think because she was squeaking about how excited she was to see her mom. My thoughts were spinning between panic and hysteria.

"Hey, guys, what are you up to?" asked Sage.

"Arie is taking me to see my mom."

Shocked, Sage looked at me. "Oh, well, that's great." She scrunched her face, questioning me.

All I could do was shrug my shoulders and follow the bouncing Energizer Bunny. "Bye," I said to Sage as I chased after Amary.

We were at the waterfall within minutes, and I hadn't put together one coherent thought. "Amary, be careful on the rocks. They're slippery!" I yelled after her. A memory of my mom telling me the same thing whizzed through my head.

I was five and beyond excited to skip rocks at Deer River. I sprinted in front of my mom and over the large rocks that made a bridge from one side of the river to the other. It was shallow enough that while standing on the rocks the water only came to my ankles. My mom yelled behind me, "Arie, be careful. Those rocks are slippery!" As I turned to tell her I was fine, I slipped and fell into the river. My mom trudged quickly to my side and picked me up. I had a little scratch on my knee, and my wrist hurt from catching myself, but other than that, I was unharmed. My mom smothered me with kisses, causing me to laugh and forget about the fall.

I was just like Amary at this age. It had me smiling until I remembered why I was here. I caught up to Amary in front of the cascading water. It always boasted different colors of the rainbow when the sun hit it at a certain time of the day. We were fortunate to be here to see it.

"It looks like a rainbow of Skittles," she said, amazed.

I couldn't help but laugh. I was so anxious that delirium was setting in. She laughed with me. "You're absolutely right. It does look like a rainbow of Skittles."

"Why don't we have to eat here? I really miss Skittles."

The innocence in her words was always refreshing. She didn't have a care in the world. She just wanted some damn

Skittles. And her mom. I needed to focus. Tivon said to trust. I took a deep breath to clear my head. "Okay, buggie, are you ready?"

"Uh-huh. What do I do?"

"Just look through the waterfall and think about your mom."

"That's it?"

"Yep, it sounds easy, but it took me—," I stopped short, completely shocked when I saw an image appear of her mom picking flowers in a garden.

"It worked. That wasn't hard."

I was still stunned. "No, I guess not."

"She looks so pretty. She loves working in the garden," she told me.

"I'm beginning to think it's a mom thing. My mom loved it, too." I put my hands on her shoulders for comfort. I think more to comfort me than her.

"Will I ever get to visit her?" she asked as she choked back tears.

"I don't know, buggie. I don't know." The image faded, and Amary's tears came quicker. I turned her around and bent down to her level, lifting her chin so she would really listen to what I had to say. "I know this is hard for you to understand right now. You're so young, and all of this really isn't fair, but you have a destiny that's bigger than this moment. You and I were meant to do something amazing together, and I promise I will never leave your side, okay?"

All she could do was nod and fall into my arms as her tears slowed down. I rubbed her back and stared off into the waterfall. An image of my own mom appeared. Her chestnut hair was flowing softly around her face as she smiled at me and blew me a kiss. My heart skipped a few beats. I smiled back, not really knowing if this was real or if she could see me too, but I wanted to believe, so I kept smiling. After all, essence never dies. Who knew how it could manifest?

My skin started to tingle, alerting me that someone

outside of my bloodline had entered.

"Why is my skin prickly?" Amary asked.

"Shhhhh." I pushed Amary behind me in protection and scanned the area. There was only one entrance to the waterfall and nowhere to hide. It was an enclosed rock cave covered with patches of green moss and flowers. It was a confined space, so I could see if someone came in.

"What is it?" Amary whispered.

"I'm not sure." I was terrified to move, but I also had that feeling in the pit of my stomach that we needed to run, but I didn't want to scare Amary. "It was probably nothing. We're done here, so let's get back to the village." I grabbed her hand securely, so she wouldn't run away from me and walked carefully but swiftly over the rocks, surveying the cave with every step. As we reached the exit, I let out a sigh of relief. I pulled us out and dragged Amary behind me quickly. I still had that weird feeling we were being watched, but I couldn't see anything to verify my paranoia. I just wanted to get Amary home safely.

As we turned the corner that revealed the village ahead, I could see that something wasn't right. People were rushing around, wildly scooping up their kids and running into their houses. It was a scene straight out of an M. Night Shyamalan movie. *What was happening?* I clutched Amary closer to me and started to run.

"What's wrong, Arie?" She sounded panicked.

"I don't know, but we need to get home." We both ran as fast as our legs would permit and made it safely to the end of the village where our house was located. Tivon came running toward us with another young man by his side.

"Are you girls okay?" he asked in a commanding voice.

"Yeah, we're fine. What's going on?"

"Sage is missing," he said.

"What do you mean 'Sage is missing'?" I was both confused and scared.

"I can't feel her. She's gone," he said admittedly.

"Oh, no. Does that mean she's—" He cut me off before I could say it. *Dead.*

"No, it just means she's been taken somewhere that shields me from being able to feel her essence. Amary, I need you to go with Heath back to the house."

Did he just say 'Heath'? As in Heath bar? So not the time to make fun of names.

I could tell Amary was reluctant as she crouched down a level and hid behind me. "I would prefer her staying with me. No offense, *Heath*, but this is the first time I've met you."

He stepped forward. "I assure you that she is safe with me," he said with arrogant confidence.

His voice was as beautiful as he was. He was a perfect blend of River and Ashe. He had dark hair, but it was longer than Ashe's and shorter than River's. He was in- between their heights, and his build was probably in-between too, not too muscular, but toned and defined. His eyes were the color of an amethyst. The only time I had seen purple eyes was the fox that visited me a couple of times in the other reality. Since everyone's eyes here were amber, it had the gears in my head working. They made me think of gems. I caressed my mom's ring nervously. I needed to look up the amethyst stone. I couldn't remember its strengths and weaknesses. I broke my stare and switched my attention to Tivon. "I promised her I would stay with her if there was ever trouble."

"I can see I'm not going to win this one. Let's all go quickly then. I need to talk with you privately."

We all shuffled into the house. As we rushed inside, the comforting tingling as we passed the entrance never felt so safe. "I'm just going to take her to her room," I announced.

"Please, be quick," Tivon said.

I ushered Amary down the hallway into her room and closed the door.

"Arie, what's happening? Who would take Sage?"

"I don't know, but I'm going to find out, and I will bring her back safely," I spoke assuredly.

"I'm scared. I thought we were all safe now. Wasn't that why they brought us here?" she pleaded.

"You're too smart for your own good. Who told you that?" I was trying to calm her down and keep the conversation lighthearted.

"The kids. They said we needed to be here to make the darkness go away. What's the darkness, Arie?"

"Wow, okay, well, this isn't the easiest thing to explain. You remember when I told you there's something in us that tells us when something is right and wrong?"

"Yes," she replied.

"Some have chosen not to listen to what's right, and their essence has become dark. Darkness doesn't belong here, so we were brought here to send them away."

"So, are they back?" she asked.

"I need to get back to Tivon to find out. I'm not really sure what's going on. You'll be safe in your room."

"What if I need you?" Her voice broke as she grabbed my arm.

"I'm going to show you something, okay?" She nodded. I brought her over to the bed and put her on it. I sat on it across from her. "We are from the same bloodline here. In fact, we are made of the same essence, so there's this neat thing we can do to communicate without talking or even being close to each other. I'm going to show you how it works."

"Okay," she responded reluctantly.

"You know how at the waterfall all you had to do was think about your mom, and she appeared? This is the same thing. Just close your eyes and picture me. Then say my name inside your head, and I will hear you. Do you want to try it real quick?"

"Yeah," she said eagerly.

"Close your eyes. Clear everything out of your mind. Take a deep breath and picture me. Then think my name." I closed my eyes and waited, hoping this would work. I didn't actually know if we could communicate this way, but I figured since

Tivon could read my thoughts it had to work for us, too. After a minute or so passed, I was getting worried. I opened my eyes and watched her as she contorted her face in concentration. "Take another deep breath and relax." She did as I said, and then I heard it.

Arie.

It worked. *I'm here, buggie.*

"It worked, Arie. It really worked!" she squealed as she jumped onto my lap and hugged me tightly.

"Will you be okay now?" I asked quietly.

"Uh-huh." She nodded her head more confidently.

I stood up. "Good, I'm going to find out what's going on then." I bent over and kissed her on the head. "I'll be back soon."

"I love you, Arie."

"I love you too, Amaryllis." I shut the door behind me and rested my body on the door for a minute to recompose myself. Hearing that from her lit a fire in my heart that burned out when I lost my mom. I loved that little girl to pieces. She was *mine* forever and always.

As I walked back down the hallway, I could hear Tivon and Heath talking. I couldn't quite make out what they were saying, though. As I approached, they became silent. Heath was leaning on the couch, but as soon as he saw me, he stood up straight as if I were his commander or something. "You can relax," I said. It made me uncomfortable that he felt he needed to tense when I was around, but he didn't budge. He also didn't look me straight in the eye.

"Arie, Heath is here to protect you. Much like River," Tivon informed me.

I was shocked. First, that I had a protector again, and second, that he threw River's name out there like it was nothing to replace him. "I get that Sage disappearing has everyone on edge, and no offense to you, Heath, but can't *you* just watch over me like you have been?" I asked Tivon, somewhat annoyed. I really didn't like that he felt he could replace River.

"I don't trust myself to do that on my own right now. I would never want yours or Amary's life in danger because I'm distracted by all of this," he said stubbornly.

"I'll agree to this if the focus is on Amary's safety." I crossed my arms to get the point across that I meant business, as childish as it was.

"I wasn't asking, Arie. Heath will make sure you are *both* safe," he responded sternly.

I knew I wasn't going to get any further with this conversation and to push it would just make me seem like a whiny teenager. I wanted to prove I was mature enough to be a part of this as much as anyone else in the village. During the night of my ascension, I proved my strength was much more than they had ever seen, so I knew I could protect myself. I just wanted to make sure Amary was protected in my absence, so for now I would play the helpless card if that's what they wanted.

"I know you're not helpless, Arie," Tivon interrupted my thoughts.

I shot him a glare.

Heath gave a strange questioning look between us. Obviously, he didn't know about our ability. I addressed Heath, "So, Heath, everyone here has amber eyes. Why are yours different?"

He looked at Tivon for permission to answer. Tivon nodded.

Oh, brother. This commander act was going to get old really quickly with me.

"I come from a nearly extinct protection clan," he said matter-of-factly.

The word "extinct" resonated sadly within me. I wondered how many of his kind were left. And were there other clans? I didn't even know there was anyone else here except for the nature spirits.

"You still have a lot to remember, my child, and in time you will remember it all. Your memories, our history, and you'll eventually learn your true purpose. I need to communicate with the other elders before hysteria runs rampant. I'll be in my office if you need anything."

He left Heath and me in an awkward silence. Was I supposed to make small talk? It probably wasn't appropriate to ask about the extinction thing. He wouldn't even look me in the eyes. He kept his focus on random spots around the room— the floor, the backyard, and the kitchen. "Why won't you look at me?" I asked in a snotty voice. His mere presence irritated me. He was, after all, replacing my best friend and potentially the love of my life.

He seemed startled by my abruptness. "Clans are not supposed to look at each other directly."

"Why?"

"Why don't you know if you are *one* of them?" He pointed to Tivon's office.

Now I was thrown off. He came off a little short. "Tivon didn't tell you about me?"

"No, he just recruited me and told me I was to protect his daughters, you and the little one." He brushed the words off quickly.

His rudeness was appalling. He was so polite to Tivon. Why did he think it was all right to treat me any differently? And why would he feel the need to be rude to me? "The little one has a name. It's Amaryllis."

"I apologize. *Amaryllis*," he said straightforwardly.

Clearly, this wasn't the best first impression by either of us, but if we were going to be spending a lot of time together, we needed to figure out a way to coexist. "Okay then, I'm just going to check on Amary." I started walking away, but turned to say one last thing. "But it's Amaryllis to you." I knew that was immature, but he was rubbing me the wrong way, and I didn't want him to get too comfortable around us. I headed down the hall.

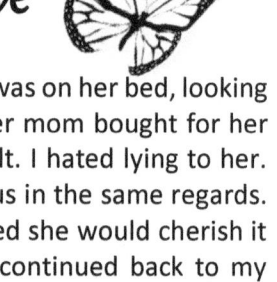

Chapter Five

I peeked into Amary's room. She was on her bed, looking through *Spirits of Nature*, the book her mom bought for her from my store. I exhaled a sigh of guilt. I hated lying to her. That book meant so much to both of us in the same regards. Our mothers gave us that book. I hoped she would cherish it like I did. I left her undisturbed and continued back to my room. I didn't know what to do with myself. I was too anxious about Sage to sleep, and I was too annoyed with *the protector* in the living room to hang out there. What I wanted to do was find Sage.

An unfamiliar sensation rolled over my body like a slow moving earthquake. I caught my breath as my heart sputtered with the waves. *What was happening?* I was trying really hard not to panic and trust in all the new sensations the universe had to offer, but this had me lying paralyzed on the floor and closing my eyes until the vibrations passed. This was the first time a sensation caused me pain. My eyes welled up as if I was chopping a raw onion. I was about to scream in agony when I heard it.

"Arrrie, help me."

My eyes shot open. It was Sage, but how...? I closed my eyes again and tried to concentrate on her voice, hoping I would hear her again and bracing for the pain. The wave washed over me again, and my body tensed. The black cloud filling my head was replaced with a foggy vision of Sage crouched in the corner of a room. Her face was hidden in her knees. I frantically tried to study the parts of the room that were clear. She was sitting on a concrete slab, and the wall behind her looked to be made out of fabricated rock. It was so dark in there. The vision started to fade. I screamed in defiance, "Noooo!" Sage's head shot up just as the vision went black. *She heard me*.

My door crashed open, and immediately strong arms flew around me. They held on to my body tightly as it convulsed the last of the pain out. When my body had enough, it went limp. As I looked up to face my protector, his eyes were fiercely purple. *He was worried.*

"Stay with me, Arie," he said as he lifted me and placed me carefully onto my bed.

My body was so weak, but his eyes had me transfixed. *How was he doing that?* And then recognition registered in my memories. The fox flashed before me, and its amethyst eyes stared at me warmly. Heath was *my* fox.

"What's going on?" Tivon burst into the room.

Heath hesitantly unlocked his hold on me, knowing I finally understood who he was. When he turned away from me, the connection was instantly severed, leaving a little ache behind and me confused.

"She's okay, sir. I found her on the floor shaking." He inched his way off the bed.

Tivon sped gracefully to my side. "Are you okay, child? What happened?"

He took my hand in his. Heath backed out of the room, but stayed in the hallway just barely visible. "It was Sage. I saw her. I *heard* her. When she called out to me, my body shook with pain, but I saw her, Tivon. How is that even possible?" I inquired.

"I don't know. It's a bloodline ability, and Sage is not of our bloodline, but there are many things we don't know about your capabilities. Did it hurt much?" he asked with a fatherly concern.

"A little, but I'm fine now. I think I know where she is." I sat up, my body's energy restored.

"Where?" Heath asked as he came back into the room.

"They took her to the same place they took me, only I don't remember exactly where that is. Ashe..." Saying his name aloud caused me to pause momentarily. "He flashed Amary and me out. I'm not sure where we landed, and I was in pseudo shock with being here in this place, so I'm not confident that I remember the way." I looked at Tivon. "She's scared. We have to get her out of there. Why would he take her?"

Heath chimed in, "To get to you. He's trying to lure you. That can't happen."

"But why does he still want me? The ascension is over. Killing me isn't going to stop anything."

"He's up to something. What? We don't know yet, but Heath is right. He's setting a trap, and you won't go." His authority came through loud and clear. "Your job is to stay safe and keep Amary safe. Let us handle getting Sage back. Understand?"

The rebellious teenager in me wanted to fight, but I had to put Amary's safety first even before Sage, so I whispered, "Understood."

"Heath, come with me. We need to gather," Tivon instructed as he left, followed by Heath who stole a quick glance back. His eyes penetrated right through me. The image of the fox popped into my head again. My mom was right about it being a male. It was comforting that a little living piece of my other home had come with me and could live here, even though I didn't know anything about him. It didn't matter. He had been watching me since I was little, and now I truly felt I could trust him. He wasn't what I needed. He wasn't River or Ashe, but I knew he would protect Amary and me with his life. I needed to find a way to visit River again, soon. After we got Sage back, I was going to do what it took to see him. I had to be able to harness this power for something other than fighting off darkness.

"Arie?" Amary tiptoed into the room.

"Yes, sweetie?"

"Are you okay?" she asked carefully.

I patted the bed. "Come up here, buggie."

A smile lit up her face as she hopped onto the bed and sat on my lap. "I'm fine. See?" I pinched the skin on my arm. "You aren't dreaming. I'm here."

"I saw Sage," she said.

I was astonished. "What do you mean you 'saw Sage'?"

"She was in a dark room. It looked like the same place we were in when the bad guy took us."

It made me nauseous to think she just went through the same physical anguish I went through. "Oh, no, Amary. Did it hurt?"

"Did what hurt?" she responded.

I turned her around to face me. "When you saw Sage, did your body hurt?"

"No."

Weird. Why would it hurt me and not her?

Amary interrupted my thoughts, "She's sad, Arie."

I pulled her into a hug. "I know, buggie. We're going to get her back."

I wanted to talk to Tivon, but he looked like he was having a pretty intense conversation with the wall, something I would never get used to, so I skated past the door and darted to the backyard. It was getting dark, and the silence was inescapable. Everyone had locked themselves up securely after they heard about Sage's disappearance. *It was my fault.* Pyrrhus was trying to get to me any way he could. Not knowing why was scary as hell.

I flinched as someone joined me by the riverbed unexpectedly. *Dumb.* Why didn't I just run into the forest screaming, "Take me"? I couldn't afford to get lost in my self-pity. Heath spoke up before I turned to identify the looming presence.

"You should really be more attentive," he commented flatly.

Yeah, thanks for pointing out the obvious. "I know," I whispered.

"Are you okay?"

Wow, was he actually talking to me like a real person with real feelings? "Yeah, I was just thinking about someone." *Someone I missed horribly. River.* He would know what to do in this situation. He always knew what to do.

"By the looks of it, it's not Sage," he suggested.

"No," I admitted guiltily. *Way to make me feel like crap, Heath.*

"River is a great person and an even better protector," he exclaimed.

I was shocked, which registered on my what-the-hell face that consisted, I assume, of a rather unattractive brow furrowing and bugged-out eyes.

"Don't look so shocked, Arie. I watched you two grow up in the meadow."

I was right. "I suspected you were my fox." I blushed. A silence built as we both let the reality of our connection sink in. We had essentially grown up together, yet so far apart. I broke the silence. "Why did you only make yourself visible the two times?" My voice betrayed me with its obvious disappointment. A disappointment I hadn't known was there until now.

"My job was to watch over the two of you and your mom and only interact when absolutely necessary."

Funny. I didn't remember needing him in either instance. "So, then why did you?" I asked boldly. The comfortable atmosphere surrounding us shifted to what I could only describe as peculiar, but in a good way. *Ugh! What was I thinking?*

"I couldn't resist," he said coolly, boundaries between us erased.

Oh crap! I can't do this! I tried, but I couldn't deny the growing affection between us. *It's not real. It's just my transition into my new skin. It's not real.* If I kept repeating this, maybe it would be true. I probably looked like an idiot just standing there unresponsive and dumbfounded.

"I'm sorry. That was inappropriate. It won't happen again," he rambled out quickly and turned to walk away.

"Wait, Heath. It was nice and refreshing to hear you say something so..." I was trying to find the right word to rectify the situation. I didn't want it to get weird. "...honest." I held my breath for his response, but he didn't say anything. Instead, he exhaled deeply and covered the short distance to the house quickly. *Dammit. What was wrong with me?*

Chapter Six

I sat on the edge of the riverbed and let the water tease my toes as it rippled downstream. The moon was captivating as always, larger than life, bright, and blue. I soaked in the rays, enjoying the warm feeling they illuminated in my veins. Meditation was my escape, but also my way to clarity. I needed to figure out what Pyrrhus was plotting. I felt bad not planning Sage's rescue, but it all came down to Pyrrhus and me. If I could figure out what he was up to, I might be able to get a few steps ahead and surprise him. *I hated this.* I knew I needed to accept my destiny. I imagined Tivon's proud booming voice, but I missed my simple life with River and Star.

I missed the days when we would congregate at the bookstore around lunch and reminisce about silly high school moments. Like the time Star tripped on a fallen branch on our way into the school from a recent storm and landed face first into a pile of mud. It wouldn't have been as funny, but she had just bragged about getting a stain out of the favorite shirt she was wearing. And she was carrying a donut she had just retrieved from her newly pronounced crush. The look of disbelief on her face was priceless and had us rolling, including her.

Who was I kidding? After my mom died, I wasn't living. *I was dying.* I was given a second chance to be something. To be *someone.* If for no one else other than Amary. As I tipped my head back, draining the moon of all its power, I experienced the familiar connection Ashe and I shared. I lifted my head and saw the orange butterfly that manifested after Ashe's last breath had landed upon my knee. I knew I wasn't supposed to, but I wanted so badly to trap this beautiful butterfly in a sanctuary inside my room. I believed he carried Ashe's essence, and I would do anything to be close to him again. I held out my finger, and he hopped on. When his legs landed, a wave of joy traveled up my arm and catapulted me into another world.

I stood in the middle of the butterfly circle in the meadow, a cloudy feeling surrounding me. I scanned my backyard and discovered fresh weeds popping their way through the dirt. The buds of all the flowers were drooping, and their dried petals layered the earth below them. The grass was several inches tall. Everything was unkempt except for the circle. It was unaffected by time and weather as it always had been. An anomaly I now understood.

I'm here. I'm really here. My cheeks burned with joy. Although things were foggy, I was home. I didn't know how I had gotten here, but I had just made my first reality jump. A laugh filled the air, and I quickly realized it was me. I spun in circles, like I had done so many times as a little girl. I knew it was silly and childish, but the euphoria building within me that I was home didn't care.

"Arie?"

I slammed the brakes on my spinning and confronted River. My heart stopped. He was here.

"River!" He looked disheveled. He had scruff growing on his face, his hair was longer and messy, and the bags under his eyes told stories of many sleepless nights. My heart dropped a few flights. He wore a faded tight-fitting tank top and his signature work-in-the-yard jeans. His tennis shoes were worn on the edges, and a hole was forming at the tops where his big toes rubbed furiously, struggling to find a way to air.

I tried to cross the threshold of the circle, but I was knocked back by an invisible force field. I yelled again, "River!"

He stepped closer to the circle, squinting his eyes. Recognition registered. He couldn't see me. When my mom came to me, her image was shadowed in fogginess, but I could feel it was her before she broke through. How did she break through?

"Arie, is that you? Please, be you." A muffled sound infiltrated the circle.

I was panicking. I wanted to reach out and hug him before I faded. My mother was never able to stay very long. It was happening. He was dissipating. No. No! I shot my arm in front of me. It worked. I could see my hand clearly on the other side of the haze. River stepped closer, so I grabbed his shirt and yanked hard. He was strong, but now I was stronger, thanks to the ascension.

River stood in front of me in the circle, just a nose length apart and clear as a cloudless sky. His smile warmed my heart.

"Missed me, I see." He winked.

"You have no idea." We latched on to each other tightly. I knew we didn't have much time, so I pulled away, not letting go of his arms. I never wanted to let go. "How long have I been gone? Everything's overgrown again."

"Three months," he replied.

I knew I shouldn't have been so surprised, because the short visions I had before I came to the new reality had me losing hours. It was more of disappointment than surprise. The longer I was there, the more time I lost exponentially with River and Starling.

"How did you know I would be here?" I inquired.

"I didn't. I came over to work in the yard."

That explained the worn clothes. His heart was larger than life. I was gone, and he was still taking care of me. "Thank you."

I trailed my hand down his arm and grasped onto his hand gently. I turned it over with his palm up and traced on his hand. Something I hadn't done since we were kids. I had a hard time expressing deep emotions aloud, so I adopted this ritual with him.

He watched carefully and then responded, "I love you, too."

I had drawn the letter "I," a heart symbol, and the word "you".

"Arie, you're fading," he commented sadly.

"I know." I could feel it. "I promise I will find my way back again, soon. Please, tell Star I love her."

His voice became distant, but I heard. "I will."

I was on the riverbed again. The butterfly had made its way back to my knee, but now suddenly flew off into the sky. A residual sadness settled inside me. I heard a bustling of voices coming from the house, so I made my way back, a little anxious about the uneasiness I had surely created between Heath and me.

Several people were congregated in the main room. I wanted to call it a family room, but that seemed so normal for such a surreal place. As I stepped inside, the buzz of my presence rushed through me. I barely felt it now. I didn't know if it was because I was becoming desensitized by the little charge of the organisms or if they were just getting sick of me. I laughed to myself. That was a strange thought.

Everyone ignored my entry, except for Heath, who glanced at me and then quickly looked away. *Awesome. Real smart to upset my protector.*

A woman with a tight strawberry blonde bun sitting on the couch spoke up. "The longer Sage is with him, the more her light will fade. We can't afford to wait."

What? How could Tivon have left that out? He was in my head again because he locked eyes with me. I searched for an apology, but his stare only gave away determination.

"My daughter has joined us," he announced.

They all turned around to me. Next to the woman with the tight bun sat a boy that looked to be a few years younger than me. I knew who he was immediately from the strawberry blonde hair and the sprinkling of freckles covering his fair skin. I hadn't been reacquainted with Sage's family since I had been back because of my comatose-like withdrawal, but there was no question of the family resemblance. The woman with the tight bun was her mom, and the boy was her little brother.

Standing in the far corner next to the fireplace was a tall burly man with long hair pulled back into a ponytail. His arms were crossed firmly in front of his chest, and he looked less than friendly. He looked more aged than Tivon. His skin was rough as if it saw too many days in the sun, and his biceps bulged with power. He adorned a semi-groomed short beard and mustache and wore a pair of faded jeans and a gray loose-fitting shirt. Across from him on the other side of the fireplace was a handsomely rugged guy with short dark hair. His tight black shirt did little to hide the muscles hidden beneath. He was more casual than the rest of the group, but no less attentive. He leaned on the wall with one leg crossed over the other. My eyes scanned his steel-toe boots, up to his fitted leather pants, and settled on the top of his head because he was staring at the ground. It just occurred to me that everyone's clothing here was pretty bland. No patterns, pictures, or lettering. *How boring.*

I wondered if these were the elders. Actually, the lack of bodily presence concerned me. As if on cue, four more people joined the group. There was one tough-looking girl in the mix, wearing a deep-red shiny skin-tight half top that stopped just under her bra line and skin-tight black leather pants and steel-toe boots. Her clothing almost replicated the casual guy leaning on the wall. He was most definitely not looking at his shoes anymore. She commanded the attention of a room when she entered. She gave me the once-over that made me feel undeniably incompetent. She was a little taller than me with dark hair and dark glistening skin that highlighted the definition on her arms and abs. She didn't look much older than me, which had me curiously upbeat. *Maybe they would take me more seriously now.*

"The rest are here. We can begin the formal discussions now," Tivon announced.

The other three guys settled against the glass wall that led to the backyard. They looked strikingly similar. They were all the same tall height with the same features— brown skin, sharp noses, thick eyebrows, and shabby black hair. They even wore the same clothes— dark pants that looked like dress pants, white polo shirts, and black tennis shoes. They had to be triplets.

"I think it's time my daughter met all of you, again." He winked.

The amount of eyes bearing down on me immediately threw me back into my high school English class where Mrs. Smith made me stand up and read one of my poems she had been raving about. My knees became weak, beads of sweat covered my forehead, and my stomach started churning up my lunch. This was before my mom died when things like that meant something. After that, I could have given Helen Keller's speech, "Strike Against War," without even batting an eyelash. *Ironic.* I didn't know why I thought about that particular speech, but here we were plotting our offensive attack on Pyrrhus. My favorite part of her speech ran through my head.

Strike against all ordinances and laws and institutions that continue the slaughter of peace and the butcheries of war. Strike against war, for without you no battles can be fought. Strike against manufacturing scrapnel and gas bombs and all other tools of murder. Strike against preparedness that means death and misery to millions of human being. Be not dumb, obedient slaves in an army of destruction. Be heroes in an army of construction.

I bore back at all the eyes glaring at me, knees intact, no sweat, and my stomach ironclad.

"Arie, these are the elders." He motioned his hand around the room.

No one spoke. You could hear a mouse scurry across the floor it was so quiet.

"And this is Sage's mom, Jules, and her little brother,

Brandt." He pointed to the couch.

It was clear no one was going to speak up besides Tivon. They were too busy summing me up, so I took the liberty of breaking the ice. *Shatter the silence.*

"It's nice to meet you all...I mean, it's good to see you all again." I looked to Tivon with a questioning look of approval.

His infectious chuckle startled everyone. "Yes, Arie, you have met all of them in your other life here."

His laugh was warm and inviting, which made the others laugh, too. All except Heath. He maintained a focused and concerned stare.

"Let's skip the formalities of names for now. We have much more pressing matters to discuss," Tivon declared.

Jules spoke up quickly, "We have to get her out of there."

The bearded man jumped in, "We don't even know where she is."

My cheeks burned with knowledge. I knew where she was, and Tivon and Heath knew it, but I wasn't sure they were ready to share that bit of information, so I stayed quiet.

"Jules, we are going to do our best to get her back as quickly as possible, but we have lost too many recently, so we need to be careful. Everything has to be planned out perfectly. No one dies!" Tivon's voice rose with that final statement.

I felt the prick of guilt. We had lost so many because of me. Because of the ascension. I couldn't help myself. "I know where she is."

Darts were thrown at the big target on my face, only they were eyes. Now my knees were weakening, and I could feel the sweat bubbling below the surface, taunting me to be released. I refused to back down. I refused to take steps backward, but I could tell Heath and Tivon were unhappy with me. In fact, they were genuinely pissed. I continued quickly, "Well, I don't know exactly where she is, but I know the place. She sent me a vision, and it was the same place Pyrrhus had taken me. Only I don't remember how to get there. But I do remember what it felt like, and I remember some of the sounds like..." Tivon's slow shaking of his head shut me up. Jules had been hanging on my every word, so she immediately looked at me questioningly for stopping short.

"Like what, Arie? What were the sounds?" she pleaded.

"That's enough, Arie. Jules, can you please take Brandt and excuse the elders?" Tivon asked politely.

She started to open her mouth to say something, but instead, stood up and quickly shuffled out with her son. The dominance in the room was all-consuming. The bearded man addressed me.

"What do you mean she sent you a vision?" he asked cynically.

Tivon answered before I even had a chance to process the question. "It seems Arie's gift of visions was magnified in the ascension. And in the future, Lance, I would prefer you didn't address my daughter so casually." The tone in his voice mimicked nails on a chalkboard.

"I'm sorry, sir," he said as he bowed his head ever so slightly.

"It's okay..." His glare stopped me mid-sentence. It dawned on me that I was interrupting a power struggle. *Duh!* I wasn't used to this kind of hierarchy game, but I needed to learn quickly if I was going to fit in and not screw up things. *And not kill anyone.*

Chapter Seven

The rest of the gathering went pretty quickly. Jules held back quiet whimpers while Brandt barely held on to his teenage aggression. I admired that he loved his sister so much. I learned he was fifteen. It was sad to think while most fifteen-year-olds were focused on sports and starting to notice girls, Brandt was worried about saving his sister. Nothing really got accomplished. Jules pleaded, and the elders agreed they needed to devise a strategically-planned attack. No one addressed me again after Tivon berated Lance. I was invisible again, like in high school, only now it bothered me, a little.

I sat on the back porch after the elders dispersed. Amary was playing with Iris and some other girls at the riverbed. Iris was her first friend here. Although she was a few years older than Amary, they had really taken to each other. I was glad she found a sister-figure around her age. I knew Iris was fond of her and would teach her how to grow up in such an enchanted reality.

"May I sit with you?" Tivon asked in his more serious voice.

I knew what was coming. He hadn't looked at me since my little outburst of information, so I knew I had done something wrong. "Of course," I replied. I scooted over, giving his broad stature plenty of room.

"I'm sorry if I seemed tough in there, but it's very

important that you and I establish an oral confidentiality agreement. The elders might assume I was intentionally withholding information, and we don't need any more darkness in our village."

I nervously picked at my fingers. I wasn't used to all this responsibility. "I'm sorry. I understand," was all I could say.

He patted my shoulder. "No need to be sorry, my child. You didn't know, but now you do."

He was still exploring the physical actions that went with being a father. His awkward shoulder pat proved he had a long way to go, but in all fairness, I hadn't really been very open to affection since I got here. Who was I kidding? I hadn't been affectionate since River left. What I had in me I reserved for Amary, and Amary alone.

"Does Jules have any other children?" I asked.

"No."

"Brandt seems very capable."

"He is. He wants to join the allegiance, but he's not old enough. I don't think we'll be able to stop him now," he responded.

"So, there's an official allegiance?" The thought of these beautiful people priming for war knotted my stomach.

"Since you were killed, a lot of things were put in place. The ones with us the night of your ascension were a part of the allegiance. They have been well-trained over the decades. While we lost some, Pyrrhus lost more."

That night haunted me every night. I never got to meet or thank those people for risking their lives for me and ultimately sacrificing it. I knew who their families were just by their mere avoidance of me. They weren't mean in any way. In fact, when I was near them, all I felt was pure heartbreak. I think being around me induced that sadness, so they eluded me to avoid it. *Makes perfect sense.*

"This is never going to end. Is it, Tivon?" I never addressed him as my dad. Not since that day in at the waterfall. *One day.*

"Not as long as Pyrrhus is out there."

That settled heavy on me. I was the reason all of this started, although I'm not so narcissistic that I would think it would have never happened. There was something in Pyrrhus that bled darkness. Something that dark had to be ingrained in his DNA. I knew everyone here thought it was jealousy that manifested the darkness, but I couldn't help to think there was more to it.

Tivon broke an ever-growing silence that had developed. "We need to start looking for that place you saw in your vision, but I think it would be best if we waited until sunrise."

I flinched at the thought of entering the shadow stalkers' territory, but I knew we didn't have much time to save Sage. "Okay."

After Tivon left, I went to the waterfall. I knew I would be safe there, and I wanted a quiet sanctuary in which to meditate. I hoped if I concentrated hard enough I could remember more details of where Sage was. Where Amary and I were when Ashe... I couldn't finish my thought. The wound was still too raw.

I climbed over the wet rocks and stole a quick glance at the waterfall as I passed by. I knew there had to be more secrets to this waterfall, and one day I would unlock them, but for now, I wanted to focus on just Sage. I took up residence on my usual flat rock that stared over the great expanse of this place. It still took my breath away. The blue of the sky was more like an aqua, and a few wispy clouds painted the horizon. The weather was always temperate here, but the sky changed just like at home. *Crap!* Like the other reality. I would never get used to calling this my home. *I didn't want to.* As much as I loved Tivon, this would never *feel* like home. Home was where I grew up. Home was in the house full of the memories I shared with my mom.

Home was with River.

I closed my eyes to shut out my surroundings. Then I drowned out the noises by concentrating on the steady and slow breaths I inhaled and exhaled deeply. I crossed my legs and rested my hands on my knees, and I brought up the image of Sage in the room on the floor crying. I could see her pain, but I couldn't feel it. I needed to dive deeper. I concentrated on the concrete floor below her and the rock walls she leaned on. They were chiseled too perfectly to be natural. To be real. *Wait!* I focused harder on the walls. There was something that didn't feel right about them. I reached out my hands as if I could touch them, and then all of a sudden I could. This had to be a fabrication of my meditative state. This couldn't be real, but the wall felt so real. It was smooth, though, not rough like I would expect rock to be. I remembered now, but had forgotten, because of the panicked state I was in.

I was touching the wall just to the right of Sage, but when I reached out, she was no longer there. I tried to look around the room, but it didn't exist. I could only see and feel what I had seen in my vision. *Where did she go?* She had to be somewhere in this room. I felt scared again. I felt trapped here again. In a frenzy, I touched the concrete floor, but couldn't move past the vision parameters. I had no control here. I couldn't break my meditative state.

I had no control.

My heart was racing now as my eyes tried hard to see past the fogginess with no success. I was really here, but now, how did I get out?

A sparkle on the wall caught my eye, so I moved closer and recognized it immediately. It was a malachite stone. It was a beautiful, green, smooth stone with circles of white that mimicked rings inside a tree trunk. While its powers included love and protection, its main purpose was to make dreams, imagination, and memories more vivid. Now that I discovered this one, I saw more scattered about as part of the design of the wall. Everything was making more sense now. These were put into the walls to summon people. Malachite particularly affected the emotional state of a person, and since I was upset about Sage, it fed on that vulnerability. I was genuinely apprehensive now. Was I here physically too' or just metaphysically? *Dammit*! I cursed myself for not spending more time studying gemstones with my mom. I didn't know how to get back to the waterfall. I had gone there alone, and I didn't tell anyone I was going. *So stupid.*

Just then, the back of my hand started burning. I gripped it painfully, thinking it would stop the searing, but it didn't. Tears welled from the extreme discomfort as the burning spread through my fingers up my arm. When I didn't think I could take it anymore, my vision became blurry, and everything went black. The pain subsided and the trickling of water and the smell of flowers filled my senses. I opened my eyes, and to my relief, I was back at the waterfall. I looked down at my hand where the burning had become impossibly unbearable to find the orange and red butterfly perched. I was astounded when recognition set in. It had pulled me from the dream.

"Are you watching over me, little guy?" I asked the butterfly.

I put my other hand out, so it could hop onto it. I raised it to my nose to get a closer look. It was still as magnificent as I remembered. The orange and red stripes were separated by black lines. They had looked like flames when the butterfly circled Amary and me the day after the ascension. A sort of hologram image of Ashe appeared. He was also as I remembered him. Beautiful amber eyes with green speckles and dark, thick, rumpled hair against his olive skin. I had to be hallucinating, but I wasn't afraid. I liked it. I liked seeing him again, even if it was just a figment of my imagination. He had tantalizing, full, pink lips that fit perfectly with mine. The image was only a few inches away from me, his lips in perfect alignment with mine. They moved in, and I imagined again how they would feel against mine. I was caught off guard when I not only imagined them, but I could also feel them. They were soft and still sent shocks of excitement through me. I had closed my eyes in the exchange, and when I opened them, he was gone. The butterfly took flight, and I was again alone.

As I lay in bed, I was surprisingly calm after the weird experience at the waterfall. It was alarming how quickly I was adjusting to this place. Things didn't shake me the way they used to. I had sneaked into Amary's room and gave her a quick kiss on the forehead as she snuggled under the sheets. We needed to sleep, but not to eat. It must be because the sun fueled our energy in place of food. And in my case, the moon also gave me energy. I was the only one who could harness both. Another anomaly. I imagined being sucked into a different location through a meditative state was my own special little gift, too. *Lucky me.* How could I protect myself if I didn't even know all my weaknesses? Yet, somehow Pyrrhus knew. He knew more about what I was than I did. Than anyone did. *How?*

I sat among the glossy green grass blades. The hybrid butterfly/dragonfly insects we called the "flying dragon" circled around me playfully. I loved sitting here alone for hours, just watching nature play. Sage was at home with her little brother, and River was working with my father. I didn't mind, though. This was my time. On cue, shivers raced up my arms. I knew he was back. He started coming around more since my thirteenth celebration, but I didn't like how he made me feel, but I also wasn't one to be unpleasant. We were all very accepting of everyone and only were really aware of the light that people carried inside their souls. I had confided in River once about how Pyrrhus made me feel when he was around, and he didn't really understand it. He didn't feel the same thing as me. He was well-liked by everyone, as we all were, so I imagined I had to be the only one who felt something off about him, but what that something was, I didn't know. I had never felt it before, so I didn't know how to define it.

"Hey, Arie," he said casually.

I felt bad feeling the way I did about him, especially when he was always so polite to me. Was there something wrong with me? "Hi, Pyrrhus."

He sat next to me, uninvited. "What are you doing?"

"Just watching the bugs," I replied.

"Can I watch with you?" he asked shyly.

"Sure." I had the urge to refuse, which made me feel worse. The negativity he brought out in me weighed on my conscience.

We sat there in silence and watched the bugs together. His presence was not comfortable like River's and Sage's. He touched my hand, and something dark consumed me. Sadness, pain, rage. I pulled my hand away quickly.

"I'm sorry...ummm...I..." he muttered as he jumped up and ran away.

"Wait, Pyrrhus!" I shouted after him, but he was gone in a flash. I caressed my hand he touched and shuddered. What was that?

I woke up in a pool of sweat and breathing hard. I looked around in the dark, confused and scared. As my eyes adjusted, I saw my room come into focus. *I was okay. It wasn't real.* I concentrated on slowing down my breathing by looking out the window and letting the moon refocus me. The rays searched me out, and when they found me, they penetrated through the open window and filled me with life. The warm tingle it created had a euphoric calming effect. It must have known I needed its light to recover from my dream.

I couldn't possibly go back to sleep after that. Pyrrhus had invaded my meditative states and now my dream states. But, at least in the dream, I was getting back pieces of my former life. *My memories.* Maybe it would help me piece things back together. Maybe it would help me find Sage. Or even better, maybe it would help me discover what Pyrrhus was up to.

I kicked off the blankets, trying to cool down as quickly as possible. My T-shirt clung to my skin. I pulled it away and over my head. It was River's shirt that he lent me the night of my eighteenth birthday when I passed out for almost a week. I never returned it, and now it was my only piece of him. It had a weird symbol on it that I meant to ask him about, but forgot in all the chaos. It looked like the lowercase "i" with a scripted number "9" on both sides, the right side being a backward number "9". It was simple, and I knew it had to have some importance to River, because this was the only shirt I remembered him owning with anything on it. He was very plain. *Because he was from here.*

I placed it carefully onto the end of the bed. I stood by the open window in just my sports bra and boy shorts and let the breeze cool me down. It felt so good. In a few hours, the sun would be rising, and Tivon and I would be off to look for the room made of rocks and dangerous gems. I contemplated telling him what happened at the waterfall, but I didn't want anything to risk him changing his mind about going after Sage. I didn't think it was in him to leave her to Pyrrhus' devices, but I didn't want to chance it. Besides, now that I knew about the gems, I had an advantage. My mom's ring was the most powerful stone of all the gems, and I could draw from its power if needed.

I rubbed the ring like a genie would poof out of it in a cloud of smoke. The last time it glowed was in proximity of the dagger at Ashe's resting place. *As if it belonged to me.* But it burned when I touched it, so I wasn't sure. It just felt right to leave it with Ashe. *It belonged to him.*

Chapter Eight

I spent the last few hours of the night staring out the window, not thinking about much in particular. I was drained from the day before, and I just needed to zone out for a while. When the sun peeked over the horizon, I got dressed in fresh boring clothes. I was still not used to not showering. We were always clean here and smelled like flowers of nature. It was peculiar. Not that I minded being clean all the time. Hell, it was an obsessive compulsive person's dream, but it was a ritual that reminded me of what it was like to be normal. *To be human.*

A short, but rough knocking at my door signaled the beginning of yet another journey. I was surprised to see Heath on the other side. I had expected it was just Tivon and I going, but I guess that would be careless now that I thought about it.

"Hey," I said. Such a human word. Everyone spoke so formally here. Maybe I needed to practice. "I mean, hi."

"Don't do that, Arie. Don't try to change for this place. Just be you," he replied bluntly.

Great! He was starting to remind me of River. That was something he would've said, so as in true fashion when I was particularly uncomfortable with something, I avoided it.

"Are you coming with us?"

"Of course," he responded.

"Who's going to stay with Amary?" I wasn't happy about

both of us leaving her.

"Iris and her family are going to come here and watch her. They were instructed to stay in the house while we were gone. She is safe here. We have several members of the allegiance watching the house, too."

I guess they had it all covered then. Of course, they did. They had been living in fear for years before I came. Nothing had really changed because I came. It was supposed to, though. I was supposed to be the answer to their freedom from the fear. Somehow I failed them.

"Are you ready?" Heath asked.

"Yeah."

As we walked by Amary's room, I stopped. "Give me a minute," I said to Heath. I popped my head inside. She was at her desk coloring. "Hi, buggie."

She hopped up and hugged my waist tightly. "Hi, Arie. Want to color with me?" she asked with a smile plastered from ear to ear.

"I would love to, but right now, I have to go with Tivon somewhere. Can I color when I get back?"

"That would be great. Iris and her older sister are coming over to play. We're going to play dress up."

"That sounds like a lot of fun. Just save some energy for me." I bent down and kissed her on the cheek and walked back to the door.

"Arie?"

"Yeah, buggie?"

"Why don't you call him Dad?"

I didn't know what to say. It was a question I had asked myself multiple times, but didn't have an answer to. It just never felt right. I walked back over to her, sat down on the floor, and invited her onto my lap. She crawled on without hesitation.

"You seem to ask a lot of complicated questions. I know he's my dad, but I only just met him."

"You just met me, and I hear you refer to me as your

sister."

She had me on that one. "True. I'm not sure how to explain it without it sounding like I don't trust him, because I do. Whole-heartedly. With you, it's easy to accept you as my sister, maybe because you're so young. With grownups, everything seems to be more difficult to define." I heard a small tap on the door. "I need to go. I'll be back soon." I hugged her and slid her off my lap. It reminded me of the day when Heath came to me as a fox. He snuggled protectively onto my lap, and then I scooted him along. I sighed deeply. *Things were always more complicated with adults.*

I joined Heath in the hallway, still perplexed at the chain of events that led me to this point.

"Are you okay?" he asked, nervous.

"Yeah, I'm fine. Let's go."

I walked with Heath and Tivon to the edge of the village where a half dozen men stood. There was one female aside from me. It was the elder I had met earlier. Well, I didn't actually meet her since I didn't know her name. Brandt was among them as well. The five men that included Brandt were all wearing black shirts, black pants, and black steel-toe boots. I wondered how Brandt had convinced them to let him come along. It seemed foolish to have someone so emotionally involved risk the scouting mission. I recognized the other five men from around the village, but couldn't remember their names. I wasn't even sure I knew them to begin with. Everyone was dressed for battle. The only weapons I saw were long thick sticks. I had seen them in action the night of the ascension. They held a dangerous amount of energy. When the sun set, so did their energy level, so they stored it inside them. *Brilliant, really.* I wondered if Pyrrhus had figured this out, too. I didn't have to answer because I already knew the answer. He didn't need the sticks since he had learned how to harness the power of gemstones, or at least I was assuming he had. The girl approached us. She looked even more menacing up close.

"Sir," she said to Tivon as she bowed her head.

"Yes, Norinda, what's on your mind?" he asked.

"Do you think it's wise to let Brandt come along?"

I shot her a surprised look. Maybe we were more alike than I thought, or I was just getting smarter the longer I was here.

"Norinda, I understand your concern, but if this is what he needs to heal, then we will give it to him."

Heal? What was he talking about?

"Yes, sir." She bowed again and walked away without a glance at me.

Tivon announced, "Let's get going. The sun is rising quickly."

They created a gap so Tivon and I could walk to the front. He turned to me. "You will lead. We will follow."

Why did it sound like he meant it more than just this situation? I looked back as all the eyes waited for me to show them where Sage was, but I had no idea where to go.

Tivon sensed my hesitation. "It's okay, my child. Close your eyes and let your heart and soul guide you."

I stood there in a tight pair of jeans and a tight black tank top, pretending to be a normal girl back at my meadow. I closed my eyes and blocked out everything except for the memory of Sage in that room. I could smell the mustiness and hear the distant trickle of water. "It's somewhere along the creek. Close to it," I declared with my eyes still closed. I tried to remember more, but I couldn't, and the vision faded. I opened my eyes and blushed as everyone stared.

"We follow the creek north," Tivon commanded.

We traveled on the path we had walked to the ascension, but then veered left through the thick of the unmarked forest. Thank goodness, we hadn't made it to Ashe's spot. I think Tivon did it on purpose. He knew it would be hard for me, and yet, I still couldn't call him Dad. *How long would I be broken?*

As always, the forest craved me as much as I craved its energy. When I brushed up against a flower or tree, my body tingled. I felt every surge I received. It was magnificent. I knew the others saw my reaction to the light touch of the forest, which made it awkward, because it was somewhat an intimate moment for me, but I knew I had to let that go. My privacy here was almost nonexistent.

When we reached the river, we chose to walk in it rather than next to it. The forest was difficult to get through in a timely manner. I pulled up my jeans as high as I could before I waded in. I heard a chuckle as I was pulling up the first pant leg. I looked up to see a stupid grin on Heath's face. Everyone was already in the water. "What?" I snapped. He was making me feel stupid.

"You won't stay wet after we get out of the water. Just like we get clean, we also dry."

"Oh," I said and pushed down my jeans. Now I really felt dumb. I blushed with embarrassment and quickly walked into the water. The rush of natural energy jolted me. I had to grab on to Heath for leverage. There was so much at once that it was almost too much. *Painful.*

"Arie, are you okay?" His voice was distressed.

"Just give me a sec," I said through broken breaths. I held on to him tightly until my body settled, and then I was catapulted into another memory.

I sat in the middle of the creek on a flat rock, smiling from ear to ear because River had just fallen into a deep hole and was covered to his chest.

He splashed water at me. "Laugh it up, Arie. You're next."
He started to push against the current to get to me.

I slid off the rock and tried to get away from him, but I was laughing too hard to make much progress. We were both fifteen and still the best of friends. Things had been brewing differently between us, though. It was fun, and I liked exploring the new feelings by teasing him whenever I had the chance. He was catching up to me, so I clawed my way out of the river and ran into the forest, giggling along the way.

"You have to catch me first!" I hollered back. He was impossibly faster than me, but I was better at hiding. I ran for a couple of minutes, looking for a good hiding place. Just as I was passing a large sequoia tree, a hand reached out and grabbed my arm, pulling me down. It was Pyrrhus. His hand burned my arm, so I swatted it away.

"Shhhh," Pyrrhus whispered.

"What are you doing?" I barked.

"I'm helping you hide."

"I don't need help." I pushed myself up, but he yanked me down again. Every time he touched me, it felt like I was being branded. "Ouch, Pyrrhus. That hurts. Let go."

He let go quickly with a hurt expression.

"Look. I'm sorry. I didn't mean to yell at you, but you scared me," I said, trying to rectify the situation. He perked up at my apology, just as River caught up to me.

"What's going on?" he asked suspiciously.

Pyrrhus cowered against the tree. I felt sorry for him, even though he gave me the creeps. "Nothing. Pyrrhus saw me running and wanted to join in."

River looked at both of us for a moment and then let it go. "Okay, sure. No problem."

"Actually, I was going to head home. I'll see you guys later." I headed back through the forest to the path. I couldn't shake the feeling that there just wasn't something right about Pyrrhus.

Tivon joined us. "It's too much for you. We should walk alongside," he demanded.

"No, it's fine. I'm fine. It just caught me off guard. It's dissipating now." It really was, but that amount of energy scared me. The memories were getting darker. What would happen if I experienced too much? I shook off the thought and started to move forward. With each step, the pain lessened. I didn't realize until we had gone several feet that I was latched on to Heath's arm. I must have done it instinctively. He held on to my hand protectively.

I was finally able to let go of Heath and walk on my own. We had been walking for a couple of hours, and although I wasn't physically tired, I wanted to stop. *I needed to stop.* I scanned the forest and felt something familiar. Followed by my entourage, I walked out of the river and took a few steps into the forest. Tivon hugged one side of me while Heath embraced the other, but no one spoke.

I pushed my way through a rather dense grouping of bushes with the help of the guys. On the other side, I knew where I was. "Can you guys stay back for just a sec?" I requested.

Tivon replied, "Yes, but don't go far or out of sight."

I continued to walk slowly forward. The dirt became soft and fought its way between my toes. The leaves of the tall foliage glistened under the sun, and the flowers bloomed proudly. Their fragrance reminded me of the nectar my mom made when we went outside to the meadow to attract the butterflies. I sneaked a taste once. It was sweet with a twinge of bitterness.

I searched the area, and when my eyes landed on my prize, I walked toward them. They were the purple butterfly flowers. I knew what would happen if I touched them, but I couldn't resist, so I reached out one finger and lightly tapped one of the blooms. It came alive and flew away. It had turned into a real butterfly. I spun around and faced everyone. "We're here."

Chapter Nine

It was difficult being back here. Ashe had rescued Amary and me, and this was where we landed. *Huh?* I didn't ask many questions after the ascension, but I wondered. "Tivon?"

"Yes?" he answered.

We were all in the same vicinity of the area with the butterfly flowers, but the soldiers... *Was that the right word for them?* It seemed accurate since they had trained as part of the allegiance. Anyway, they were combing the outskirts of the area while Norinda and Brandt stayed closer to Tivon, Heath, and me. "Can anyone here fly?"

He looked at me curiously. "Why do you ask?"

"When Ashe rescued us, he touched us, and then there was a blinding light. A moment later, we were here. Did he fly us here?"

Tivon's inquisitiveness disappeared, and a scowl accompanied by furrowed brows replaced it. He was troubled.

"Is there something wrong?" I asked to break the silence. Heath was eavesdropping and had stepped closer to us.

"No, Arie. No one we know can fly," he said with an insistent period to end the conversation.

He had never shut me down like that. He was always so careful with his words and trying to make sure I was comfortable with delays in answers, but it was clear he didn't want to speak about the matter, which of course, made me want to know even more. I knew it wouldn't come from Tivon.

There was always Heath, though.

The five men came back and stood in silence, waiting to be addressed.

"Did you find anything?" Heath asked.

"No, sir," the taller of the group replied.

Sir? Since when did Heath earn the title 'sir'? Things were happening, and I was definitely not in the loop. The thought angered me. What else weren't they telling me? Heath turned to me.

"Arie, these men have searched everywhere and have found nothing," he said coldly.

I glared back. "Maybe because they're looking with their eyes," I snapped. *Dammit!* I shouldn't be mouthing off to him in front of the group. I bit my lip apologetically. "What I meant to say was they are looking with the wrong sense." I closed my eyes and inhaled deeply. The noises faded, and the air stilled. I entered the in-between state my mom referred to as 'transcendental awareness,' a place where the physical didn't exist. I could only explain it as feeling weightless and a complete separation from body and mind.

I was in the room again, surrounded by the beautiful green stones. They were out of place in such a dark and cold setting. I took on my physical form and rushed around the room for any other clues to where it could be hidden. I could hear the water, smell the mustiness, and feel the rough rock beneath my feet, but nothing new. Then I heard a loud scream that had me clawing at my ears for relief. It was a high-pitched scream that one might hear from an animal being tortured, only it sounded vaguely familiar. I couldn't place it, but I knew the person the scream escaped. When the screaming stopped a few moments later, I removed my hands and prepared to awaken from my meditative state, but then a bright light shone in the back corner. When it fizzled out, I covered my mouth to keep myself from crying out. Tears rushed down my face, and I shook my head violently to remove the image from my mind. It had to be a hallucination. It had to be.

This couldn't be real.
This wasn't real.
I wasn't here.
He wasn't here.

Ashe lay in an unmoving lump on the ground. My heart pounded painfully in my chest, and my core burned. I walked carefully toward him, not knowing if this was a trick.

But I knew.
I knew it was real.
He was real.

Suddenly from behind, an arm wrapped around my stomach and forced me back. I tried to rip it off me. As my feet lifted off the ground, I kicked violently to get free, but I wasn't strong enough.

I wasn't strong enough to save him, again.

"Arie, you need to come out of it."

Heath's troubled voice became my only anchor to my senses. Everything else disappeared.

"Arie, you need to come back to us."

Now it was Tivon's voice I heard. It was powerful, and it had a pull that Heath's did not. A dim light appeared, and slowly things started to come into view. As my vision became clearer, the sounds of the forest surrounded me. I saw Tivon standing above me as I lay in Heath's lap.

"She's back," Heath proclaimed.

He brushed the side of my face methodically as a person would love a pet absentmindedly. I admired the red specks that glowed within his purple irises. I wondered if that was a reaction to a certain emotion.

"Welcome back," Heath whispered.

"Thanks, I think." I didn't want to leave Ashe, but I could feel I was in danger. The scream I had heard was Ashe's and something I never wanted to hear like that again. I could only imagine what they had done to extract that sound from him. It haunted me. The image of him lying lifeless infuriated me. My cheeks got hot, and I knew they were bright red.

"What's wrong, my child?"

I wasn't ready to tell them about Ashe. They were already shutting me out from information, and this would only push me further out of the circle. "I heard someone screaming. It distracted me. And then Heath pulled me back. It was too soon. I need to go back." I sat up and started to ready myself.

"You're not going back in!" Heath ordered. His voice was sharp.

I gave him my best death glare. "She needs me."

Tivon jumped in, "And we need you. Your breathing became...unsettling. We will try again later."

When Tivon spoke, everyone listened. There was no arguing with him. I wanted to, but I was still playing by the rules. Something I wasn't sure I could do for much longer. If Ashe were alive, I would save him. I would save them both, even if it cost me my relationship with Tivon.

I didn't want to admit it, but I was exhausted after my metaphysical jump. I went straight to bed after they took me home. I felt better as the sun rose the next day, but I was starting to feel different. Whatever the ascension had kick-started, it was pumping through my veins more ferociously as the full moon closed in. Time moved slower here and so did the moon phases. At home, the moon had a twenty-eight day orbit. Here, it was much longer. I wasn't even sure if it was on a regular cycle, but the tension that built inside me with every sunrise told me it was getting close, and something was telling me things were about to get more complicated.

A few days passed with no progress toward finding Sage. The elders were around the house so much it was almost as if they had moved in and always talked behind closed doors. Tivon filled me in on the details every night, but I still wasn't invited to the meetings. I was restless. I needed to get away. I needed to be alone.

I was sitting on Amary's floor playing tic-tac-toe with her. She was so creative. Instead of drawing the table onto a piece of paper, she made a board out of sticks she painted bright pink and tied together with peeled strings of bark. She collected rocks to use as markers.

She was beating me, mainly because I was so distracted by my thoughts.

"I won!" she shouted cheerfully.

She snapped me back to the game. When I looked down to congratulate her, the winning stone caught my breath. It was one of the malachite stones. "Where did you get that stone?" I was probably being silly, because for all I knew, these stones among many others could be everywhere, but I was starting to be a pessimist about coincidences.

"By the waterfall." She smiled.

"Can you show me?"

She nodded enthusiastically. "Can I see my mom again?"

"Sure, buggie."

We left the game untouched and set out on our well-traveled path to the waterfall. I hadn't brought Amary here since that day she saw her mom in the garden back home. It was a lie, but her heart showed her what she wanted to see, so I let it ride.

Somehow we managed to get away without an escort. Ever since Sage had been kidnapped, Heath had been on our heels. He did his best to keep his distance since his less than comfortable confession. I tried not to think about it. It wasn't hard now that I knew Ashe was alive, or at least I strongly suspected he was.

Amary ran ahead inside the waterfall cave. I knew she would be safe out of sight for a moment.

"Hurry up, Arie!" she yelled over the crashing water.

Before I entered, I walked around the entrance, carefully investigating all the stones. Most were ordinary river rock with some more unique brightly covered smooth stones, but I didn't see any other malachite stones. A screamed filled the air that had my feet sprinting and my blood pumping in a split second. I raced through the cave and found Amary staring at the cascading water with a blank stare. *Did the scream come from her?* I rushed up to her and grabbed her in my arms. She wouldn't break her eyes from the waterfall. I looked but saw nothing but mist, and then she went limp in my arms.

"Amary." I shook her gently as I held back the fear fighting its way to the surface. "Amary, wake up." I put my ear to her chest. Her breathing was shallow, but regular. I knew where she was. "No. No, Amary. Snap out of it. Come back. *Now*!" I kept shaking her gently. *How did Heath get me out?* I was starting to panic. I knew what I needed to do. I put her head upon my lap and caressed her cheek softly. *I could do this.* We were connected. If I just focused, I could get where she was. Just as I was closing my eyes, an image of River filled the mist. His back was to me, but I could feel his pain break through the shield that separated our realities. He stood up and turned toward me. He was cradling Starling in his arms. She was limp. "No, no, no. This can't be happening." I didn't feel any different. I couldn't have taken her essence. I didn't want it.

My thoughts froze.

My body froze.

I looked down at Amary. Her skin was emitting a soft glow now. Oh, no. This wasn't fair. How could this be fair? How could she live knowing Starling died for her?

She couldn't.

I cradled her limp body in my arms and stood and faced the waterfall. River and I looked like mirror reflections. We locked eyes. We felt each other. I knew he could see that Amary was the reason. I knew it would bring him some comfort, but not enough. He was alone. He loved Starling like a sister, as I did. Another loss to a greater cause still unknown. "I'm sorry," I said aloud, not knowing if he could hear me.

He bowed his head to Star's forehead and kissed it. I half expected her body to be replaced by butterflies like Sierra's, but I knew better. She was like my mother. River would have to lay her to rest.

A surge of power blinded me and catapulted me into River's thoughts. I threw back my head and succumbed to his pain, his memories, all flooding me in rapid flashes.

River and Starling were in the back of her boutique eating lunch and laughing. Star began to cry, so River reached out his hand and placed it over hers. A spark ignited between them for the first time. River rescinded his hand and clumsily jumped up. He knocked over a soda can and cleaned the spill haphazardly with Star. Then he rushed out of the shop, leaving Star with a look of confusion and guilt.

It was dark, and River was standing outside of Star's apartment. He was pacing and shaking his hands nervously. He took a deep breath and knocked twice. Star opened the door and invited him inside. They sat on the couch at opposite ends and watched a movie as stiff as mannequins.

Star and River stood at my mother's gravesite for a few moments and then walked to the butterfly circle in the meadow. They sat down and talked as the sun set. Star cried again, and River put his arm around her for comfort. He kissed her head innocently.

It was pouring outside, and River and Star were running from our spot at the park to his car. He was holding her hand and trying to shield her from the rain. When they reached his car, she kissed him. The moment was suspended in time.

The power drained from me, and the images were lost, but the months of emotions between River and Starling remained. I felt their guilt, their nerves, their happiness, their love, and finally River's loss. In the blink of an eye, I was crushed.

The image of River holding Star was gone from the waterfall, and I was left with just Amary.

"Arie?"

Amary had woken up.

"What happened?" she asked.

"Nothing, buggie. Everything's okay. Everything's going to be fine."

"Can I see my mom now?"

"It's getting late. We need to get back. We can come back tomorrow."

"I'm really tired," she whispered as her eyes blinked heavily.

"I'll carry you. Just rest." She leaned her head on me and closed her eyes. My chest was tight. So tight I could barely breathe. It was taking all my strength not to break down. Not to mourn my best friend. Not to mourn for my other best friend. To stay strong.

I needed to be strong.

I would be strong.

Chapter Ten

I slept beside Amary that night because I didn't want to let her out of my sight. I didn't know what happened at the waterfall or how it would affect her, so until I knew more, I would stay by her side. Heath had questioned us when he saw me carrying her, but I just brushed him off. So much was happening at once, and I needed to decompress. Why would Amary need Star's essence? She was only five. I sank my head further down on the pillow.

I felt guilty because what was bothering me the most was the one thing I was trying to avoid thinking about. River and Star together. I should have been mourning the loss of my friend, but instead, I was replaying the brief moments River shared with me. In my absence, they had fallen in love. I shouldn't have, but I felt betrayed, and I hated myself for it. After what I did to him with Ashe and even before that. I had rejected his affection for so long that really it was only a matter of time before he moved on. I should have been happy it was with my best friend. They needed each other. Together, they would have thrived, and now River had to endure another loss. First me and now Star. How much more could he take? How much love could he lose? How much until life broke him? Or did I already break him, and Star was his salvation? And now she was gone.

When insurmountable pain consumes someone, it weighs down their chest so much that breathing is a struggle. Almost to the point where they just want to give up and let fate have its way. But I wasn't ready to give up. This was just another moment, and it would pass. I had to believe this was all for a reason. That all the loss would lead to a love unimaginable by the human soul. Too much for a human to manage. I wasn't human, though. I was more. I could handle it.

Enough was enough. I stormed into Tivon's office the next morning. Norinda was there with the gruffy-looking elder that I remember Tivon referring to as Lance.

"It seems my daughter has something to say."

Norinda was standing in the corner, and Gruffy was leaning on the desk. Tivon was sitting behind the desk.

"You can't keep leaving me out of this!" I was huffing like a child, but I didn't care. "Where's Heath?"

"He's out. And to be fair, you are keeping things from the elders, too."

He stared at me, as he would a defiant child. He had me on that. "Fine." I threw myself into one of the chairs. I knew which chair to evade now. "You first," I said.

"Norinda," Tivon encouraged.

She sighed loudly, not hiding her annoyance for my sake. "We think we might know how Pyrrhus is jumping realities and bringing back others."

I leaned forward. "Gemstones," I blurted out. Everyone stared at me, dumbfounded. "What?" I snapped. "Are you all shocked that I'm not as stupid as you took me for?"

"No one has ever thought you were stupid, Arie. You are seen as fragile," Tivon countered.

"Not helping," I responded.

Gruffy spoke up. "I think what he's trying to say is that we need to handle you with care. You're our only hope."

His words were short, but profound. I had been looking at all of this wrong. *I was being a child*. They were shielding me from the big bad wolf. I felt horrible. I made eye contact with Tivon and declared, "I'm sorry."

"It's okay."

The room remained quiet while we all digested what happened.

"Arie, do you have some things to tell us?" Norinda prodded carefully.

"Yes, I already mentioned that I have visions, but when we went looking for Sage, and I stopped to meditate, I projected into the room where she had been. It wasn't a vision. There were malachite stones planted in the walls around the room. Are you familiar with the powers that gemstone carries?"

Tivon answered, "We all know everything there is to know about nature and its power, so you may continue."

"I believe the power released by the malachite stones is making my memory of the room real again. It's hard to explain. Because I have a memory of that place and because it still exists, the stones are able to pull me into the room at any given time."

"So, what you're saying is you were there in present time?" Gruffy asked.

"Yes. Exactly."

Tivon paced nervously behind the desk.

Norinda addressed Tivon. "What is it, Tivon?"

"When Pyrrhus discovered he could use the stones to lure the dark ones here, he realized he could lure anyone anywhere."

I chimed in, "Not anyone. Me. He's trying to lure me. We already know he wants me, but we still don't know why."

"I do." Heath leaned on the doorframe.

He threw something at me. I opened my hands just in time to catch my mother's ring. I had never taken it off, but I did last night because I didn't want to accidentally scratch Amary while we were sleeping.

"They don't want Arie. They want that ring," he said coolly.

I sat on the back porch as I caressed my mother's ring. Everything was starting to piece together. It all happened so fast it was hard to process. This ring was more powerful than I had ever imagined, and in the wrong hands, it could wreak unimaginable havoc. It terrified me, but I was relieved that Amary was no longer a target. I knew gemstones were powerful back home, but it was mainly to ease mild psychological and physical pain. Here, it was so much more. Stones were highly coveted, but never a threat. Not until Pyrrhus, at least. In the short, intense discussion with the elders, I discovered the allegiance had been scouring the land collecting the stones. Tivon was the keeper, which made his leadership role that much more important. While they tried to keep the hierarchy at a counsel level, it was obvious to everyone that he was the top of the food chain and someone everyone respected and trusted with their lives.

I told them about the malachite stones in the walls of the cave or room or whatever it was. They all shared a look of understanding that was lost on me until Heath explained. The reason we couldn't locate the room was because it was under the protection of the stones. The only way it could be found was in a dream-like state. Something I apparently was the only one capable of doing. I was fine with it, but Heath and Tivon were less than thrilled. I think slightly enraged would be a better description of it with white knuckles and red faces.

I would be lying if I said I wasn't scared, but knowing everyone I loved was safe, with the exception of Sage and Ashe, was a huge relief. I knew a lot about the stones and their specific powers, which empowered my confidence. That and the rise of power within me that increased as the full moon approached. We had decided the best time to attack was the second day of the full moon. This would give my body a chance to absorb the maximum amount of energy and me a chance to recover since the transfer of energy was draining, and what I had recently discovered in the river, slightly painful.

Now that we had a plan in place, my thoughts went to River and the loss of my friend. He needed me. I wanted to be there for him, but I still hadn't been able to reality jump, and I knew Tivon would not show me with the tension rising.

The river!

I jumped up and ran around the house to the path that led me out of the village. I found the broken branches where we trudged our way to the riverbank. I followed it again, causing more damage to the forest and making a clearer path. When I reached the river, I halted. My heart was pounding. The pain the last time I jumped in here made me hesitate, but it was worth it. *I could do this.* I took a deep breath, closed my eyes, and walked bravely into the water.

The surge of power knocked me to my knees. I felt them scrape against the rock and then heal. The real pain came from within. It burned my chest and stung in my veins. I focused my thoughts on River back at the meadow. Everything was cloudy. *Dammit!* I wasn't trying hard enough. As if squeezing my eyes shut tighter would manifest my will, I did it, along with clenching my hands into fists. My nails dug into my skin, but the pain dispelled quickly as my accelerated healing kicked in. The current was strong and cold, trying to drag me down, but I had a secure stance in a fighting position. I was fighting with the water. What a silly thing!

I took another deep breath and let the painful memory of River holding Star lifeless in his arms overwhelm me. I couldn't tell if the mist of the water was soaking my face or if it was tears, but if this would send me home, I would endure.

The water stopped rushing, the forest sounds ceased, and my heart stopped. I was freefalling to the ground with no control over my limbs. *Were Pyrrhus and his crew taking me again?* This felt vaguely familiar, like the night in River's backyard when they had taken hold of me and were carrying me into the forest until Ashe saved me.

Ashe.

No! This wasn't the time. River. That's where I needed to be.

When the floating sensation stopped, my body buzzed to life, and once again, I had control. I hesitantly opened my eyes, worried it didn't work, but a part of me knew something had transpired because I was no longer surrounded by water. I opened my eyes.

I did it!

I spun around, soaking in the meadow, my house, and my mom's resting spot. Laughter filled the air, and I realized it was me. I was spinning and laughing and letting the sun warm my skin. The way it tanned my skin felt different here. It felt natural and real.

I was home.

River!

I ran to the house and up the porch steps. The door was locked. Of course, it was. I was gone. No one expected me to return. I wasn't exactly attire-ready to sprint to River's house, as I looked at my bare feet and sundress, but it would have to do. I jumped off the porch, skipping all the steps as I had done so many times as a little girl, but now it hurt. A pain shot through the bones in my feet. *Right!*

I could feel here.

I could feel everything.

A sly smile rose to my cheeks. When I ran over my gravel driveway, I laughed as the rocks cut my feet. It would elicit a strange reaction from anybody watching if I didn't live in the middle of nowhere. Nobody here to witness my strange behavior. Who knew I would miss feeling rocks cut me like glass?

By the time I reached River's house, I was panting hard, and sweat beaded on my forehead. I stopped a few feet from the front porch to catch my breath. I found myself feeling self-conscience for a second. I brushed down my dress and ran my fingers through my knotted, thick, dark hair. I didn't have to worry about brushing it...*what the hell do I call that place?* It just occurred to me that no one referred to it by a name. Maybe I would call it Neverland. I giggled to myself like a psych patient pacing a white padded room.

"Arie?"

His voice could still freeze my limbs and warm my soul. I turned around to face him.

"Are you really here?" he asked gingerly.

I still couldn't move. I was overcome with emotions. Other than my mystical visit, it had been so long since I was face-to-face with him. I could touch him and hold him. And I did. I jumped into his arms and cried. The tears caught me by surprise, but to feel and smell him again broke down every wall I had. He squeezed me tightly into his chest and held a fistful of my hair as he pressed his lips onto mine. It was so fast, but I instinctively reciprocated.

I was home.

It was hard to let go, but I slowly separated from his lips. We took each other in as time stopped for us. His eyes were still bright blue with floating specks of hazel, but something was different. Red spider veins cracked across the white plain. It reminded me that Starling was gone, and he was left alone. It broke my heart. He saw the shift in my eyes.

"I can't believe you're really here."

"Me neither."

"How did you do it? Did Tivon show you?"

"No, he has no idea I'm here. I didn't even know I could do it, but I had to try. I had to be here."

He sighed deeply and sat on the edge of the porch steps. He leaned over his knees heavily as if defeated by the world. I wasn't sure what to say or what to do. He didn't know that I saw his memories with Star, and I wasn't sure if I wanted him to know. I didn't want him to worry about how I felt about it. I just wanted to take care of him like he had done for me for so long. *It was my turn.* I sat quietly next to him and just listened to his deep breaths as his chest heaved them in and out. It was a soothing sound.

"How long do we have?" He broke the silence.

"I don't know. Tivon told me he was able to visit sometimes for only moments, while other times he was around for days. I'm new at this, so I can only assume not long."

He hung his head down. Seeing him like this was killing me.

"It's hard being here without you. Without Star."

I put my arm around his waist and rested my head on his shoulder.

"It's hard without you, too," I whispered.

I didn't know how long we sat like that without talking, but it didn't feel like long enough. The sun dipped below the horizon.

"River?"

"Yeah?"

"How long have I been gone?"

"Nine months and five days."

My jaw dropped. It had only been a couple of months in Neverland. He was counting my absence like my mom used to do for Tivon. I was hurting him. I didn't mean to, but he was waiting for me. He would always wait for me, like my mom did for Tivon. Remorse rushed through me and settled in the pit of my stomach.

"I'm sorry, River. I'm so, so sorry."

He looked up and studied me hard. "Don't ever be sorry. Ever."

Chapter Eleven

River and I stayed outside until the moon was well in the sky. Only when my teeth started chattering did he insist we went inside.

"Do you want something to drink?" he offered.

My mouth suddenly went dry, and my stomach started growling viciously.

He started laughing. "I see you have acquired a new talent."

I blushed. "I'm a little hungry."

"I can hear. Well, let's fix that then," he said as he handed me a glass of water.

I guzzled it down and went to the sink to get a refill as he threw together a huge Italian feast. It reminded me of the night he made me dinner before everything started happening. When everyone was still here.

"Are you okay?" he inquired.

He always knew when my mood changed. "I was just remembering the last time you made me dinner."

"Yeah," he said. His face reflected my nostalgic sorrow. He turned away and tended to the boiling pasta.

I wanted to catch up and tell him everything that was happening in my new home, but the silence was so comfortable and inviting that I saved it for another time. I just wanted to listen to him breathe and watch the slow movements of his body when he moved around the kitchen. I wanted to memorize every inch of him, every movement, and every unique mannerism that made up *my* River.

After dinner, we snuggled on the couch to watch a movie. It was one of my favorites. I wasn't even born when it came out, but I had seen it playing on TV once, and it instantly went on my list. I didn't watch shows much. My mom encouraged playing and reading over anything else, so when I did watch something, I really had to enjoy it.

"It's nice to see you haven't lost your love for *The Breakfast Club*," River said.

"Nothing could ever change that."

"What is it about these rebel movies that you love so much?"

I never really thought about it, but I did tend to favor the rebellious love stories, like *Pump Up the Volume* and *Grease*. The sappy love stories were kind of lame to me, but the ones where the main characters were trying to find themselves first and then found love always melted me a little. "I don't know. I guess I like when love finds the outsider. I feel like they deserve and need it the most."

I didn't know why, but my chest tightened, and tears fought to surface. Then River said it, and it all made sense.

"Because you feel like an outsider, Arie. You always have."

I scooted as close as I could to him, without jumping onto his lap, and rested my head on his shoulder. He put his arm around me and held me. Another thought surfaced and darkened my mood down another level.

"River, I know you loved Starling. I mean, more than just friends." I felt his body stiffen. "It's okay. I understand. She was hard not to love, and I was gone." He remained quiet. I wanted to say more, but I didn't know what. I knew he felt bad because he felt like he betrayed me, but he was also still mourning her, as I was. There was too much. It was too much, so I let the silence continue until he was ready.

I enjoyed the warmth of his body and the security of his embrace. My lids were heavy, and instead of fighting it, I allowed myself some peace, thinking it might be my last chance at it for a long time.

When I woke up, my head was in River's lap. His head was resting on the back of the couch. From the sound of his breathing, deep and rhythmic, he had fallen asleep, too. I listened to the gentle growl that rose and fell with his chest. I sat up gently and watched him. He was beautiful. This is how he looked before my mom died. He was just River, my best friend, not the protector. His breathing changed, and he rolled his head over to face me. I rested my cheek on the back of the couch and let myself get lost in his blue eyes. He stared back and smiled. I instantly felt transported back to the meadow in the butterfly circle where we shared our first kiss. When there was nothing but us and my heart knew he was the one. Before Ashe.

I reached out and caressed his cheek, the new stubble tickling my fingertips. I didn't expect what I did next, but I was letting my heart lead, right or wrong. I leaned in and kissed his lips. They we still soft and inviting like I remembered them. As my lips lingered and took in the memory of a lost time, I wondered if he would recoil, thinking of Star and Ashe or if he would give in to the moment.

When his lips pressed back, I knew we were both giving in and flying free. It was slow and soft and perfect. I could barely breathe as I inhaled the magic his energy had over me. My heart fluttered, sending tingles out like a tsunami. My hand slid from his cheek, down his jawline, and to the back of his neck. He shifted his body so his chest pressed up against mine, the kiss still sensual and innocent as he held my cheek in his grasp, not letting go of the hold he had on my heart. Something that was always out of reach, but slowly being reeled in.

A burning began deep within and made its way to the surface, breaking through the epidermis and searing my lips. The pain forced me from River's lips like a blow to the gut. As I floated backward in slow motion, I heard the distant pleading of River's voice. What he was saying was lost between his mouth and my ears. I drifted with the emptiness that surrounded me like a plane among the clouds.

I inhaled deeply, trying to catch my breath, only for my lungs to fill with water. Panic rose in my chest as the burning in my lungs increased. A familiar cold bit at my skin.

The river.

I was in the river.

As recognition finally hit, I forced my body to remember, too. The current was hitting my body hard as I shot open my eyes. I was fully submerged under the water, but my dress had tangled up in something that kept me from floating with it, the force of the river's anger slamming into me to free me. I needed air, but my face was just below the surface, and my dress was keeping me from breaking through. I tugged at it as hard as I could. I felt it giving as the fabric started to tear, but I was already losing strength. Any moment I would lose consciousness. I mustered all the strength I had left and pulled hard. The fabric ripped free, and my head bobbed to the surface. I sucked in a deep breath. The burn of life in my lungs hurt but came with a sense of relief. I waded to the edge of the river and found my footing on the rocks and climbed out. My energy quickly restored as my last limb left the water's grasp. I watched in disbelief as the current calmed instantly to a light drift. *What happened?*

"That was stupid, you know."

I looked back to see Norinda leaning on a tree with her arms crossed. Her confident stance irritated the crap out of me. "Thanks for your help," I shot back at her.

"You looked like you had it under control."

Jerk.

She pushed herself off the tree. "Besides, you're supposed to be the most powerful one here. Why would I think you needed help from little old me?" she said mockingly.

"Whatever." By the time I stood up, I was dry, as if the river trying to swallow me whole had never happened.

"No, but seriously, that was really careless. With the amount of natural energy a current of water produces, you should know better than to mix it with whatever is juicing through your veins."

I hated that she was right, but I was desperate. I needed to see River. I needed the affirmation that our connection was still there even with the distance that existed between realities. "I know," I grumbled under my breath.

"Look. I get that you miss your friends, but you have a little girl who needs you, and doing stupid crap like that—"

I jumped up and cut her off, "Don't tell me what Amary needs, and don't assume you know the first thing about my friends or me!" I yelled. I could feel a storm building within me. "I'm here. I'm here for you and Tivon and everyone else. I'm here because you needed me with no choice of my own. My mom died because Tivon chose her to carry a burden she never asked for. I'm here while all my friends, while everyone I love is slowly taken from me because *you* need me. So, don't tell me anything! I am here!" I stomped past her, clipping her shoulder with mine.

As I broke through the branches to find the path, I ignored the tingles of energy feeding me and silently sulked for the peaceful moment with River that was ripped from me by the natural pull of this place. It had sunk its claws deep into me and wouldn't let go without a fight. It needed me as much as everyone else did. All I wanted was to go back to River, but I knew that life was over. It was time to face the facts. I was no longer a stupid teenager barely holding on to life. I was their redemption, and in order to be the person they needed, I had to let go.

Let go of my mom.

Let go of Starling.

Let go of River.

That last thought of River ached a little, but I pushed it aside and hardened the shields around my heart, hope, and love. Anger flowed through me like the current I had just fought against. The fire within would be the only hope for balance again, so I let it spread. I let it take over.

I walked through the village with purpose, not making eye contact with anyone. I could feel energy seeping out of me, and so could they. I pounded up the steps to the house and shoved open the doors with a wave of my hand. It should have shocked me, but I could feel the power I had now. There were no limits. I made no attempt at stopping for anyone as I walked through the house past the elders gathered in Tivon's office to the backyard. I locked eyes with Amary chasing butterflies by the river. I walked up to her and took her hand in mine.

"I need you to come with me."

We walked quietly back into the house as I led her to her bedroom. When I let go of her hand, she jumped onto her bed and grabbed her giraffe and hugged it tightly.

"What's wrong, Arie?" she asked softly.

"We aren't safe here."

She gasped, surprised. We had been sheltering her from the truth for too long.

I continued, "You need to learn how to use the power this world has given you. I know you haven't ascended yet, but it's there waiting to be summoned, and I think if you concentrate hard enough, you can tap into mine and use it until your ascension."

"Why would I need it?" she asked more confidently.

I swear she had matured several years since we had been here. It wouldn't surprise me. Nothing here surprised me. Everyone seemed older than what they looked.

"I'm leaving, Amary."

The shock on her face pained me, but I had to continue. I had to be strong. "I'm going to find Sage, and I'm going to put an end to all of this now. I won't lose anyone else."

She crawled over to the edge of the bed where I was standing and wrapped her arms around my neck. "I know you can do it, too. I love you, Arie."

I hugged her tightly. "I love you, too, buggie," I said as I petted her hair. I pulled back slowly and absent-mindedly brushed her hair behind her ear as my mom had done so many times with me.

"I'm going to get us back home, Amary. This isn't our home. It never will be. I promise I will find a way. When all of this is done, I will find a way."

She returned the gesture by brushing my hair behind my ear.

She grabbed my cheeks and said, "I know."

My heart melted in only the way she could melt it. I would do anything for her, even if that meant giving my life. I gave her one last hug.

"Stay close to Heath, and remember whenever you need me, close your eyes, and you'll find me. I'll always be here. And remember what I said about using my energy. Don't even hesitate. If you're in danger, take it."

"I will."

I searched her eyes for any doubt, but found none. She had definitely matured quickly here. She would need it.

I went to my room and threw off my dress. I tugged on a pair of jeans and plain fitted gray V-neck shirt. I wiggled my bare toes, and after a quick glance of determination in the mirror, I left the house without a word just as I had entered. I got as far as the end of the village when a hand gripped my wrist harshly and whipped me around.

"Where do you think you're going?" Heath asked as he faced me with fire in his eyes.

I yanked my arm, but couldn't get his hand to let go. "Let go!" I said slowly so he felt the purpose with which the words were meant.

"No," he countered with just as much force.

We were having a standoff and neither one of us was yielding.

"You will let me go, or I will force you to let me go." I branded the words into his stare.

"Try it," he challenged me.

A soft growl I had never heard before escaped my mouth as I closed my eyes and concentrated on releasing his grip from me. He was strong. I opened my eyes and saw the fight his entire body was putting into his hold on my arm. The pain on his face should have affected me, but it didn't.

"Arie, stop," he gritted through his teeth.

I didn't respond. My arm broke free, and he fell to his knees, struggling for composure. I didn't know what I did to him, but it was damaging to say the least. "Don't try to stop me again," I warned.

I turned away and left the protection of the village and Heath.

Chapter Twelve

The full moon arose in the sky as I trotted through the forest looking for Pyrrhus. It would give me the strength I needed to defeat him, but it would also feed him energy. I stopped to gather my senses and let them lead me. As I shut down the noises around me, I heard a crunching of leaves nearby. I stayed still as it got louder. When I heard it right behind me, I whipped around, quickly swooping my arm in front of me and forcing back everything, including throwing down Norinda. *Great! Someone else trying to stop me.*

"Damn, Arie," she snapped.

"What do you want, Norinda? Why are you following me?"

She jumped up and brushed herself off. "Well, someone had to. I saw you take down Heath, so he was in no shape."

I felt a twinge of regret. "You should have taken the hint. Now go back."

"Look, Arie. I can see you're pissed, and you're determined to take down Pyrrhus, but it would be naïve for you to think you can take him down at the same time as all his followers. I'm not here to stop you. I'm here to help you."

I studied her for a moment. She was telling the truth. "Why?"

"'Why' what?"

I clarified, "Why do you want to help?"

She hesitated. "Because Pyrrhus killed my father," she

said bravely.

Dammit! I bit my lip and tried to keep a strong stature. "The night of the ascension?" I asked, bringing the flare in my tone down a notch.

"Yes." She held her head up high.

"I'm sorry." I wouldn't let the fault of her father's death weigh me down. Not right now. "Well, then let's go." I didn't need to look back as I continued. I knew Norinda was following closely behind. I shoved the guilt to the far reaches of my conscience where so many other things cowered, waiting for the moment they would be unleashed on the unsuspecting.

As I walked past Ashe's resting spot, I grabbed the dagger out of the ground without hesitation or an explanation to Norinda. I heard her gasp behind me, but I ignored it. The butterfly flowers immediately wilted. When I handled the dagger before, it had burned my skin, but now it felt cold against my skin. I shoved it into the back of my jeans as I moved forward, keeping my emotions at bay.

My ring started glowing slowly, and with every step, it accelerated. It was leading me to Pyrrhus. I knew it was senseless letting my fury lead me, especially without a plan, but this was the first time I felt my true strength, and I now had the confidence to use it. *And the anger.* I had learned from my initial introduction to Pyrrhus that shutting off my emotions left me vulnerable, so instead, I would mask the pain with hatred and revenge. He was the reason all of this was happening. He murdered me, which resulted in so many deaths, including my mother's, River's parents, Starling, Amary's mother, Ashe, and Norinda's father apparently. It wasn't *my* fault.

I stopped abruptly, causing Norinda to run into me.

It wasn't my fault.

It was such a simple sentence, but distinctly insightful.

I had finally forgiven myself.

"Are you okay?" Norinda cautiously asked.

I ignored her and started walking again as I repeated the revelation to myself.

It wasn't my fault.

It fed my determination. I went from an agitated tigress protecting her cubs to a ravaged beast. I was unstoppable.

My ring stopped pulsing and remained brightly lit. "We're here," I announced.

Norinda looked around, unconvinced. "'Here' where? All I see is the forest."

She was right, but also blind at the same time.

"You're not looking the right way. Close your eyes and feel," I responded, as I did the same.

The sound of a squirrel nibbling on its acorn faded along with the buzzing of a grouping of bees. The only sound left was the nervous beating of Norinda's heart. Mine was surprisingly calm. My skin heated up while my thoughts diminished. I took Norinda's hand in mine and whispered, "Are you ready?"

"Yes."

She squeezed my hand firmly as the heat sizzled off both of us, and a light overwhelmed us.

"I feel like I'm floating," she muttered in amazement.

"Because you are," I replied.

At that moment, gravity settled back into our bones, and the light dissipated. The ground beneath my feet felt cold and damp, and the air was crisp and musty. I didn't have to open my eyes to know where I was. A gasp jolted me out of the last of my trance. Norinda dropped my hand and ran to a body on the ground. It was Sage.

"She's alive, but barely," Norinda informed me.

"You should get her back home."

"You mean *we*," she said sharply.

"I'm not finished here." I hadn't told anyone about Ashe. He was here, and I wasn't leaving without him.

"Then I'm not either." Norinda stood up.

"There are things here you may see that you won't

understand. You have to let go and just trust me. I'm starting to understand why I'm here and what I'm capable of. It didn't make much sense before, but it's starting to now."

"Like the dagger?"

I raised an eyebrow to her question. I wasn't in the mood to form sentences for my thoughts.

"I know the legends of the dagger. We all do, but are you aware that it's the only thing that can permanently kill one of us? It's not a toy, Arie. That dagger, and only that dagger, decides the fate of our essence."

I approached her. I must have looked intimidating or even slightly out of my mind for Norinda to step back. She was intimidating in her own right. "Why do you think I have it? I'm the only one strong enough to take on Pyrrhus, and I plan on plunging this dagger into the vacant space where a heart should be. No mercy."

"All I'm saying is if it gets into the wrong hands—"

"I understand," I interrupted her. There were consequences in life you faced for actions you could never take back, but sometimes the risk was a necessary burden.

"How do we get out of here? The room looks solid." Norinda expressed her apprehension as she surveyed the rock-tight room.

"The malachite stones are veiling the door. The stones are blurring the lines between reality and dreams. Just imagine the door as being real, and the power of the stone will be broken. This hideout, this place isn't in some mysterious corner of the land. It's right outside the village. Pyrrhus is using the stones to mask it within a dream-like state. You can break the veil if you see past reality and into the realm of the dream world. It's brilliant, really. I don't think any of you realized how much power gemstones could have if put together like he has done. These walls are covered in malachite stones, as I imagine the rest of the place is."

"I wonder what other stones he has." Norinda sounded fretful.

"I don't know, but what I do know is I have the most powerful one," I lifted my ring that was still glowing as I continued, "and I have the dagger. I know how the gemstones work. This ring can absorb the power of any gemstone. That's why he wants it so badly. If he has this, he will be unstoppable."

"I don't get it. I've seen that stone before. It's not like it's the only one."

"I thought the same thing until I realized the combination of the diamonds and my mom's essence makes it one of a kind. She had to die in the ascension for her essence to survive within this ring, giving it the strength of a thousand gemstones. Tivon made this ring for my mom, knowing that if anything ever happened to her, she would always live on inside it. Like me, he wasn't willing to let our essence join the natural state of the universe."

"How do you know all of this?"

I turned away from her, shielding the pain on my face. "I saw it," I said quietly.

When I caught the ring that Heath tossed to me, it burned in my hands. The burn numbed my senses until I was no longer in the office with the elders. Tivon was in the center of a dark room lit only by the glow of beautiful gemstones of every variety in jars placed on shelves. He was sitting on a stool, leaning over a wooden carpentry table. The room smelled like him. A gentle musk that attracted my sense of smell. I walked around the table to see what he was doing. He was setting an opal into the center of a circle of diamonds on a band. I couldn't see his face, but a tear landed on the table, spreading outward and then was absorbed by the wood. His hands were shaking slightly. When the opal was set, he tightened the prongs and lifted it to admire it. His face was broken, and his pain radiated stronger than the glow lighting the room.

This was is it.

This was the moment he realized Ariana was going to die.

He put the ring into a simple cloth pouch and squeezed it

safely into his fist. I watched as he looked at the gemstones around the room. Aside from the pain I felt from him, there was an immense amount of guilt. He had been entrusted with the stones, and he was violating that by making this ring. A ring that would keep my mom with him forever.

With us.

"Arie?"

Norinda touched my shoulder, and I was instantly back in the center of chaos, rage, and hurt. I wanted to kill him. It singed the fibers of my core. I wiped away a tear and answered blankly, "I'm fine. Let's go."

We walked past Sage who was still in a coma-like state on the ground. I spun around to face Norinda. "This room is our way out. Whatever happens, get back here, and take Sage. Just remember this is all a façade. We are in the forest outside of the village. Close your eyes and imagine it, and you will be there. Don't wait for me! Got it?" I barked.

"Got it, Arie. Now back off. I'm not the target."

She was right. My rage was blinding me. "I'm sorry," I said as I spun back around and walked through what looked like a wall. As soon as I broke the mirage, Norinda followed me. We were inside a structure made of stone. The walls and floor were cold to the touch, and it smelled musty like the room Sage was in. It was dark and quiet, but not a normal silence. It was stale. We walked slowly along the wall. I could only see a few inches in front of me. After a few minutes of walking in complete darkness, I spotted a faint glow ahead in the distance, allowing me to make out the area around us. We were walking through a tunnel.

Norinda whispered, "Do you ever wear shoes?"

"I don't need to, and the more exposed I am, the easier it is for me to get the energy from things."

"You really are an anomaly, Arie. Thank you for helping us."

All her tough walls lifted to show me a frailty she had probably lost long ago. It should have warmed me to hear that, but instead, it stung. Her statement had left me as the outsider once again. Only here to help, and then what? Leave?

Yes, I wanted to leave.

As we approached the light, faint voices could be heard coming from somewhere. I had two goals.

Find Ashe.

Kill Pyrrhus.

In that order.

We reached a staircase that spiraled up out of sight. The gemstones in the wall lit the way. We climbed vigilantly as it spiraled around twice. The top was open and illuminated by the moonlight. This looked more like a house than where we were. A grand house at that. The staircase led to a vast open ballroom furnished with old world couches, coffee tables, and lamps.

How cliché.

The floor was still the rough natural concrete as downstairs, or I guess, it was the basement. I confirmed the only light was from the moon pouring through the skylights that spanned the entire length of the room. *Smart.* There were two exits to the room. One on the right and one on the left.

Norinda was beside me now. "I know what you're thinking, but I think it's a bad idea, Arie. I don't think we should separate."

"It would take too long if we didn't. The moon is almost at its highest peak. We need to get out of here before then." I was confident that Pyrrhus was no match for me, but I didn't want to risk Norinda's life. Everyone would be juiced up to the max.

Her lips pursed, and her forehead wrinkled in frustration. "Fine, dammit, but you better not confront him. If you find him, then come find me first. Got it?" she retorted.

"Likewise," I replied. I wasn't looking to pick a fight with Pyrrhus until I found Ashe, but I wasn't going to tell her that.

"Which way do you want to take?" she asked.

I pointed to the far corner on the left. I could feel Ashe's energy screaming since we arrived here. I knew he was that way.

"Okay, then. Good luck, Arie. I'll meet you back here before the moon peaks."

She took off jogging through the other doorway. She was graceful, so her footsteps in those heavy boots were barely audible. "Good luck," I whispered after her.

I paused for a moment and inhaled a deep breath as I gripped the dagger for reassurance. It was still cold to the touch. I traced the engravings meticulously and then pulled it out and made my way across the ballroom. I was quiet, but nimble. The excitement of seeing Ashe again was escalating. I had missed him so much, and it hadn't really sunk in that he was still alive. To be honest, I wasn't sure what I saw was real, but I could feel him, and that couldn't be faked. Not with us.

My ring was pulsing again, and my need to find Ashe was barely containable. I listened as I quietly entered a hallway. I could hear voices echoing from somewhere, but I ignored them. All I was following was the instinct in my gut telling me Ashe was alone and needed me. The hallway was dark, but illuminated by more stones. They weren't malachites, though. They were diamonds. *Herkimer diamonds.* I was awestruck. I had to stop to touch one of them. I had read about them, but I had never seen one. In fact, my mom told me they were impossible to locate. She was a gem collector and tried for years to track them down. She also said they could be dangerous.

I looked down at my ring. *Were these Herkimer diamonds?* They looked like regular quartz diamonds in small sizes because quartz are cut and formed like a Herkimer. It would be easy to confuse them, but Herkimers were naturally perfect in shape no matter what size, and these were large. They had eighteen facets and two points. Quartz diamonds had to be cut; otherwise, they would look like a clump of glass-like rock. The naturally occurring flawlessness of the

Herkimer diamond was a mystery. Their cores were soft and held an unparalleled power. The natural double points made it a super power gem, and alongside the opal with its own super power...the thought of that much power resting on my finger made me shudder.

I took in the extensive hallway. There were so many diamonds. How did Pyrrhus find this many? And where? This should have knocked down my confidence a few notches, but it didn't. It was unwavering with the thought of Ashe. I continued down the hallway, passing one closed door after another and listening to each one before moving on. Some of the openings didn't have a door and led to other parts of the house, but my ring kept me on this path. As I reached the end, I became discouraged. It was a dead end, but Ashe's energy was strong where I stood. I closed my eyes and shut down my senses.

He was here.

"Arie."

My eyes shot open, and the dead end that stood in front of me disappeared and revealed Ashe sitting on an old twin bed. One that could be found in a prison cell. The room was a stark contrast to the rest of the house. It was plain and small.

As I stared at him, fear settled in my bones. I tried to hide it, but couldn't anymore. I was scared he wasn't real. I was afraid to get my hopes up, only to find out this was a trick. So, my hesitation was founded, and my feet remained plastered to the floor.

"Arie, it's me." His words were exhausting him.

"I just...I saw you die, Ashe. You died in my arms, and then your body turned into butterflies. This place hides a lot of secrets, but it's hard for me to believe you're really here."

"Then don't take my word for it," he said as he stood up.

My heart skipped a beat. He was coming toward me. *He was going to touch me.* I had spent countless hours remembering what his touch felt like. How it sent tingles throughout me. How my core burned. It had kept me from moving forward.

His walk was wobbly as he stumbled over. He had been hurt. I met him halfway. "You shouldn't be walking. You're hurt." His face was shielded by shadows before, but then he stepped into the light from the hallway. His eyes had lost their glow, and his face was pallid and sunken. "What did they do to you?" I was horrified.

"Nothing. I was dead, Arie. This is what happens when you're brought back from the dead and not fed energy. They have been starving me of it. Keeping me locked up in here."

We were only a few feet apart now. My skin was sizzling so damn hot now that I could feel the perspiration building on my face. My breath was getting shallower and my vision foggy.

"Arie, you can't be here. Look what I'm doing to you," he said, distraught.

"What are you doing to me, Ashe?" I asked. Or did I say it in my head? I was having a hard time focusing.

"My body needs energy, and you're juiced to the max. It's stealing it, and it'll take it until you're drained of all of it. You have to go."

"No." I tried to collect myself to stand firm. "I'm not leaving you here. I thought I could live without you, Ashe, but I can't. I can't live, so take it." I launched at him before he could move out of the way. I latched on to his arm, and as soon as we connected, sparks flew. I heard a scream of pain and realized it was me, but I wouldn't let go.

I would never let go again.

I was losing consciousness. The light that surrounded us was different. It swirled with a rainbow of colors. My energy started to return along with my vision. I looked up and stared into the amber glow I had missed. Ashe was holding me in his arms. I reached up and touched his cheek.

"You saved me again," I whispered.

"I don't know how you're doing this, Arie. You should be dead. This kind of energy transfer should have killed you."

"Do you feel better?" I ignored what he said.

"Yes."

"Good," I muttered right before I passed out.

Chapter Thirteen

"Arie. Arie, you need to wake up. Arie."

I could hear his voice. It was so beautiful and warm, but it was a dream. Not a dream, a nightmare. One that repeated in my head night after night. My stomach balled into knots so tightly that I would wake up from the pain and the tears.

"Arie, please, I need you."

My heart stopped. That wasn't Ashe's voice; it was Amary's. The fog lifted instantaneously as I jumped up. After a second, my senses returned, and I could see I was still in the room I found Ashe in, but I was on his bed.

"Arie, you're awake," he said as he raced over.

"Amary. She needs me," I sputtered out so quickly I was choking on my words. The familiar panic that started in my stomach was quickly creeping up to my chest.

"Arie, breathe."

Ashe sat next to me on the bed, but it wasn't lost on me that he was careful not to touch me. "You can't touch me. Can you?"

"No. I don't know. I don't want to risk it. I can't see you in pain like that again."

"I need to find Norinda and get back to Amary." I jumped up. I felt light as I landed on my feet.

"Are you sure you're okay?" Ashe questioned.

I looked at my ring. It had stopped glowing, but I knew it was responsible for protecting my essence while I gave Ashe what he needed. "Yeah."

"You go to Amary. I'll find Norinda."

I was torn. I had come here for Sage and him, and now I was leaving Norinda along with them. "Sage…"

"I will make sure we all get out of here."

He stood in front of me. I could tell by his dark irises he wanted to touch me. He wanted to give me that comfort.

"I'm sorry, Arie. I'm sorry I can't comfort you the way I want to."

"Don't be. Having you alive is enough. For now."

"Let's go. I'll get you to the stairs, and then I'll find Norinda. If Sage is still down there, take her with you."

"Thank you, Ashe. You don't owe me anything, and yet you're willing to risk your life again for me."

"When will you realize we don't owe each other anything? I love you, Arie. We were meant to be together, and when the time is right, we will be."

I soaked in the truth that emitted from his eyes. He felt what I felt. We were connected in a way that only made sense to us, and not even death could keep us apart.

I led the way back out of the hallway. My ring pulsed as we passed its sister stones and then faded again. The house was quiet. I couldn't hear voices anymore, which bothered me more. Nighttime was their lurking period. When we got to the grand ballroom, I observed the full moon was dangerously close to the highest point in the sky.

"You know it's the honey moon," Ashe whispered.

"What? Oh, no!" I had been so consumed with life here that I hadn't really paid attention to dates. The honey moon was a rare event, revered by those who believed in nature's power and the dates that made them gain or lose strength. The honey moon was a full moon that occurred on the thirteenth day of the month that fell on a Friday. It was also considered the most powerful full moon in the spirit community. "I have to get back to Amary. Something's not right."

I padded across the ballroom quietly and down the corridor that led to the stairway. I paused for a moment and turned to Ashe. "I'm sorry."

"For what?" he replied.

"She will always come first," I said shamefully.

"As she should."

He turned and disappeared in the direction that Norinda had taken. My heart ached, but I knew I would see him again. I ran down the stairs and burst into the room. It was empty. *Crap!* I had a moment of second-guessing myself, but I knew in the end I would always choose Amary.

I closed my eyes and concentrated on the sound of my breaths entering deeply and expelling slowly. After a moment, I felt the shift in my surroundings. I opened my eyes and was back in the forest. I didn't hesitate as I took off running. A scratching on my lower back as I moved reminded me that the dagger was still secured in the back of my jeans. I couldn't bring it back to the village. The elders would sense its power. As I passed Ashe's former resting spot that was now nothing but shriveled up blooms and dead grass, I launched the dagger into the ground without stopping.

I made it to the village in no time and picked up speed when I saw our house. I didn't even have to wave my hand this time. Just thinking about the door opening caused it to crash against the interior wall. After flying through, I was caught by a pair of arms and flung back. I tried to break free, but something was blocking my power.

"Stop struggling," Tivon said in a deadly voice.

I froze. He had never spoken to me like that.

"Are you calmed down enough for me to let go?" he asked harshly.

All I could do was nod my head. His grip loosened, so I stepped away and faced him. "How did you..."

"Suppress your power?" he finished.

I nodded.

"Don't you get it, Arie? You might be the most powerful

being here, but you aren't invincible," he scolded as he opened his fists to reveal dark blue sodalite gems.

I was speechless. I hadn't considered the stones that could disarm my energy. Sodalite stones were used to create inner peace by calming the energy and increasing the physical strength of the person in possession of them.

"You can't run off like that again, Arie. We have to assume Pyrrhus is in possession of every gemstone in existence. We can't be careless."

As the shock diminished, I remembered Amary. "Where's Amary?" The panic rose again.

"She's in her room with Heath."

I sprinted to her room and threw open the door. She was sitting at her little table coloring with Heath. I didn't understand. She called for me. "Amary, are you okay?"

She faced me and smiled, but I could tell there was more she didn't want Heath to know. I nodded in understanding. "Heath, may I spend some time with Amary alone, please?"

He glared at me. He was still pissed about earlier. "Thanks for letting me play with you, kid." He ruffled the top of her head and walked past me, grabbing my arm.

"We need to talk," he gritted through his teeth as he pulled me into the hallway. He slammed me against the wall. "Don't ever do that again."

His anger bothered me. It made me feel guilty, but I was determined nothing was going to stop me. I loosened his fingers on my wrist one by one. "I'm sorry."

"Fine, but you can't let yourself lose control like that again. It's dangerous. You're dangerous."

His words hit home. They were viewing me as a danger. *What had I done?* I had lost their trust.

"Amary started screaming out of nowhere. I found her pounding the bed in her sleep. She says she doesn't remember anything. I didn't want to leave her until you returned."

His voice had softened with the mention of Amary. He

cared for her. "Thank you. I'll talk to her."

He started to walk away and then turned back. "How did you know there was something wrong with her?"

I wasn't sure how to answer that question. I didn't want anyone to know how deep our connection was. I needed to keep it a secret for her safety. Not that I didn't trust Heath and Tivon, but I felt better knowing we were the only ones who knew. "I could just feel it."

He accepted my answer with a nod and disappeared down the hallway. I went back into Amary's room and shut the door. She immediately smashed into me and wrapped her arms around me. "What's going on, buggie?" I held her tightly. She started whimpering, so I knelt down to her level and took her in my lap. "Buggie, what's wrong?"

She sniffled and finally found her voice.

"There was an old woman in my dreams. She was trying to take me."

"Take you where?"

"I don't know, but I was scared, so I yelled for you like you told me."

"But you were dreaming?" I asked her. I don't know why I was so surprised. Dreams were a powerful way to communicate. I used the dream-like states to break through Pyrrhus' illusions.

"Uh-huh. She said she knew your mom, and she was taking me somewhere safe."

Chills ran down my spine. "My mom? Are you sure about that?"

"Yeah. And she had purple eyes like Heath."

What was she saying? I was so confused. My mom had never mentioned anyone but Sierra, Hudson, and the orphanage warden. She said she was like a mother once. Surely that couldn't be the same woman. But why not? Heath came to me as a fox. Was it possible she was put there to watch over my mom? If so, that would mean someone knew all of this was going to happen. That I would be murdered.

That my mom was special and would be the vessel to carry me into a new life. My head was spinning. All the assumptions overlapped and drowned out critical thinking.

"Arie, are you okay?" Amary asked as she stared at me.

The fuzziness in my head was making me weak. I felt like I was going to faint, but her voice helped me keep it together. Someone was lying to me, and the only person I could think of was Tivon. "I'm fine. Will you be okay if I leave you for a little bit? I can have Heath come back?"

Someone knocked on the door. "Come in." It was Iris.

"Can Amary play?" she asked politely.

"Amary, would you like Iris to stay with you instead?"

She beamed. "Sure."

I gave her a kiss on the forehead and left them to play. Her innocence returned when Iris sat down to color with her. I shut the door and leaned against it as I tried to figure out my next move. Ashe, Sage, and now Norinda were still in the hands of Pyrrhus, and I had just learned that my whole existence in both realities was planned out way before me. Then there was the old lady with purple eyes. Maybe I would start there. I needed to find out more, and Heath had to know something about her. I also needed to get back to Ashe, but I knew Tivon and Heath wouldn't let me out of this house, and now they had the tools to stop me. *Dammit!* I rolled over and pounded my forehead on the door. *What the hell was I going to do?*

"We really need to talk, Arie."

I scrunched my shoulders to my ears and shriveled at the anger in Tivon's voice.

"Follow me," he ordered.

When I looked up, he was already leading me further down the hallway past my room. I followed like a good little girl, for fear of seeing the true wrath with which he was capable of emanating. He led me into his room. This was the first time I had seen it. He always kept his door closed, and I wasn't one to snoop. Well, not in his stuff, at least.

It wasn't much bigger than my room, and it also had an adjoining bathroom. The colors were subdued with dark grays and creams. It was soft, but masculine. Sometimes it was hard for me to decipher between the two realities, because this one replicated so similarly. Tivon opened a door that I assumed was a closet. The clothes hanging in front of me confirmed my suspicions. It was a minimal amount. The shirts were all dark colored and plain. On the right there was a small shelving unit that held his neatly folded pants. If he weren't in such a bad mood, he would be chuckling at the sheer confusion written all over my face. I almost said something sarcastic when the clothes started to fade and one single step down appeared against the back wall. It was a reminder it was less than normal here. He turned on an interior light that illuminated the now empty closet except for the one step leading to nowhere. Tivon entered the closet and put his foot onto the step. This caused another step to appear.

"That's a nifty trick," I blurted out.

"It only works for me. It works off my essence. Now follow closely behind, or it will recoil on you. It doesn't like strangers," he said curtly.

He was referring to the steps like they were alive. I thought nothing surprised me anymore, but this was off-the-rocker strange. I carefully took my place on the step behind Tivon. My foot instantly sank into it a little. It was made of some sort of organic material, not solid. Now it made sense. It *was* alive. It doesn't make it any less strange, but I had to admit, it was kind of cool. It felt weird as it squished around my feet.

"It's not going to swallow me. Is it?" I asked playfully, but kind of seriously at the same time. Who knew!

"It might if you don't stay right behind me," he replied with a straight face as he studied my reaction.

I must have reflected my horror all over my face because his chuckle filled the air. "Are you messing with me?"

He stopped laughing. "Maybe."

He started walking again with no further explanation. Step by step the staircase appeared out of nowhere. If it weren't for the stonewalls secured around us, I would have been slightly less comfortable. At least I could hold on to a wall for leverage. The organic material of the steps was hardly easy to navigate.

As we went deeper, I felt like we were traveling through a tunnel. The steps led us sideways rather than up and down, although it still felt like we were descending. It was hard to tell with steps appearing only one at a time.

We walked quietly for a few minutes. I could sense by Tivon's tense shoulder stance he was still upset, but all I could think about was Ashe and the others in danger. I was afraid to tell him Norinda had joined that list.

"I know about Norinda, my child," he said without pausing.

"Of course, you do," I mumbled under my breath.

Tivon stopped. "We're here."

I looked past his shoulder, but only saw a wall. I frowned in bewilderment. "Ummm, okay?"

He touched the wall, and it faded away to reveal the gemstone room that I had seen in my vision. It was even more miraculous in person. My ring pulsed with excitement as I fawned over the pure beauty of the room. The multitude of colors the different stones emitted created a vortex of swirls similar to the Milky Way galaxy. The same carpenter wooden table and stool furnished the center of the room while the gems were protected inside the glass-enclosed jars.

"Why are we here?" I asked.

"By now I assume you understand the true power within that ring?"

"Yes."

"And you know that the real power comes from adding your mom's essence?" he inquired.

I had a feeling he already knew the answer to that. I looked down at the ring. The pulsing had stopped, but a soft glow remained. Thinking about my mom stirred up an ache that was trying to find the comfort of a cave deep within me. "I had a vision. I saw you...when you were making it."

"I was in a bad place. I had just learned the truth about your mom's fate, and I panicked. I didn't want to lose her. I know I broke an oath by making that ring, but I was desperate. I wasn't thinking clearly. Much like you today."

"I didn't mean to..."

"You could've killed Heath, Arie. Dammit." He pounded the table hard with his fist, causing me to flinch. "You, we, have no idea how powerful you are...what you're capable of. We don't know why you were prophesized to save us. We don't even know what you're supposed to save us from. You can't let your emotions rule you."

I interjected, "But you did when you made this ring for her. You did the most amazing thing by us. We will always feel her presence. She will always protect Amary and me. *This* was not a mistake." I was raising my voice near the end.

Tivon put his head down in defeat. "Yes, it was."

His hand had taken hold of my heart and crushed it. My eyes filled with tears. "How could you say that?" My lip trembled.

"Because that ring, you, are what cause the destruction of the fabric that keeps our realities in balance."

I shook my head in disbelief. What was he saying? My thoughts were muddled in pain and truth, and tears blurred my vision. My hands quivered as I tried to cover my face in shame. I fell to the ground as my knees buckled. Tivon raced over and put his arm on my back. I let him for a moment. I let him act like a dad. That was what he was, right? My dad. Someone who was supposed to teach me how to pump my legs on a swing, ride a bike without training wheels, fly a kite by the river, skip a stone, and protect me. *No!* He didn't get to pop back into my life after I had survived my mother's death and years without him. He didn't get to just be my dad. He had to prove it.

"Don't touch me," I gritted through my teeth. The fire was bursting every blood vessel in my body. He let go and took several steps back. "I won't be a victim anymore. I won't be the reason why people die. I won't be the reason this place falls apart. I won't take the blame. *You* are to blame." I pointed at him dangerously. "You shouldn't have stolen my essence when Pyrrhus murdered me. You shouldn't have tricked my mom into falling in love with you so she could be a vessel for my rebirth. You shouldn't have given her this ring."

"Arie," he pleaded.

"No! You are to blame for all of this. You should have let it be. Let me be. But *you* let your actions be guided by emotions, and now we are here, in this predicament. I have been beaten and torn down more than any normal child should be, and I won't let it continue. I'm going to do right by Amary and Ashe and Sage and Norinda and everyone here. I will fix this. By myself."

I didn't give him a chance to stop me. I spun on my heels and raced out the opening like a butterfly escaping a predator. I was moving so quickly through the corridor that led us to the room that the steps couldn't keep up, but I kept going. My feet floated above them, and I instinctively spread my arms to the side, and a pair of extraordinary amethyst wings appeared. They were *my* wings, and they were magnificent. The purples faded into hues of blues, and the black outlines of the patterning created an abstract geometric block pattern. Their wingspan was impressive and filled the blank space between the gem room and the world on just the other side. I closed my eyes, shut off the pain, and let go.

To fly was to be free.
To fall was to be real.

Chapter Fourteen

I wasn't sure how I landed at my childhood hiding place. I was flying through the hallway, and then it just vanished, and when I opened my eyes, I was here. I must have been in shock because I hadn't moved from the rock I sat upon for some time. The tingle in my shoulder blades remained with my wings.

Wings.

I had wings.

And they weren't just any wings. They were butterfly wings. I tried not to think of what I would look like to others. What they would call me?

A freak. I was a freak. I couldn't hide what I was anymore. I knew I shouldn't be ashamed. They all said I was special, but I knew the outsider culture, and this had publicly branded me.

I had hidden my head in my knees for so long my vision was blurry when I finally looked up. My thoughts had frozen in time back at the gem room with Tivon. I was empty. I had spilled everything I had been feeling, and now the dust was settling between the synapses that had dimmed after the confrontation. I felt naked. As the world became crisp again, I spotted a design on the bridge of my left foot. I traced it with my finger. It was the same nature spirit symbol that adorned River's T-shirt that I coveted, and it was now permanently tattooed on me. The wings and now the mark.

I was evolving.

I was like nothing they had ever seen. No one had ever spoken of a hybrid before. I had butterfly wings, the energy of a thousand nature spirits, and yet was still human to the core. I was the one who would destroy walls between realities, yet also be the only one who could replace them. How many knew why I was here? Why I was created? Is that why the elders glared at me? They knew I was the cause of imbalance? Who was the old lady with purple eyes haunting Amary's dreams? Why are there always so many unanswered questions? If they were just straight with me, this would be a lot easier, but they were hiding things from me, and there had to be a reason.

The large glossy foliage serving as my cover started moving unnaturally. I tensed. I had nowhere to run. As Sage peeked in, I jumped up. "Sage!" I wrapped my arms around her neck. "You're okay."

"Miss me?" She giggled with a twinge of guilt.

"You have no idea." Her presence was just what I needed right now. I pulled her into my spot. "Where are Norinda and Ashe? Are they okay?"

"Norinda went back to the village," she responded hesitantly.

"And Ashe?" I pressed.

Tears filled her eyes. "I'm sorry, Arie. He didn't make it out with us." Her head fell in shame.

"But he's okay, right?" She didn't respond. "Right, Sage?" I asked more forcefully.

"Yes, he was okay when we got out. Pyrrhus found us just as we were escaping. Ashe covered for us, but he never came out."

My mind and heart were competing as they battled through the possibilities. "I'm sure he's fine. Pyrrhus wouldn't hurt his own brother." I paused for a moment as I forced myself to believe it. "How did you find me?"

"I returned to the village. When I couldn't find you, I asked Amary. She said you were here."

How did she know? Our psychic connection must be growing. "Is she all right?" I asked, feeling the concern well up.

"She was playing with Iris out back. Why? Is there something going on with her?"

"What isn't going on? Everything is a mess! I'm just glad you and Norinda are safe."

"You're going to do something stupid again. Aren't you?"

She read it on my face. She knew I was going back for Ashe, but first, I needed to know what I was dealing with. I wasn't about to let fate be my demise. I could change things if I knew what I was up against. I could do things differently and write my own destiny. "Sage, I need you to listen to me very carefully." I inched closer to her.

"Okay?" She swallowed hard.

"I need you to take care of Amary and not question my intentions or actions. There's more going on here than the elders are telling us, and I'm going to find out what it is. The pieces aren't fitting together from the bits of information they are letting us be privy to. And don't trust anyone."

"What about Heath?"

Yes, what about Heath? My gut was telling me he was safe, but I also thought that about Tivon, and now I was questioning that. "Keep your trust at arm's length with Heath, okay?"

"Geesh, Arie, what the hell did I miss?" she inquired nervously.

"A lot."

I walked back to the village with Sage to find Heath. The sun was setting, but I found him out back watching Amary. I sat on the porch next to him. "I'm sorry about earlier."

"Okay," he replied.

His posture was stiff, and his voice was sharp. He had shut me out, again.

"I don't want it to be like this. I just—"

"What do you want from me, Arie?" he interrupted.

"I was just trying to..."

"'Trying to' what? Get in my good graces again, so you can give me the third degree? What do you need to know now? I assume that's why you're here?"

He hadn't even looked at me yet. He just stared out like he was watching Amary play. His words were harsh, but I couldn't argue. He was right. I was here for information, and shamefully enough was the reason why I was being so nice. "I guess I deserve that." I wanted to get up and leave. I wanted to give him that, but I couldn't. It was wrong, but time just wasn't on my side anymore. "You remember earlier with Amary?"

"Yeah."

Quick and to the point. This was going to be harder than I thought. "She told me she had a nightmare."

"That's not abnormal for a child, Arie."

"No, but it was what the nightmare was about that bothered me."

"Fine, I'm playing. What was it about?"

"An old woman was trying to take her."

"That's it? Why would that upset her so much?" he inquired.

"She had purple eyes like you." I watched him for any sign of a reaction. The muscles in his shoulders had tightened slightly, and his jaw clenched. He knew her. "Do you know her?" I asked carefully.

His muscles relaxed, and he hung his head down. "I have an idea."

I waited for him to lead the conversation. I didn't want him to feel like the only reason I came around was to pump him for information. I really did like him. He had a tough exterior, but he had watched over me and was now watching over Amary. He was more of a protector than Tivon ever was. He was like a brother to me.

"If I'm not mistaken, it's my grandmother."

I was stunned into silence. I didn't know what to say. His clan was basically extinct. Was his grandmother one of the last survivors? And if so, was she Amary's protector? I knew this was hard for him to divulge. I had tried to ask him about his family once, but I lost the courage. I knew how painful it was to talk about my mom and the others I considered family, so I didn't want to drudge that up for him, too.

The sun had fallen below the horizon as we sat there in silence. I was thinking about my mom, and he was probably thinking about the family he had lost. It was a comfortable silence that we both needed. Amary had run inside when it got dark, and Iris went home. It was just the two of us.

"Do you want to talk about it?" I finally asked.

"There's so much, Arie. I wouldn't know where to start," he said dejectedly.

This was the first time he had shown me his vulnerable side. He was letting me in. He needed me, but not like the others needed me. They needed me to save them. He needed me to heal him.

"Why don't you start with your grandmother?"

"Can I just show you?" he requested.

"Sure, but that might be more painful for you. You'll be reliving whatever you show me."

"I know," he said defeated.

When he looked at me, I noticed the rawness in his eyes. He was tired, and it looked like he was almost out of fight. "Are you sure?"

"I'm sure."

I turned toward him as he did the same and placed my hand gently upon his cheek. He closed his eyes, and the kindness of his essence filled me. He nestled into my hand and placed his hand over it. I didn't know if I would ever see him this placid again.

A blood-curdling scream shrouded me, blinding my thoughts. When the terror in my bones ceased, I found myself in the middle of an unknown village in a forest that looked similar to the forest that surrounded the nature spirit's village, only less modernized. It was simple, with wood structures that all replicated each other. The only difference was the color variation of each door. The structures were small, maybe equivalent to a two-bedroom one-story house, and they blended into the forest butting up against trees. It looked like a peaceful place to live, but then I saw people hidden under cloaks emerging on the village. There were so many. All I could see was darkness swirling around the houses. More screams filled the air. Women, children, and men were being seized. I caught a glimpse of a younger boy about ten years old hiding within a hole of a tree. As I moved closer, his purple eyes caught my attention. It was Heath.

More screams tore me from the little boy. Some of the protectors were able to escape in the forest, but not many. When I looked back at Heath, the older woman was pulling him out of the tree. She stopped for a moment and made eye contact with me. I was startled. I peered behind me to see if there was something else she might be looking at, but there wasn't. When I returned my direction, they were running into the forest.

The village was empty within minutes of the attack. Either people were taken or they fled. The only thing left was the insurmountable fear that suddenly hit me like a punch in the gut. No, no, no. Babies crying, kids shaking, women trying to protect their little ones, men trying to protect all of them. I felt all of it. It was too much. My hands were shaking, my face was wet with tears, and my heart was broken. How could anybody do this? How could someone take children? I balled over and tried to control all the chaos that consumed me.

This wasn't real. This wasn't real. This wasn't real. This wasn't real.

The flood of emotions stopped suddenly, and my stomach settled. I opened my eyes and focused on Heath, who was still sitting across from me with his hands gripping his knees, revealing the whites of his knuckles that told the story of his childhood. The pain in his eyes could crush walls made of steel. My heart crumbled like a stale cookie. I wanted to reach out and take him into my arms. Be *his* protector, but I couldn't. Our relationship was undefined, and this wasn't the time to assault susceptible emotions.

I was scared to say anything. He had just let me into the hardest moments of his life, revealing his scarred soul. What do you say to someone after that? 'Hey, it's going to be okay?' or 'I'm sorry for your loss'. Or even better, 'It'll get better with time'. They were all equally awful clichés, and there was nothing cliché about what he went through. His scars were still pink. There weren't enough years in a lifetime to turn them white. So, I stayed quiet and waited. Waited for the horror to fade from the glaze over his eyes. And then he spoke.

"It never gets better. Does it? I see it in your eyes."

He searched my eyes for hope that I wanted so badly to give him, but mine had drained from me so long ago I didn't know how to put up a façade for him. "I'd like to think it will," I said softly.

"But you don't believe it," he pressed.

One stab to my heart.

"No."

"I didn't think so."

The protective beauty in his heart faded a little.

Second stab to my heart.

"Will you ever love me like you love them?"

His question tackled me from left field. I stumbled to expel thoughts, but they wouldn't formulate into coherent words. An awful gurgling spilled out instead.

"It's okay, Arie. I get it. I understand. I've always known. One owns your heart, and the other has your soul. There's nothing left for me."

Third stab to my heart.

"I, uh, Heath, I don't know what to say right now. I'm sorry." A cliché. *Figures.*

More silence.

Only now it was filled with tension. The smart thing at that point would have been to walk away from the situation, but I still needed to know things. "Is your grandmother still alive?"

"Yes, she lives secluded in the forest."

We eased back into a somewhat normal conversation for us. "She protects Amary. Doesn't she?"

"Yes, but she also protected your mom."

My stomach dropped to the floor with the mention of my mom. I wondered if that would ever change. "How? Really? Did she ever talk about her?"

"We weren't allowed to talk about the ones we protected. We weren't even supposed to identify whom we were assigned. It could compromise their safety."

"But she did. She told you?" I asked eagerly. I didn't know much about my mom's younger years, and this was a window into the past.

"She loved your mom. It was hard for her to watch her grow up knowing she was being raised as a sacrifice. It made her mad. I overheard her arguing with my grandfather about it a lot."

It was nice to hear she loved my mom. "What is your grandmother's name?"

"Malin, but everyone called her Mali."

"That's pretty. Why does she stay hidden? I would love to meet her."

He hung his head. "You'll never meet her. She's ashamed for not doing more for your mother. She tried to save her from her fate once. My grandfather stopped her."

My eyes perked up like a puppy's ears hearing the mention of a dog treat. "What did she do?"

"I'm not sure. She didn't talk about it, but she changed after that. She wasn't the carefree grandmother she once was. She started wearing a mask of disdain. She tried to take it off when it was just the two of us, but it didn't matter. She changed."

I found myself feeling sorry for her, even though I didn't know who she was, but she loved my mom enough to be affected by her death in a way very few understood.

"How did she get assigned to Amary if she stayed hidden?"

"She requested her. You were already assigned to me, but when Amary was unexpectedly conceived, she wanted to try to make it up to you and your mom for not saving her. They granted her the request because they knew how passionately she would protect her. They knew she would give her life for Amary, and that's what was required with both of you. After what happened at the village, many weren't as willing to be protectors of that caliber because they had their first taste of despair and death. They were no longer naïve. They were scared."

Having a look into Heath's life was sad, but inspiring. His purpose was to protect, and he did that with pride and without question. A shift was starting within me. Heath was more than just a man. He was a martyr. I didn't know what that would take from a person or what price a person would have to pay, but I imagined that was why he held up such a tough front. To protect his heart from bursting. To protect me. "Your grandmother sounds amazing."

"She is," he responded solemnly.

He didn't have to say it. I could tell how much he missed his family. It was concealed in the tone of his voice when he talked about them. "We need to find her, Heath. I need to know more about my purpose, and it sounds like she might know. My father won't tell me, and I have a feeling the elders are in on something having to do with it. I need to find out quietly."

It was pitch-black outside now. The full moon had passed, and the new moon had taken its place. This was one of my favorite times in the phase because I could see the flashing lights of the fireflies filling the space. It was mesmerizing. I let them serenade me as I waited for Heath to respond to my request.

"Arie, are you ready for the full truth? It might not be pretty," he finally said, unsure.

I thought about what he said. I knew he was right. In fact, I knew the truth was going to be ugly, and things were going to get messy. Why else would it be so well protected? People only hid dark secrets. Secrets that hurt. Secrets that would destroy a person or even a community. His question was more than valid. *Was I ready for the truth?* "I don't know, Heath, but if it means keeping Amary safe, then it's a necessary truth."

He studied me for a few moments. Normally, it would have made me uncomfortable, but I knew he was just trying to gauge my intentions. When he seemed satisfied with what he found, he watched the fireflies with me as they blazed swirling trails in front of us.

"Things used to be simple and peaceful here, Arie. You would have loved it." He penetrated the silence.

"I remember a little when I was younger here. It was lovely..." I trailed off. "I hope one day it will be like that again. I would love Amary to experience it. To feel safe and enjoy the true beauty this reality has to offer." I wanted to protect her from the evils of the world like my mom had done for me for so long. For sixteen years I lived in ignorant bliss. I wanted that for Amary.

Heath stood up and put his hand out for me. "Well, what are we waiting for then? Let's go find Mali."

A gleam filtered back into his eyes. He wanted to see her again, too. I reached out and put my hand in his. He felt safe again. He felt like River.

Chapter Fifteen

It was internal torture not to know what was happening with Ashe, but after seeing how it affected Pyrrhus when he thought he had killed him, I knew he wouldn't hurt him. Ashe was probably safer there at this point.

Heath and I decided it was best not to waste any more time, so I said goodnight to Amary, and we left in search for his grandmother only minutes after our talk. It was our first real bonding moment, and I doubted it would be our last. Tivon hadn't attempted to talk to me since our falling out, which I thought was best for both of us. I was waiting for the elders to descend on me after Tivon told them about my wings, but they hadn't, so I assumed it would remain a secret between us for now.

I told Amary about Grandma Malin. Then I asked her to tell Grandma Malin we were looking for her, if she appeared in Amary's dreams again that night. It was amazing to me how much Amary accepted and understood. She gave me a longer than usual hug before I left. It had me pining for quality time alone with her. I was the closest she had to family, and I wanted her to feel confident in that relationship. I never wanted her to question whom she could come to when she needed someone.

I looked back at the house before we started on our mission.

"She'll be okay," Heath reassured me.

"I know," I said, but I wasn't so sure.

"You may not see Mali, but she's watching over her. She always has been. She won't let anything happen to her."

I sucked in a deep, cleansing breath as if it would fill me with confidence and strength. "Let's go."

I followed Heath deep into the forest. It sizzled to life as I breezed past. I had never been this far from the village, but it felt familiar. Then I realized it was because of the vision he gave me. We had made it to his old village. Everything had changed and nothing at the same time. All the structures were there, but they spoke years of neglect. Probably left untouched since the raid. I wanted to know more about what happened, but I knew it was too soon.

Heath stopped in front of one of the houses. The past had grabbed him, and he was entranced by years of pain.

"Do you know why your village was raided?"

He didn't flinch. "Not fully. Grandma Mali told me it was because they were trying to stop a prophecy. You know what's ironic about it all?"

"What?"

"You didn't even exist yet." He shook his head in disbelief.

I felt small. My existence had caused so much destruction even before I was me. *How could I feel responsible for that?* I shouldn't, but I did. I slunk to the ground and sat on a tree stump. I had finally realized this was bigger than me. A destiny, my reason for being here, was in place, and nothing was going to stop it. "What am I thinking, Heath? How can I possibly stop the destruction of balance? How can I stop a fate that is written in the stars with a permanent marker? The only reason any of you know about it is because the wrong person found out about me." I could hear Pyrrhus' name scratching at my ears.

He joined me at the stump, squatted down in front of me, and pulled up my chin. "There's a reason we found out, Arie. Because someone had hope it could be stopped. Because someone believed in you."

My heart warmed, and I held back tears.

A crunching noise had us both on our feet and on high alert in a split second. Heath stepped in front of me and put his arm out protectively. It reminded me of how both Ashe and River did this with me, too. Did I deserve so much protection? Were they protecting me because they cared about me, or was it because I was the chosen one? Questions that would continue to haunt me.

An old lady stepped out of the cover of the forest into the village.

"Amary told me you were looking for me."

Grandma Malin was definitely aged, but still breathtaking. Her long, thick, silver hair hung down to her waist, and her matured skin was smooth and glowing. She was tall and heavyset with a thin smile, but she stood proud and strong.

Heath's shoulders relaxed, and he dropped his arm to his side.

"Hello, Arie. I'm Malin."

"Hi," was all I could manage. Her presence was slightly intimidating, but I knew she wasn't a threat by the way Heath was standing.

She walked up to him and put her hands on his shoulders. "Hi, Son."

Heath melted into her arms. She held him tightly as she giggled with remorse. I felt like I was eavesdropping on a private reunion, so I backed up quietly to the house that had Heath frozen in a moment. I assumed it was his childhood house. I went around to the front door and stared at it, still deciding if it was all right for me to enter. All the doors in the village were a different color to signify their ownership. Heath's was a deep turquoise. It felt warm and inviting, but the emptiness radiated off it. I placed my hand onto the wood before I reached for the handle. The physical interaction tingled the palm of my hand. *It was organic.* It fed me energy like a mother feeding her baby. I pulled my hand away quickly, feeling guilty for stealing an energy that didn't belong to me. I grabbed the handle and pushed open the door. It revealed an open room with no windows and two hallways on either side that led to more rooms. Much like Pyrrhus' house, the roof was wall-to-wall skylights, which would light up the room brightly by the sun and moon, both of which were absent right now so the darkness was thick. Luckily, my ring was emitting a soft glow.

A couch was pushed against the back wall, and a table lay on its side along with a couple of chairs, some with broken legs. Nothing had been touched since the day this village had been taken by storm. The fear still lingered in the air.

"Hey."

I spun around to face Heath. I felt guilty for invading his privacy. He looked past me and took inventory. "I'm sorry. I should have asked first."

He looked back to me. "It's okay, Arie. I haven't been able to come here since that day."

He had never mentioned his parents, and I didn't even know if he had siblings. He would talk about them when he was ready, so I decided not to push. Malin walked in behind him.

"We need to talk," she said as she closed the front door. She raised her hand and chanted something inaudible as she placed her hand onto it. When she was finished, we all helped pick up the room, so we had somewhere to sit. I sat directly across from Malin at the round table. Heath was closer to me on my right, so he could have quick access to the only entrance to the house.

"You look just like your mother," she said thoughtfully.

"Thank you." I smiled shyly.

"Did your mother ever tell you about me?" she asked.

Heath sat stationary and just listened. He was leaning on the back two legs of his chair with his arms folded across his chest. He seemed calmer and more at ease around his grandmother.

I shook my head at her question. "Not really, I'm sorry."

Unconvinced, Malin looked at me. "She never told you about the old lady that raised her at the orphanage?"

Recognition registered on my face. I had a feeling it was her, but I wasn't sure.

"I thought so," she said in response to my reaction.

She was Jenny. "She said your name was Jenny?" I was leaning forward across the table now.

Her chuckle occupied the room with much needed life. "That's right. The one and only, but here I am Malin."

"I can't...this is...unbelievable," I rambled. I was rendered speechless. My mom had told me *everything* about Jenny. She loved her like her own mom, and she said Jenny had raised her like she was her own daughter. Something wasn't quite right, though. My lip curled as I tried to put my finger on the problem.

"What is it, Arie? Your mother had the same look when she was trying to figure out something." Her chuckle had transformed to an amused giggle.

That's it! "Your eyes," I blurted out suddenly. "They aren't the right color."

Her giggle changed back into an infectious chuckle. Heath joined in. I looked at both of them dumbfounded. *What was I missing?* They didn't stop laughing, so I joined them. It was that delirious laugh people get when they're stupidly tired that ends in crying. It felt good to laugh like that again. Heath was laughing so hard he fell off his chair he was leaning back on, Malin's cheeks were bright red, and my face was drenched with happy tears. We had let the moment take us on a rare rollercoaster ride high into the sky where nightmares didn't exist. Once we regained our composure, it took me a minute to remember what had set us off in the first place.

"My mom had said your eyes were a rich maple syrup amber color," I stated.

"Your mom was right. We have the ability to change our eye color to disguise that we are protectors. Purple eyes are the trait of our kind only. We don't like for people to know what we are. I changed them for your mom because I don't believe any humans have purple eyes. That would seem a little strange. Don't you think?"

"Yeah, I guess so." I liked Malin. She was straightforward and kind. She treated me like her own granddaughter. I guess I kind of was in a way. "Malin, will you tell me what you know about me?"

Heath had made his way over to the couch after his fall. His eyes were closed, but I saw them twitch. He was definitely awake.

"Please, call me Mali," she requested. "I know more than most, but I don't know it all. Unfortunately, I learned it too late."

She glanced over at Heath. He still pretended to be asleep.

"He said you saved him," I reassured her with a knowing smile.

"I did, but I was too late to save his parents and his baby sister."

I felt the wind knock out of me and the knots in my stomach tighten as if opposing teams were playing tug-of-war. Did she just say 'baby sister'? I felt a panic attack coming on as I started feeling dizzy and breathing quickly thinking about Heath losing a baby sister. My cheeks became hot, but my heart pounded as anger took the place of the attack. I leaned over the table toward Malin and gritted through my teeth in a low voice, "What kind of person could kill a baby?" My cheeks were wet again, but these were tears of wrath, not weakness. I was very close to a blind rage episode. Malin placed her hands over mine, and I could feel the anger swim out of me immediately. I locked eyes with hers, looking for answers to what she just did. As if I asked aloud, she answered.

"I'm a protector of everything, Arie. Not just the physical."

It made total sense. Heath had tried to do this when I was enraged, but I had been too strong. He needed the stones to balance me.

"You're strong, Arie. Stronger than anyone ever imagined. That could work for us. Your strength will give us an element of surprise."

"What else do you know?"

"An innocent soul would be lost and reborn into the purest essence the universe has ever bestowed upon us, and she would soar through the sky with the wings of an angel, destroying the balance by the love in her heart and restoring it with a sacrifice of hate, pain, and betrayal."

I digested what she said rapidly. Everything had transpired from me dying and being reborn to flying with my butterfly wings. The next thing was the destruction of the balance, but she said I would destroy it with the love in my heart. How could love destroy anything?

"What else do you know about me?" I inquired.

She kept her eyes locked on mine. I knew there was something she wasn't telling me. She was protecting me. No, that wasn't right. She was protecting Amary. "What is it, Mali? You need to tell me." I was heating up again, my voice shaky. I was afraid.

"There's something you need to understand, Arie. That was the whole proverb, so there were a lot of interpretations of what it meant, which caused chaos. It's been known for longer than anybody remembers, passed down from village to village. You know we all have extended lifetimes, your father being one of the oldest. It was dismissed when many generations failed to see it unfold. And then you died and word got out about your rebirth. The few elders that remembered the fairy-tale proverb met and resurrected the possibilities of its truth. They started picking it apart, each coming up with their own interpretation. The lack of certainty started a domino effect of fear.

"Your father came to me when your mother was born and asked me to protect her. He knew she was the one that would carry you. He swore me to secrecy. No one else knew. I didn't question his request, because in return, he promised to help protect my family for his lifetime, and that was good enough for me."

Tivon *did* know everything and always has. Malin had confirmed my suspicions of his treachery.

"The elders couldn't decide if they should kill you or protect you. If you were dead, you couldn't destroy the balance, but they were afraid their actions would cause the destruction of the balance anyway."

"I don't understand. Their reasoning seems logical about killing me," I replied.

"There were so many uncertainties, and messing with fate is considered the darkest of evils, even above murder. They were fearful. But it was too late for my village when they had a pang of regret. They had raided it and tried to take everyone that would protect you and your sister. They realized their mistake years later. Only a few of us escaped, so they made Heath your protector, and then I volunteered to watch over Amary after your mother. I didn't trust anyone else."

Malin was practicing full disclosure with me. It was refreshing. I was tired of the secrets and questions. To be honest, I was exhausted not being able to trust anyone. There was more, though. I could feel the tension building. The swirling was stirring in my stomach, and goose bumps were making trails on my arms. "There's more. Isn't there?"

She broke her stare for the first time and took a deep breath. Whatever she was preparing to tell me wasn't easy for her. That much was obvious.

"They don't like that there are two of you, Arie. Two of you with the same powerful essence. They think they can control *one* of you."

I searched for the next words she was going to mutter, but I didn't need to. I knew what she was going to say. They were planning on killing one of us. Heath had sat up. He was actively listening now. He was hearing this for the first time.

"As soon as they discover who is the true chosen one, they will kill the other."

It was like she left a bomb on the table and had finally detonated it. I knew who the chosen one was, and so did Tivon. I had sprouted wings less than twenty-four hours ago when my anger consumed me as his lies started to unfold. And for whatever reason, I think Malin knew, too. I didn't know how, but if she knew, then others might also. We exchanged a knowing glance lost on Heath. "You'll keep Amary safe." It was more of a statement than a question.

"With my life," she responded.

Heath stood up. "And yours with mine."

Chapter Sixteen

The three of us stayed up all night plotting and telling stories. We had accomplished a lot. It was late, and we needed to energize for the morning, so Heath showed me to the bedroom that was his when he was little. Like the rest of the house, it was simple. The walls were white, and his bed had blue sheets. The only other furniture was a maple dresser across from the foot of the bed. There were no windows, but again, the roof was a skylight. It made me curious as to why our house didn't have skylights. We all fed off the sun's energy, so everyone had designed their houses for constant exposure. Except for us. *Odd.*

He didn't come into the room. He just stood in the doorframe. I felt bad for him. I knew how hard this was for him to be in his house again. He was going to sleep on the couch. He said it was because he wanted to stand guard at the door, but I knew the real reason. It was just too difficult for him. Something I understood. We connected on a different level tonight.

We knew the same pain.

I sat down on the bed and watched him absorb the memories of his childhood room. "Are you okay?"

He leaned on the frame and hung his head down. "Trying to be."

It was such an honest and raw answer. "Do you want to talk about it?"

He sucked in a deep breath. "Does anyone ever want to

talk about something painful?" he asked quietly.

"No, I guess not." I hated talking about my mom's death, but I loved talking about her and remembering her. Heath hadn't said a word about his parents or his sister. He was still closed off. Maybe one day he would be ready. "I'm here, though, when you want to remember them."

"Until this is all over at least," he mumbled.

That hurt. I knew he didn't mean for it to, but it did. He wasn't one to sugarcoat things. He just told it like it was. I went over to him and forced him to look at me. I put my hand on his chest. "I will never abandon you, Heath. We understand each other in a way no one else can. You're my friend. It might not be what you want from me, but I love you like family, and I will always be here for you. I'm not going anywhere." I rested my head on his chest. When he gave in to my affection and wrapped me in his arms, I sank into him. Being held like that made me miss River.

Heath whispered into my ear, "I'll take what I can get."

He kissed me on top of my head, a signature River gesture.

We stayed like that for a few minutes, and then he headed back to the couch. I slipped off my jeans and shirt and shimmied under the sheets in my bra and undies. I was exhausted, and once my head hit his pillow, I fell asleep.

My dreams plagued me with unclear premonitions. It was difficult to decipher any of them. River and Ashe were there, along with Amary and Tivon. Chaos ran unchecked, but the hardest part was the insuperable pain I felt. It was so heavy on my chest I could barely breathe. Pyrrhus was there, too. Laughing. I didn't know how to stop all the visions and emotions. I was spinning in circles, and then I shot up in bed, suddenly awake. The room was dark with the lack of moonlight. I wondered if Heath got scared as a child while he slept in a room so dark. I needed to sleep, but my head was too busy, so I just lay in bed and stared at the stars.

I needed to get the target off Amary. The only way was

showing them my wings, but I didn't know how they worked. They had come and gone on their own in my moment of blind rage with my father. I had other moments similar to that, and they didn't manifest. I didn't know what the trigger was, but I needed to figure it out. Yesterday, it seemed so much easier. Kill Pyrrhus. Now, it was more. This went deeper than him. The elders were being fueled by fear, and they wanted one of us dead. I imagined after I restored balance they would want both of us dead. Malin said they feared how much power we had.

They would never let us live.

My thoughts drifted to my fight with Tivon. It was more like a falling out. We hadn't spoken since it happened, and the degree of the exchange seemed almost impossible to repair. I was upset with him, but deep down, I knew his intentions were good. He just loved my mom that much. We both did. The more I thought about it, the worse I felt. I missed him. We didn't talk much, but just feeling his essence close by was enough. I missed Starling, too. I had been trying not to think about her death, but it was creeping into my wild mind now. I was hoping I would never need her essence, but it had never occurred to me that Amary would need it. My ring started pulsing, and the effect in the room was like a strobe light at a birthday party. Whenever it glowed, there was a purpose. Maybe it was mourning the loss of my best friend also. *Wait! What if the ring was the key to my wings?*

They were too big for this room, so I threw on my clothes and tiptoed down the hallway and peeked into the front room where Heath was passed out on the couch. Malin slept in her old room down the opposite hall. I imagined myself as light as a feather as I reached the door and slowly opened it. Once I slipped outside, I let out a sigh of relief. I wanted to test my theory, but I didn't want an audience. Not yet at least. I hoped they wouldn't be mad at me for keeping this a secret.

I went around the house facing toward the center of the village and sat down on a patch of grass. My ring had stopped glowing as soon as I left Heath's room, so it was dark again, with only the light of the stars. I had felt distant from nature because of all the mayhem, so my body relished in the moment of peace. My body molded to the ground, becoming one with it as the grass blades wrapped themselves around my toes. I could finally feel the energy from the light breeze that frequented this reality. It felt like little kisses from nibbling fish on my exposed skin. I let my long hair hang naturally and could feel it lift off my shoulders when the breeze kicked up from time to time. I rested my hands on my lap in a meditation pose and opened myself to the natural power around me. I knew the creek was close because I could hear a fairly large animal lapping up water. The water was calm as I heard only a light trickle as it navigated over rocks and pebbles. The leaves rustled, and the night creatures sang softly. I missed these moments. They were my favorite once upon a time. When life was simpler. When I was naïve to my destiny. I needed to do this with Amary more.

She needed this.

I needed this.

The thing about letting go and giving in to nature is relinquishing control over the mind as well as the body. Starling's mischievous smile was the first thing that popped into my thoughts. My memory had captured her perfectly. Her long blonde hair tumbled over her shoulders, and her crystal blue eyes smiled. Her lips started to move, but were muted. It reminded me of the time my mother tried to talk to me.

My heart jumped.

Like my mother.

I opened my eyes, and Star was standing before me. She was almost transparent, but she was there. My heart palpitated, and a shaky feeling filled my chest as I reached for her. She reached out her hand in unison. My ring glowed softly as our hands touched. We both looked at each other, surprised.

"Arie?" Her voice was unsteady.

"How...Star? Are you really here?"

Her presence solidified as the moments quickly passed, and then she was here. All of her. She was here. I watched as she studied herself in disbelief.

"Arie, is this a dream?" She looked at me for answers.

I shook my head. "No, Star, I think you're really here," I said, laughing and crying at the same time. My emotions were jumbled and out of whack. I was bordering delirium seeing my best friend again. My sister. Star was still patting herself down when I launched at her with a tackle hug. She screamed and hugged me back as we rolled around on the ground like little playmates again. She had joined me in my indecisive emotional delirium.

A sudden screech of shock from Star tore away the innocence, and I pushed off her as she looked behind me in what appeared like astonishment combined with a little bit of horror. I glanced back, and that's when I saw them.

My wings were back.

"Star, it's okay." How do you explain this to someone that's not from here?

She sat back. "They're magnificent, Arie."

I smiled. I could always count on her support no matter how much of a freak I was.

"And huge," she finished.

I couldn't help but laugh. They were huge. They could wrap around my entire body and hide me in a cocoon.

After we stopped giggling together, she inquired about her presence. "Am I alive here now?"

"I think so. That's what it looks like at least."

"Is this what happened to your mom?"

"No," I responded sadly. She had, but I had to choose between her and Amary's mom, Misty, in the ascension. Maybe now that both of them were gone, it made it possible for Star to be here. This just reminded me how much I still didn't know about this place or myself. Not knowing made me hesitant to put all my trust in Star's resurrection. I couldn't take losing her again, if this was only temporary. Something I would keep to myself.

She stood up and spun in place, giggling loudly. "Arie, this is amazing. I'm alive again."

I smiled to myself as I watched her enjoy her rebirth, but it was half-hearted. I wanted to give her this moment, this happiness even if it turned out to be false.

She stopped spinning and fell to the ground in front of me. "Does this mean I get to be here with you now?" she asked, gleaming.

"I don't know what it means," the voice of reasoning coming out, "but I'm glad you're here."

"Can I touch them?" She eyed my wings.

"Of course."

She inched closer and gently petted the side of the forewing, which was the top portion of the wing.

"They're so soft, and the colors are so vibrant," she said in awe. "Purple was always your favorite color." She looked at me and smiled. He smile faded as she studied my expression closely. "Are you okay?"

"I'm starting to be," I reassured her. She awkwardly took my shoulders in a hug, my wings making a full embrace impossible.

"Things are going to get better. They already are. I'm here."

She had no idea what was brewing, but she would soon find out.

She pulled back. "River needs to know I'm alive. Is there a way to tell him?"

Remembering their relationship and my last encounter with him butted heads. However, my love life, or whatever it was, took a backseat to the foreshadowed hell quickly approaching. "Yes, but right now isn't the time, Star. I'm sorry. There's a lot happening, and the best thing would be to get you somewhere safe before things get dangerous."

"What's going on, Arie?" Her innocent bliss stripped.

"It's safer if you don't know. It's frustrating, I know, but you just have to trust me for now. I want to keep you safe."

"I do trust you. I just want to make sure you're okay. You always take care of everyone else and forget about what you need."

"Thanks, Star. I'm glad to have you back." I wanted to say more, like her being gone crushed me and made it hard to breathe, but I couldn't. I needed to stay focused for what was about to come. I needed to be strong. For everyone.

"What are you doing?" Heath's voice was bitter.

My wings had disappeared before he saw them. I looked at Star and whispered, "Don't mention the wings to anyone, okay?"

She nodded obediently.

I stood up, pulling Starling with me. "Starling, this is Heath. I imagine you already know who Starling is?" I directed at him.

"I do," he responded.

Star looked back and forth between us. "How does he know me?"

"I'll tell you on the way to Tivon's," I said to her.

"I think that's the best place for her," Heath agreed. "And maybe on the way, you can fill me in on how she got here."

"Deal. Should we wake Malin?" I asked.

"She's already gone. She went to Amary."

The plan was in place and already in action. "Good."

Chapter Seventeen

This was the longest walk back to the village ever. My stomach was in knots thinking about the confrontation with Tivon and having to face him again. I knew he would be angry with me. I overstepped my bounds. He might have been my father, but he was also the superior of the elders and talking to them informally or inappropriately was forbidden. They were such a forgiving community I didn't really know if they actually punished anyone for anything, but I guess with their sweet nature, they probably had never encountered the situation before. Until me, of course. I was like the bad rebel teenager who turned everyone's lives inside out and upside down. I wasn't making myself feel any better. I wanted to prove I was mature like them, but in reality, I wasn't. Before I came here, I was a seventeen-year-old girl just trying to survive, living on my own. Now, more than a year had passed and I was the chosen one who would save everyone and was responsible for a five-year-old girl who acted more mature than me at times.

I started laughing.

Heath and Star looked at me like I was losing it, but I couldn't help it. Everything I was thinking would sound so ridiculous if spoken to someone in the other reality. I would be thrown into a padded room and heavily medicated. They had no idea what lay just beyond their mind's reach. They had no idea that other realities existed with magnificent creatures created in fairy tales, and I was one of them now.

I distracted myself from my thoughts by filling in Starling on everything that had taken place since she returned home. I also explained how Heath was a fox in that reality and watched me grow up, so he knew her from that. I filled in Heath on Star's sudden reincarnation and my assumption that she was able to stay because Misty and my mom were gone. I honestly had no idea, but it sounded good.

The dirt beneath my feet heated up as we reached my village entrance. My body must have been warning me it was time to face off with Tivon again. Only I didn't want to fight with him. I wanted to apologize, but I was also afraid he had a part in destroying Heath's village. In my heart, I knew it wasn't true, but Heath and Malin wanted me to stay cautious, especially because the elders communicated telepathically, so who knew what they could eavesdrop on.

The village was energetic that morning, but the usual carefree nature was lacking. Everyone was on edge knowing another battle was coming soon, and the air was thick with the tension. Even Starling noticed it.

"What happened here? It seems—"

"Weird," I jumped in.

"I was going to say off, but yeah."

It was hard to admit that such an enchanting world I entered not so long ago was now forever changed. "I guess nothing lasts forever," I threw out as I started leading us to my house. Sage came around the corner of my house as we approached.

"Arie, you're back." She swung her arms around me and hugged me tightly.

I stiffened slightly, but hugged her back. Word must have gotten out about my fight with Tivon. She peeled herself off me and looked at Star.

"How is she back?" Sage asked, confused.

"It's a long story." I turned to Starling. "Would you mind explaining? I need to go find Tivon."

Star responded, "Sure."

I started up the steps to the front door when Heath interlaced his hand with mine and whispered, "I'm coming with you."

It felt good to be close to someone again. I smiled to myself. I didn't have to do this alone, although this meant he was about to find out about my wings. He should know anyway. I stopped him. "There is something I need to tell you."

"You're back. Thank goodness you're safe." Tivon had thrown open the door and taken me in his arms in a matter of seconds. His concern was genuine as he spun me around into the house. He dropped me to my feet and approached Heath with his arm stretched out. "Thank you for bringing her back."

Heath took his hand timidly. "I didn't. It was her idea."

"Oh, well then, thank you for making sure she got home safely. You have exceeded my expectations as her protector, and for that, I am forever indebted to you."

"It's my honor to protect your daughter, and not because you asked me to, but because I care for her."

The room was deathly silent. The tone in Heath's voice was even, but it felt like he was challenging Tivon, so I interrupted, "Tivon, we need to talk. Privately." I raised my eyebrow and looked toward the hallway that led to the secret room.

"Aw, okay." He nodded in understanding. "But Heath can't come. I won't allow it, Arie."

I knew this was a battle I wouldn't win nor expected to. It was a sacred place, housing the most powerful gems in the universe. I'm glad he kept it so well hidden for everyone's sake. I pulled Heath aside. "He's right. You can't come where we're going."

"Then go somewhere else." He was seething under his breath.

"We can't. It's the only place I know that is safe from prying minds. I'll be okay. He's my father, Heath, and I would feel it if he was a threat to me."

Heath bore protective eyes into mine until he finally relented. His shoulders sagged in defeat. "Fine, but I'm not happy about this."

"I know, and that's why I love you," I said as I brushed his cheek lightly. "Thank you for taking care of me. Would you mind checking on Amary while I'm gone?"

"Of course." His voice softened.

I felt guilty for saying 'I love you,' but I was very clear about how I loved him, so I hoped he didn't take it out of context. He was like a brother to me, and I would always love him unconditionally as family should.

"She's out back playing," Tivon spoke up.

I dropped my hand, and he went in search for her.

Tivon and I headed down the hall, into his bedroom, and through the mysteriously growing closet, into the gem room. It looked the same as when I had stormed out, or rather, flew out. I tried to say something, but my throat was dry. *I was nervous.* I think he was too because he kept his back to me as he leaned on the carpenter table. *The air was so still in here.*

When he finally turned to face me, I was startled to see how everything was weighing on him. He no longer held the poise of a fighter. I wondered if this was what all dads looked like with naughty teenage daughters. *What a silly thought.*

"Who else knows?" he asked sullenly.

I knew he was referring to my wings. "Starling. She's the only one. She just appeared, and they were there. I was meditating. I was trying to gain control of them."

"Starling. Yes, that's another thing." He sighed.

"Did you know? That she would come here?"

"I wasn't positive, but I had a feeling. She carries some of our essence, which is why she was chosen, but it's not like River's, so I wasn't sure."

"Did Sierra or Hudson come here? I mean, if she did and she was similar to them, wouldn't they have come here?" There was hope in my voice. Hope that I might see some of my loved ones again.

"No, Arie, they didn't come here. I don't know why Starling was given a life here, but she's here, and I know you need her, so the universe was listening."

I pondered that for a moment. Was the universe catering to me? "I know what has been said about me being here. Malin told me." I waited for a reaction, but he just stood there, blank.

"She's been watching over Amary," he stated.

"Yes, I shouldn't be surprised you knew that."

"So, you know there's more to it then?" he asked.

"I do. She ran through speculations, but she said you knew the whole truth. That you knew what was going to happen."

"Did she? Huh."

I was trying to keep my emotions neutral, but he was holding back. I could feel it. "I need to know, Tivon. I need to know everything."

He pushed himself off the table he had been leaning on and walked around it without a purpose that I could see. Maybe a nervous twitch type thing. Then he waved his hand in front of a spot on the wall that was free of the shelves holding the jarred gems. I was baffled. Maybe awestruck was a better word. Either way I was stunned. Engraved inscriptions carved their way through the stonewall. The scrolling was reminiscent of my mother's. The curvature of the lettering was exquisite.

"This is what you are referring to," he said as he stepped away.

I couldn't help it. I stepped closer and traced the words like braille. Traces of light trailed after my finger just like a trailing sparkler at Fourth of July. I stepped back again to get a better look.

She will live, die, and ascend, soaring high above the mind's reach. Her love will destroy the walls that confine and protect, and she alone will be the one to restore balance through a sacrifice of life.

"This is it?" I couldn't hide my disappointment. No wonder there were so many assumptions. It was vague and seemed incomplete. It didn't really even imply that I could fly. That was a stretch for sure, but I guess it was accurate. "This doesn't help me at all. How am I supposed to prevent this destruction if I don't know what *not* to do?" My frustration was accelerating.

"Even if you knew, you wouldn't be able to stop it, Arie. You would never go against your heart. It's not in you," he said proudly.

"Dammit! I just want this to end! Why does Pyrrhus want the veils lifted so badly? I don't get it. All for power? For control?"

"Power can be a dangerous thing."

"I know. I get that. But why? It's just not adding up. He retreated to the shadows when he murdered me, so what? He wants back in the clique? He wants to be the leader? It seems so trite. To have power over people who will surely hate you."

"Why do you think there are wars in your old reality? It's all for power and money. There's no underlying reason. Don't be naïve, Arie. People will kill for less than that."

I wasn't naïve. I was a believer in the light that everyone had within them. Even with the darkness, there was still a goodness trying to push its way through.

"He loved you, and you didn't love him. It drove him mad."

That struck a nerve. Hadn't I been doing that to River? And now Heath? They loved me, but I couldn't reciprocate in the way they wanted. Would they go mad too and turn on me? Turn on Amary? But they had so much light. That had to be the difference between Pyrrhus and them. They had more light to begin with. I shifted thoughts.

"Malin told me the elders would kill Amary or me when they discovered who the chosen one was. How can I trust any of you?" I snapped.

"Malin is right, which is why I have kept Amary and you under my protection. Before you came here, they had tried to keep you under the protection of the allegiance. I didn't trust them. I knew what they were thinking. Love and greed aren't the only things that breed darkness. Fear has been building in the elders. It has been eating their light. I've been watching it, feeling it. It's only a matter of time when they lose control. Then they might just kill both of you."

"Fear of what? I don't understand. There's no balance right now. They need me."

"They fear your power. Amary's power. They are afraid of the unknown. When Amary ascends, she will be just like you. She will hold the same power. They are afraid if you turn to darkness you will destroy all the light. That our reality will be no more."

It was crazy, but it all made sense. I couldn't fault them for their fears, but to kill two innocent people to ensure those fears didn't turn into a reality was even worse. *They had to see that.* "We need to get Amary out of their reach. We are going to hide her with River in the other reality."

"You have to harness a whole lot of power to do something like that. I was only able to stay at most a couple of days with your mother, and that was draining. It took me weeks to recover. She's too young, and she hasn't ascended. You could kill her."

"What choice do I have? Leave her here and she could be killed. At least with River over there, I know she will be safe, and he will be able to tell me when she's fading. I can do this, Tivon. You just have to trust me. I'm a lot stronger than you know."

"I will always trust you, my child."

"Thank you."

He came to me and pulled me into a hug. I still hadn't apologized, but his warmth consoled my guilt. I was still staring at the engravings as they faded and just the plain rock wall remained. "Has anyone else ever seen this?"

"No, I stumbled across it when your mother died. Your mother here."

He observed me guardedly. I tried to maintain focus, but everything was fuzzy like white snow on a broken television.

"Are you okay?"

The feeling in my body was fading. "I need to sit." A strong hand wrapped around my arm, leading me to the carpenter table. Tivon helped me sit on the bench. My head felt heavy, so I rested it on my arms sprawled out on the tabletop. I couldn't think clearly, so I concentrated on my breathing.

In. Out. In. Out.

It was simple enough. We did it by instinct, but the mention of my *other* mother had made it difficult, a chore to keep me alive. The wood was cool on my arms, helping lower the sudden spike in my body temperature.

In. Out. In. Out.

It was becoming easier. My limbs became heavier as tingles brought them back to life.

I wasn't so naïve that I didn't know I had another mother. That Tivon had loved someone before the only mother I remembered. But no one spoke about her. No one alluded to the idea that I had one here first, but I knew and was too afraid to let my mind wonder about her. To taint the love I had for the only mom I knew. When I learned about my first life here, I had a moment where I wondered where she was. Why she wasn't here to greet me. I was in desperate need of my mother and her love that for one brief moment I hoped I had a second chance. Then the guilt lurked into the crevices of my heart and vanquished all thoughts of the possibility, but Tivon lifted the veil. There was no more hiding.

"I'm sorry, my child, but if you want to know everything, you need to know about Genesis."

Was that her name? Genesis? I wanted to like it. It was a pretty name, but the guilt nipped at me. I stayed quiet. I still didn't have the energy to speak. I was still processing.

"When Genesis died, I fell apart. We were supposed to have more time together. We were supposed to have many lifetimes to love each other. You were just a baby." He choked on his words, but then continued, "I knew I couldn't live in the same place without her. It was too hard. I am one of the oldest here, and our people needed a strong leader. One day when I was out reflecting on where to build a new house and life for us, I stumbled across this rock. It was massive and unusual. When I touched it, that's when it revealed its secret, but not like this. Not by an engraving. I was overwhelmed by butterflies, and when they flew away, Genesis was standing in front of the rock. She was more like an enchanting dream. Her lips were moving, but I couldn't hear what she was saying, so she touched the rock, and that's when the engraving appeared. I watched as it scrolled across the rock like pen on paper. When it was done, your mother leaned over and kissed my lips and then was carried away with the flurry of butterflies that had brought her to me.

"I didn't know what it meant then, but I knew it would be important, so I kept it safe. I built this secret room and used the gems as my cover if anyone discovered the room. After your death, I came down here to make the ring, and for the first time since Genesis left, the engraving appeared again. I still didn't understand it, but I knew it was connected to us. To you. When I came across your mother, Ariana, she felt like Genesis. In every way, she was your mother. That's when I realized what the inscription meant. That's why I left for so long. I was trying to protect you. I knew if I kept going to visit that someone would catch on. I was trying to keep you hidden for as long as possible. All of this was to protect you and your sister. That's all it has ever been about."

Tears were streaming down my face, and my arms were now sitting in a puddle of water. It hurt like hell to hear about Genesis. It hurt even more to hear she was dead, too. No second chance.

He was letting me in. He was telling me everything. I wished I could do the same, but now it was my turn to protect him. I gave myself time to collect my exposed emotions, piling them up into a neat stack and tucking them away into a pocket of my heart. When breathing became a natural part of living again, I stood up. "I need to go." I avoided the tale of my existence...for now.

"How can I help?" he pleaded.

"Stick with Heath. He'll need you. I'll join you guys when I have Amary safe with River."

He flashed a new smile at me. One I had never seen. His eyes were soft, and his lips curved up gently. "Your mother would be so proud of you."

"Thank you for saying that. I think she would be, too." We left the privacy of the room together and joined Heath and Amary upstairs. They were waiting on the back patio. Amary jumped up and down when she saw me.

"Arie, Arie. Heath told me you were taking me to see something special to celebrate my birthday." When I got close enough, she lunged at my legs.

"He did. Did he?" I said playfully. I bent down and tapped her nose. "Are you ready to see where?"

"I am."

I loved seeing her like this. Like an innocent five-year-old should be. We didn't celebrate our last birthdays. To be honest, I didn't know we had missed them because I wasn't used to how fast time flew where we were born in comparison to here, so it was important that we made up for it and it made a good ploy for leaving. "Go get your favorite blankie, and we'll be off."

"Okay," she said as she darted into the house.

Tivon stood just behind me with Heath across from me. "You two need to play nice while I'm gone. Got it?" I was directing the words more toward Heath who still looked uptight with the situation.

"Got it," he said grumpily.

"Agreed," Tivon added.

"Great. Just like old times. Now, where is Starling?"

"She's in your room," Heath replied.

"I'm just going to say goodbye to her. I'll see you guys tonight," I said as I walked back into the house and headed to my room. Star was cuddling my blanket. She put it down quickly as soon as she saw me in the doorway.

"I'm sorry. I didn't mean to..."

"It's fine, Star." I smiled to help reassure her.

"It's amazing how much this is like home. The blanket just made it seem so much more real. It still smells like home," she said mournfully.

I sat next to her on the bed. "You miss him. Don't you?"

She gave me the 'deer in the headlights' look. It made me giggle. "I know about you guys. I saw it in a vision when you died."

"Oh," was her only response.

I failed to tell her that I visited him, and we kissed, but I thought I would keep that to myself for now. It didn't mean what she would think it meant. I just needed him in that moment. We needed each other.

"Are you leaving now?"

I was relieved she changed the subject. "Yeah, but you are going to stay here. You can stay in my room. We'll figure out everything else later."

"It's good to see you as *you* again, Arie. You're strong and kicking ass."

"It's good to have you back, too."

We did a little bit of the ugly cry while we hugged, and then I left.

It was time to finish this.

Chapter Eighteen

Amary and I walked hand in hand out of the village. She had chosen to bring her ridiculously large 'Giraffy,' so she had it tucked under her free arm. She skipped and smiled all the way, which made me feel awful. She was under the false pretense of a special birthday getaway, and instead, I was taking her to the woman in her nightmares. I had a bad feeling about this.

Heath stayed behind with Tivon and Starling. At that moment their job was just to listen to the chatter of the elders to see if anyone was making a move before us. What Tivon was doing could get him banned from the village. He was taking an enormous risk, which was one of the reasons I was keeping him out of it. He insisted, though, which I admired. I knew we had a better chance against Pyrrhus if we were united.

I led us to the river. We would need that kind of energy to bring the two of us through the veil at the same time. When we broke through some thick brush, Malin was standing at the edge of the water. Amary's hand tightened on mine as she scooted behind me. "It's okay, buggie. She's here to help us." I bent down and eased my hand out of hers, so I could protectively wrap her in my arms.

"That's the lady from my dreams." She whimpered into my shoulder.

"I know, but I have a little secret for you." Her eyes widened. "She's your protector."

Recognition washed over the fear she wore. "Like Heath?"

"Yes, like Heath. In fact, that's Heath's grandma." A squeak of shock escaped her lips. I even saw a small glimmer of excitement.

"Really?" She was returning to the calm girl that walked into my bookstore long ago.

Malin stepped forward. "Yes, Amary, I am Heath's grandma and your protector. My name is Malin, but you can just call me Mali," she said in a sincere grandmotherly sweet voice.

"Can I call you Grandma Mali?" Her voice escalated several octaves.

Mali chuckled. "Of course, you can."

The previous tension had melted away with that. Things were going to be all right.

Amary tugged my arm for attention. "Are you leaving?" she asked, uneasy.

"Oh, no, buggie. We're going to visit River. Mali is just here to make sure we get there safely. Is that okay?"

Fireworks lit up her expression. "Yes, yes, yes. I miss River. This is the best birthday present ever."

She jumped into my arms, and I carried her to the river. "This is going to seem odd, buggie, but the rushing water holds a lot of natural energy, so it makes a good way to get to River. We are going to get wet, but just for a minute."

She nodded and snuggled her head into my shoulder.

When we passed Mali, she touched my shoulder. "I'll be here when you get back."

"Thanks, Mali." My gratitude could never be enough for what she had done and lost to protect Amary and me. Nothing could bring back her daughter and granddaughter.

I stepped carefully into the river. It was cold as it slammed up against our skin. I was smart enough not to wear any loose clothing this time. I tightened my grip around Amary and held a deep breath until we were in the center. I could feel that Amary was scared. Her nails were digging into my back for secured leverage that she wouldn't be washed away. This was where the river flowed the fastest and was the deepest. The stronger the current, the more energy that was produced. And we needed a lot.

I closed my eyes and cleared my head of everything except for River and my house. I rifled through memories of lying in the meadow with River at night watching the fireflies blink their way around us. I flashed to a moment when we were younger and chasing butterflies around the yard in our bare feet. The grass tickled my pads, and the dirt stuck between my toes. A lightning bolt interrupted my memory of our passionate embrace at the park on my eighteenth birthday. The light blinded my thoughts, and I heard Amary scream, and then it was quiet.

The flapping of wings aroused my senses. I popped my eyes open and discovered a whirlwind of butterflies circling us. I was still holding Amary firmly in my arms. My back adorned a dull ache where she had dug her nails. No healing quickly here. I rubbed her back gently. "Hey, buggie. We're here," I whispered. She lifted her head and surveyed her surroundings.

"Is this your house?" she asked.

I totally forgot she had never been here before. "Yes." I smiled.

"Are these all yours?" she asked as she held out her hand to the butterflies. They hopped on and off freely.

I started giggling at that. "No, buggie. They aren't mine, but they sure like to hang out here a lot."

"I love butterflies."

"Me too." We sat there for a few more moments and watched them flutter around in the morning light. Their beauty would never be lost on me. My ability allowed me to witness their magnificence in slow motion as their wings opened and closed gracefully, creating just enough momentum to keep them in flight. In a blink of an eye, the essence of all the lost souls held within them revealed themselves to me, like witnessing a spinning carousel of ghosts. Their essence filled me with warmth and courage.

"Do you feel that?" Arie asked.

"I do." We were being protected, and they were announcing their presence. We would never be alone. "Let's go find River." I pushed her up off my lap, causing the butterflies to scatter around the meadow. We had manifested in the butterfly circle from the river, bone dry, as I had been before.

We walked the mile dirt road to River's house. The forest continued to feed us energy as we grazed upon it, but at a lower intensity than in the other reality. "You know, Amary, we really need to give our other home a name."

"What do you mean?" she asked as she shuffled along the dirt.

"Well, I still call this place home, but when I think about the other reality, I don't know what to call it. I stumble on my thoughts a bit."

"Oh! I call it Serendae!" she shouted elatedly.

"Serendae?" I laughed. "Where did you come up with that?"

"I didn't. That's what Iris calls it."

"Oh. Well, that's very pretty." We had made it to River's driveway. "I've never heard anyone call it anything."

"Iris said they saw it written on a rock by the river, so they started calling it that."

"Huh." I wondered where that rock was. "Serendae, it is."

River's feet pounded the dirt as he jogged into sight from a trail behind his house. His bare chest glistened with sweat, a sign he was out running. When he saw us, his face lit up, and for a moment, mine did too, but then I remembered Starling. How was I going to tell him she was in Serendae now? He ran up to us with his arms spread out for Amary.

"River!" she yelled as she smashed into his stomach, taking him down.

"Wow, buggie, you sure have gotten big." He laughed lightheartedly.

He glanced up at me and gave me a longing look. One that said I love you, and I missed you.

"How big?" she squealed.

"So big."

I loved watching them. It made everything seem normal. *Feel normal.* He stood up easily with Amary in his arms and pulled me into a group hug.

"I missed you," he spoke softly.

"We missed you, too."

He ushered us up the driveway and into the house. To a normal guest, everything would seem the same, but not to me. I could feel the emptiness without Sierra and Hudson. River put Amary down, and she took off running around the house. I imagined she was checking out every room like a child moving into a new house. We stood across from each other silently. He stood still while I fidgeted, remembering our last moment together. The kiss.

"Thank you for bringing her."

"About that."

Amary darted into the room. "Which room is mine?"

River gave me a quizzical look. "Room?"

"Yeah, sorry. I would've called, but no cell service on the other side," I said playfully.

"Ha-ha. Funny, Arie."

"Hey, buggie. Can you give us a few minutes?"

"Can I play outside?" She jumped anxiously.

"Sure, but stay right out back."

She was running out the back door the next second.

"I guess you have some filling in to do," River stated.

I walked to the double glass doors that led out back. I watched as Amary discovered the tree house River and

Hudson had built when he was younger. She climbed the ladder and disappeared inside. "I need you to keep her hidden, River. Until everything is over." I turned to him. "Can you keep her safe for me? Find somewhere to go where Pyrrhus can't find her?" I requested. I was surprised at the quivering in my voice. He glided to me and embraced me, giving me the support I needed.

"Of course, but you need to tell me what's going on. I need to know everything."

I nodded my head against him, the smooth sculpture of his chest rubbing on my cheek tenderly.

I led him back into the family room and nestled on the couch, pulling my knees to my chest. "Crap."

"What?" River sat beside me.

"My feet are disgusting," I exclaimed.

"That's what happens when you walk around barefoot," he joked.

I was so used to being mysteriously clean all the time that it didn't occur to me to wear shoes here.

"When did you get that tattoo?" He was staring at my left foot where the tattoo had appeared after the butterfly wings. "It's the nature spirit symbol."

I brushed my hand over it. "I know. There's so much to tell you."

"I guess so."

"Would you mind if I cleaned up real quick?"

"Sure. I'll check on Amary."

We both got up at the same time, River heading out back and me down the hall to the bathroom. I closed the door and placed my feet into the bathtub. The warm water felt divine. I had forgotten what it was like to wash myself. I longed to take a hot bath, but without knowing how long I had here, I couldn't risk it. I grabbed the body wash and scrubbed off the grime hastily.

When I was done, I washed my face in the sink. The reflecting eyes looked like the deathly hollows of the future.

My mom's crystal blues had been erased and replaced by a honey brown.

"You okay in there?" River asked through the door.

When I opened the door and saw him standing there, I wished that life were normal again. I sighed and brushed the hair off my cheek. Should I start with Starling or Amary or the tattoo? What about Ashe? My stomach churned. This was going to be an interesting conversation. "Can we go out back?"

"Yeah."

We sat on the bench while Amary stayed hidden in the playhouse. Giggling, she peeked out a few times. Never too old to play peek-a-boo. I twisted my fingers in my hands.

"I know something is up, Arie. I can tell by the way you're fidgeting."

He was right. I could never hide anything from him. "Starling is alive." I glanced over and saw his eyes light up with happiness. I put my head back down in defeat. *He loved her.*

"How? I don't understand. Where is she?"

"She came to me. She's there. She can't live here anymore, River." That was the bombshell I was dreading. Not only did I have to tell him the girl he loved was alive, but also that he couldn't be with her. It was the same scenario with us...well, kind of. I was fairly confident Starling didn't love Ashe.

The intensity of thought was written all over his face. She was alive, but he was still alone. "I'm sorry."

He ignored my apology. "What's happening with Amary?"

And the wall rose again.

Cut off and protect.

"The short version. My mom before Ariana was a woman named Genesis. She proclaimed to my father after her death that I would cause the ultimate destruction between realities, but that I would also restore balance. The elders are little pansies and afraid for the power Amary and I possess, which has put a target on our heads after I bring peace back to the natural order of things. Apparently, Pyrrhus has a sick obsession with power and wants to kill us, so we can't restore balance. So basically, everyone wants us dead in the end. I don't care about me. I just want to keep Amary safe."

River rubbed the exhaustion from his face. "That's a lot, Arie."

"Yeah, I know and that's the edited version."

"How are you holding up?"

"Okay, I guess, considering."

"I'm not really sure I understand the complexities of what's going on, but my job has always been to protect you, and if that means protecting Amary, I will."

"Thanks." I put my hand on his. He wrapped his hand around it and squeezed.

"I love you, Arie. Please, don't get yourself killed. Whatever your plan is, just come back to me, to Amary."

"I will."

"I do have one question, though," he said.

"Sure."

"How is Amary able to stay here? I thought you just disappeared when your energy was drained."

I cringed my shoulders. I was really hoping he wouldn't ask because I knew he would worry when he heard the answer.

"What, Arie?"

"She is feeding off my energy. As long as I keep it up on the other side, she will be able to stay here. I taught her how." Please, don't ask how.

"If she's using your energy, then how much are you left with?"

I tried to hide my face.

"Arie, tell me." He raised his voice a few decibels.

"Not much, River. It doesn't leave me with much, but I have to do it. It's the only way."

He jumped up and started pacing on the porch.

"I don't like this. Pyrrhus is strong, Arie. You saw how strong."

He was right. It was risky giving anything to Amary, but I couldn't worry about her while facing him. "I can do it, River. I won't be alone. I have help." I stood up and hugged him. I wondered if my embrace did the same for him as his did for me. He held me tightly and kissed my head.

"I feel like all I do is worry about you," he whispered.

"I know." Something I felt awful about. I just wanted him to be happy, and he was with Star. He had it all. One way or another I would figure out a way for them to be together again. "I should say goodbye to Amary before I vanish like a dandelion in the wind." I pulled away and called for Amary. "Amary, I need to go. Come give me some love."

She peeked out the door of the tree house and made her way down the ladder. She launched up into my arms, and I hugged her tightly while I carried her through the house to the front door. "I'm going to miss you, buggie, but River will keep you safe. I promise."

"I know," she answered. "I have a secret," she whispered.

I dropped my voice to a hush. "And what is that?"

"I'm going to protect River for you," she said seriously.

I rubbed her back. "Thank you." I gave her one last squeeze and passed her to River. She looked perfect in his arms. He would make a great dad one day. "I'll come back as soon as everything is over."

"Okay."

River was trying to put on a strong front, but I could tell this was killing him. I knew he thought this might be the last time we saw each other, and there was nothing I could say to make him feel better. I just knew Amary was in good hands, and if I didn't return, he would make sure she was safe with someone else in Serendae.

They remained at the threshold and watched me drift down the driveway. I didn't turn back to look. I couldn't. It would be the demise of my strength. I trotted through the overgrown grass in my back yard and to the butterfly circle. This was my first attempt at getting back on my own instead of being forced. It usually sucked me away before I was ready. Not that I was ready now. I wanted to stay here forever and play house again.

I sat in the center of the circle and closed my eyes. It was funny how hard things seemed after my mom died. All I wanted to do was escape. To get away from myself. *Careful what you wish for.* If I could change things, I would. Change how I saw the world as a parentless child. Try to make the best of it. Try to be a better friend to both River and Starling. I would change it all.

An icy chill rolled over my toes and trickled up my legs. When it reached my lungs, my heart froze. I tried to take a breath, but I couldn't. My chest wouldn't move. Fear consumed the last of my regretful thoughts.

Chapter Nineteen

Searing hot hands burned my shoulders. The last of the energy within me threw them off. Once my vision caught up with my other senses, I registered that I was in the river, Amary wasn't with me, and Malin was lying on the rocks on the riverbed. *Oh, no!* I sloshed across the river to her side. Just as I reached her, she was sitting herself up and laughing.

"Mali, are you okay? I'm so sorry." I grabbed onto her arm, helping her up.

"I'm fine. That was electrifying." She chuckled.

I fell onto the ground next to her, exhausted by the traveling experience. Sadness over leaving behind Amary set in.

"She's safer there," Malin said.

"I know." I didn't share with her that I was scared that was the last time I would see her. She pulled herself up. I was seriously underestimating her strength.

"Let's go," she commanded.

I snapped out of my dismal thinking and followed her through the forest to meet up with Heath and Tivon. Little sparks flared on my skin as the natural energy of the forest restored my power. It hurt more than normal. A fairly powerful shock had me scream, "Ouch!"

"You're drained," Malin announced. "We need to wait until you're at full strength again."

"It's going to be tough with Amary tapping into some of it," I replied.

"Did your father ever tell you one of the special gifts that gem combination on your ring has?" she asked as she forged forward through unmarked trail.

Had he? "I don't think so."

"You have one shot to pull from all the power of the realities when you need it, but in the process, it will destroy the ring."

It didn't even take a millisecond to process what that meant. It meant losing my mom's essence. I didn't know if I could do that if a time called for it. This was all that was left of her. "What happens when someone's essence is destroyed?"

"You mean instead of released into the universe?"

"Yeah," I pressed.

She stopped and turned to me with a dark expression that pierced my heart.

"It's gone. Only the dagger of life and death can destroy essence. When anyone here is killed, their essence is released into the universe, and until it's consumed, it is in danger of being trapped. It drifts aimlessly between realities until the universe takes it. Unfortunately, most gets trapped in the darkness where the energy pull is the strongest."

The thoughts swirling around were making me dizzy. "Why would the pull be stronger in the reality where the dark resides?"

"Because Pyrrhus wants it. He seeks power and essence is energy and energy is power. Where do you think all those shadows come from? We all come from somewhere. Unfortunately, they become only a shell of what they used to be once the darkness claims them. They can't come back. They don't want to. They don't know any different. They are followers controlled by a supreme source of darkness."

The revelation was astounding. There was no way I would use the ring if it meant my mother would become one of them. We kept walking as I mulled it all over. There were so many shadow stalkers, which meant that people were being killed and their essence trapped like Tivon had done with my mother's. "What gemstone traps the lost essence?"

"It's not a gemstone, Arie. Gemstones are positive in nature."

"Right. Then how does he do it?"

"Titanium is used to capture the drifting essence. The one who traps it has control of its fate."

I had been developing a theory during our walk that I wanted to bounce off her, but time flew, and we were already at the edge of the forest where I had found Pyrrhus' grand palace. Heath and Tivon were resting on some large boulders streaked with silver and metallic, unmoving and silent. I had caused the tension that now passed between them. I would have to resolve that after this was all over.

Heath jumped up when he sensed me.

"Is she safe?" he asked.

"Yes, she's safe," I replied. *And I miss her.*

Tivon stood up, no longer concealing Norinda's presence. I hadn't noticed her before.

"We are it," Tivon declared. "We can't trust anyone else."

"To be honest, I thought it would only be Heath, Malin, and me, so this looks way better." It would be better with more, but many had already died, and many were questionable alliances. The less that knew what we were up to the better.

"I brought something to help us." Tivon shoved his hand into his pocket and pulled out a little black cloth. He opened it and hidden beneath the fabric were five black, speckled, smooth stones. They were gorgeous. "These are Nuummite stones. They are the most rare and most potent power gemstones. Keep them on you, and they will allow you to access your deeply rooted innermost gifts. Ones you might not even know you have."

Norinda gasped. She looked like she had just seen a boy skinny dip for the first time.

"I thought those were non-existent?" she questioned Tivon.

"They are. These are the last of them," he responded.

The exchange was awkward. Norinda's eyes became slits, probing whether she should believe him or not. Tivon's response to her subtle rebellion was a glare that made *me* cower with fear.

"I am the keeper of the gemstones. I do not need to disclose what is in my possession." His voice was deadly, as if daring her to press the issue further. Instead, she grabbed one quickly and backed off.

We all followed suit and took our rocks. The second I made contact with mine I could feel the swirling of the blood around my muscles. They were getting ready to release something I hadn't discovered yet. It made me nervous when it should have made me feel more confident with the fight that lay ahead. "I need to tell you all something," I proclaimed. Here it goes. They all stared at me blankly. "Ashe is alive."

I expected more from the declaration, but everyone stood, unfazed.

"We know," Heath spoke up.

"I told them," Norinda admitted. "We couldn't go into this without full disclosure of what we were up against. We don't know if he is truly with us or if he's siding with his brother."

I could feel my swirling blood start to bubble. *What the hell was she saying?* "Are you kidding me, Norinda? He saved your ass! You would be dead if he hadn't helped you." I stepped closer to her. My body was tingling. Heath grabbed my arm.

"You need to calm down right now, Arie. We can't trust anyone. She was right to tell us."

I yanked my arm from him. "Fine, but how do we know we can trust her?" I spat out.

"We can only hope that we all have the right intentions here," Tivon countered.

The dust settled quickly.

"Once we get inside, Arie, you find Ashe. You'll need his

help to get to Pyrrhus. We'll start taking out what shadow stalkers we can," Tivon barked orders.

"What? No!" I shouted desperately. "Those shadow stalkers were once your people. Our people. We can't just kill them. There has to be another way. Malin, tell them. Tell them we can save them."

Malin sighed deeply.

"Malin?" Tivon addressed her.

"She's right. Their essence is trapped, but not lost forever. If we can find where he is keeping their essence, we can regain control of them, but Arie, you need to understand something. Even if we rescue their essence, it's not for us to take and keep like Pyrrhus, or else we are no better than him. There's a special ritual we can do to help them find their way to peace."

Norinda jumped in, "This is ridiculous. You want to take out Pyrrhus and now go on a needle in the haystack mission to find the lost essence? They're gone, Arie. All of them. They aren't who they used to be. You're trying to go through too much trouble. Is there even a guarantee you'll be able to restore their essence?" she asked Malin.

"There are never guarantees, but a lot of those shadows are my people, my loved ones, and if Arie is willing to do this, then I will help her."

That shut up Norinda. And just a little while ago, I was starting to like her. That ship has now sailed.

"So, Arie, you find Ashe and where Pyrrhus is keeping the essence, and the rest of us will scatter to find Pyrrhus. Once we have him, we'll need the dagger to finish him. Do you know where it is, Arie?"

I nodded reluctantly.

"Good. Go get it," he directed.

I backtracked quite a distance into the forest. When I reached the dead blooms of Ashe's former resting spot where I had left the dagger, I looked around urgently for it. It was gone. How could it be gone? I dug into the ground frantically.

Dammit! If they knew I didn't have it, they may not want to move forward with the plan. I would have to lie. And lie well.

I looked around the surrounding area and grabbed a piece of bark that looked to be the same size of the dagger. "This will have to do." I shoved it into the back of my jeans and raced back to the others. They had congregated in a tight circle.

"Did you get it?" Norinda asked.

I pulled up my shirt to show them the bark and then covered up quickly. I didn't dare speak the lie, not trusting my skills. Plus, if I didn't say it, doesn't that mean it's not really telling a lie?

"We are ready then. Arie, join us in the circle," Malin instructed.

She shoved me in closely. They all had their stones in their palms in the middle, so I took mine out and did the same without question.

"This will get us all there with minimal energy waste," Malin explained. "Now, close your eyes and believe."

As I surveyed the room within Pyrrhus' dungeon, I looked over our meager little group. We were powerful, but substantially outnumbered. I soaked in the comfort of the rocks hidden beneath our clothing.

"Heath, go with Arie to find Ashe. We'll meet back here at high noon," Tivon stated.

Heath fell in line behind me as we climbed the stairs to the hallway that led to the huge open room. Everything looked to be in the same place as when I left. I wondered where Ashe was. Sage said he had to fight off shadow stalkers to help them escape, which meant he was on Pyrrhus' radar as a traitor. I bet he was locked up in that room again. I looked back at Heath and whispered, "I think I know where Ashe is. Follow me." I guided him across the room to the door that led down the hallway with the Herkimer diamonds.

"Are these...?" Heath's voiced trailed off in awe.

"Yeah, clever, right? I think everyone has been underestimating Pyrrhus."

"'I think so."

We walked a few more yards through the dark hallway lit by the diamonds. It was bright in the large room we came from because of the skylights letting in the light, but there weren't any here.

"This is a dead end," he said.

"That's what you're supposed to think. Hold on." I held out my hand with the ring, and the wall vanished, revealing Ashe's former prison. I ran inside, but it was empty. There were drops of blood on the sheet. I clutched some in my hand and tried to refrain from freaking out.

"Where is he?"

"I don't know." I had an awful feeling in the pit of my stomach. *Pyrrhus wouldn't.* A terrifying scream filled the house. I didn't think twice before I started running back through the hall.

"Arie, wait!" Heath yelled behind me.

I could hear his voice at a distance, but I didn't care. I knew that scream was meant to get my attention. I knew who it was. I soared through the house gracefully, my wings fully extended. I turned many corners, not knowing where I was going, but trusting my wings. They directed me to a far corner of the palace and out iron doors to a courtyard. Darkness had taken to the sky, masking the sun's rays. I wondered if that was done intentionally. Blocking our source of energy. The temperature had dropped below the standard comfort level I had become accustomed to here. Norinda was tied to a pillar on the far side of a luscious landscape, blood trickling down her fingers and staining the ground below.

I heard the gasp before I saw Heath. My wings were fully protracted, exposing their brilliance. A dramatic slow clapping sound filled the courtyard, followed by the nail biting sound of Pyrrhus' voice.

"This is wonderful," he cackled.

I couldn't see him yet, and his voice seemed to bounce off the walls, closing us in.

"Congratulations, Arie. You have fully evolved," he continued.

He revealed himself just above Norinda on the two-story wrap-around balcony.

The tone in his last statement sent chills through my bones. He almost seemed happy about my evolution.

Heath came around my right side and stood tall next to me.

"Where is Ashe?" he hissed to me.

"Did I hear that you are looking for my big brother?" Pyrrhus laughed.

I cringed every time I heard his voice.

"I'm here."

I looked across the courtyard and saw Ashe stumbling out into the clearing holding his side. He looked feeble. *He was dying.* Heath grabbed my wrist, knowing my gut reaction was to run to him.

"Don't. It could be a trick."

I looked back between Norinda and Ashe.

"It seems you have figured out your dilemma, Arie. Who will you choose to save? Someone you barely trust or someone you love?" Pyrrhus taunted.

"Shut up!" I yelled.

Heath murmured, "Look."

I followed his stare over to Norinda. Tivon was cutting her loose.

"Go," Heath urged.

Without another thought, I took off across the courtyard, my wings gliding me forward effortlessly. Out of the corner of my eye, I saw shadow after shadow jump off the balcony. Heath and Malin fought them off while I raced for Ashe. I knocked into him.

"Hold on," I whispered as he fell lifeless into my arms. I could smell death on him. "You have to hold on for just a little longer," I said as tears streamed down my face.

Our feet left the ground as my wings flew us out of the courtyard into the darkened sky.

Chapter Twenty

The clouds had only accumulated around the palace, so as we flew further away, the sun's light found me and fed me feverishly as I carried Ashe's limp body. He had passed out and still hadn't awoken. It was probably a good thing, though. I'm not sure how he would have handled waking up miles above the ground. I held him closely to my chest, sharing the warmth of our bodies. Seeing the world from above was magnificent. There were gushing waterfalls all around, spilling into the massive river that rushed to the ocean that seemed to expand endlessly. As I passed through sporadic delicate clouds, the moisture layered my skin. Everything was bright green and wisped together with the speed we were traveling. A flock of redbirds surrounded me, getting into a V-formation behind me. For the moment, they had chosen me to lead them to an unknown destination. A rumbling sound alerted me that Ashe was waking up. I whispered into his ear, "Do you trust me?" I was holding him so he was facing me, his head cradled upon my shoulder.

He opened his eyes wide and locked with mine. "Always."

My heart fluttered with my wings, and I moved in and kissed him softly. When we separated, a powerful pulse of energy passed between us. His muscles came alive, and the color returned to his skin. I took in his magical beauty. He spun his body around carefully, so he could enjoy the view as I was.

"Look over there." He pointed to the far right to a barren

forest full of tall, dead trees that looked more like sticks than trees. "That's the dead forest."

"What happened?" I asked.

"Pyrrhus. The Warrior clan lived there. He flushed them out by burning their land."

"That's terrible."

"Yeah, it was." His voice dropped.

"Did you know them well?"

"We all live cohesively, so we have a natural connection. We felt when they were destroyed. Same with The Protector clan."

I could hear the pain in his tone. We flew silently for a few moments in remembrance of the ones lost. It occurred to me that I didn't know what clan Ashe and Pyrrhus originated. "What clan are you? You don't have to tell me."

He hesitated. "No, I want to tell you. You should know."

The way he said those words made me regret asking.

"We are from The Love clan."

"What..." I was stunned speechless. How could Pyrrhus be associated with anything like love? He was pure evil. After reading my thoughts, Ashe spoke up.

"His heart wasn't always black, Arie. He loved deeply, but when we lost our mother, it changed him. I lost him to something more powerful, darkness."

I didn't know what to say. I couldn't say anything positive about Pyrrhus after what he had done, but I wanted to believe there was goodness somewhere inside him that could change him. Make him what he once was. For Ashe. He was all he had now.

"You're wrong, Arie. I have you now." He penetrated my thoughts.

"How did you do that?" I was so thrown off by his mind-reading proclamation that I almost dropped him.

"Every time you feed me your essence we become more connected."

I let that digest. I didn't think it was possible for us to be more connected than we already were. I loved him with every part of me already.

"Look over there," he said. "I want to take you there one day."

He was pointing to a billowing cloud of white steam straight ahead. "What is it?"

"It's where the accumulation of energy is the strongest. It's also believed to be the source of transition when we die. It's called Geyser Valley."

Talking so casually while soaring through the sky was unreal. I didn't even have to concentrate on our destination. My wings seemed to have a mind of their own, or they were just like any other muscle and worked off the electrical impulses of my brain stem. An automatic response that didn't need anything but instinct. "We should go there now." Our trajectory immediately steered us in that direction.

"Sure, why not?" he responded.

One by one the birds broke from formation and continued with their flight path. I wondered if they were afraid to go there. It looked so serene, but I had no idea what was beyond the thick wall of white. My wings fluttered tirelessly through the steam vents, lowering us carefully onto a thick bed of marsh. I let go of Ashe and brushed myself off nervously. The magnetism between us seemed to increase as we got closer, and it was peaking beyond the brink of control.

"Do you know how to put those things away?" He was looking at my wings.

I giggled like a little schoolgirl. "I have no idea."

"Maybe if you concentrate on it hard enough?" he added.

"It's worth a shot." My voice was shaking. The fact we were alone for the first time since our last kiss at the waterfall sanctuary was not lost on me. I sat down on the wet, spongy marsh in my meditation position and tried to erase all thoughts of Ashe, which was more than difficult. It was as if this place was meant for us.

"See, that wasn't hard," Ashe said.

I was still concentrating on making his presence evaporate that I didn't even notice my wings had disappeared. When I opened my eyes, I saw his hand reaching out in front of me to help me up. When I grabbed for it, a zap forced us both back. We were thrown onto our backs a few feet opposite of each other. It scared me, but it had me laughing uncontrollably. He joined in as we picked ourselves up.

"Maybe we shouldn't touch while we're here," he suggested.

"Yeah..." My voice tapered off. I couldn't hide my disappointment. I caught a sinful curve of his lips in the corner of my eye.

"Come on. Let's go to the center. My mom used to tell us stories about a magical stone. The one that helped our essence transition from death into nature."

He instinctively reached out his hand to take mine and then tucked it into his pocket instead.

"Best not to make that mistake again." He winked.

He still melted my heart. "Best not," I replied. I followed him through a thicket of moss-covered trees. This was the fairyland every girl imagined—green trunks from layers of moss, towering trees, and a cute boy in the lead. It was hard to believe that only a short time ago he was near death in my arms. He glided through the forest without a falter in his step. I think I even saw him skip. His muscle definition had returned to his arms, making me blush at his perfection. *He was perfection*. Not only my sight confirmed this, but also the buzzing through my body. Something had been scratching at my thoughts, so I moved up close behind him to talk to him better. I was careful not to touch him. "Ashe?"

He stopped and turned to me, the green speckles glowing amongst the hazel of his eyes.

"Yes?"

"Sage told me that we weren't supposed to be together. Actually, that we *couldn't* be together. Do you think that's why *that* happened earlier?" I rubbed the palm of my hand that had adorned a swiftly healing burn mark from the encounter. He pressed close to me, forcing me to step away until I backed into a tree. His warm breath tickled my lips and teased my heart. His lips were only inches from mine, challenging the forces of nature to try to separate us again.

Slowly and seductively, he whispered, "Whether we're not supposed to be together or can't be together, we are and I will make sure nothing pulls us apart again."

His lips remained close to mine, the little sparks building up to an explosion, but it remained to be seen if I would explode from anticipation first. Breathlessly, I whispered back, "I need to kiss you." His breathing became harder and warmer as he remained as motionless as a rock being hammered by lightning.

"I know," he said as he broke the deadly connection, taking a few steps back and then continuing our journey toward the center of Geyser Valley.

I stumbled back in line behind him, still trying to regain my composure. I loved River so much, but this was different. This was celestial. Our connection was made from the natural energy of the universe. It was our fate to be together.

My ring was an eruption of colors from the moment we came here. If the tingling on the surface of my skin weren't enough to tell me we were in a charged environment, my ring would be the telltale sign because it rarely glowed like this.

"Ashe, I feel a little strange." He spun around and stared at me. I could tell he was trying to hide something. "What's wrong?"

"Nothing, I think. It's just your eyes. They're blue again."

The announcement startled me, but it also made me happy. I wished I had a mirror. To see my mom through my eyes again was all I needed to get through this. "Are they beautiful?" A tear released.

"Yes. Very. Just like they used to be, only brighter," he informed me.

A light breeze whizzed past us, rustling a purple flower that caught my eye just past Ashe's shoulder. He turned to see what I was looking at.

"We're here," he stated.

He disappeared after a few steps. I rushed to catch up with him. When I pushed through a particularly thick patch of branches that swallowed Ashe, I froze. I couldn't speak. What lay out in front of me was beyond anything I could have ever comprehended. Ashe reappeared by my side.

"It's beautiful. Isn't it?" he asked.

"I...words don't exist to describe this. I would never have imagined something this enchanted could be real." As I soaked in the scenery, my heart ached, and my knees became weak.

We stood at the top of a cliff looking down into a valley. A bright aqua river flowed gently through it, and ornamented on either side were white, layered, cutout hills covered in bright purple flowers. Some were attached to the white rock absently, while other blooms adorned towering trees and oversized bushes. In the distance were snow-capped mountaintops with traces of purple still visible.

"Your mother was a brilliant artist."

I covered my mouth as tears streamed down my face. This was one of my mom's favorite paintings because it was simple but stunning, and here it was. It was real. I started shaking my head in disbelief. "I don't understand. How is this possible?"

"How is any of this possible, Arie?" He swept his hand around the landscape. "You have to let go of the human way of thinking. Only then will you see beyond logical thought and live in the world of imagination. The world that exists beyond what the mind is capable of. You have physically ascended, but now you need to spiritually ascend."

I was still skeptical, but the ring and my eyes didn't lie. It made sense this was my mother's sanctuary, and I was meant for it as much as it was meant for me. I was starting to see. I was starting to let go of my first eighteen years of humanity and accepting the rest of my life as an evolved species. To be the first.

"The stone is down below, hidden deep beneath the canopy of flowers in that rock over there." He pointed to a rock wall below, just a short distance from where we were.

"Let's go then." I scaled a narrow stairway cut out of the cliff below us. It was steep, but my fear of heights was surprisingly gone after taking flight over the world. Ashe followed behind me as we made the sharp descent. I watched the area buzz to life as our movement disturbed its quiet serenity. The tiny flying creatures blended with the landscape, skillfully hiding from predators. I wondered if my mom had them hidden in her painting, and that's why they looked the way they did. Here by the hands of their creator. The water was breathless from above, but up close, I could see the river bottom covered with glistening stones and colorful fish. "Are those all gemstones?"

"Yes, a rock is not just any rock here. They all carry a unique power."

Seeing all these stones set off an alarming thought. "Does Pyrrhus know about this place?"

"Of course, I do," Pyrrhus cackled as he jumped out from across the river.

The river was at least fifty feet across, so I felt somewhat safe. Ashe jumped in front of me.

"Let it go, Pyrrhus. She's gone, and she's never coming back."

A horrid screech left Pyrrhus' mouth, forcing me to cover my ears from the piercing pain. Ashe was doing the same.

"Enough!" Ashe yelled.

Pyrrhus closed his mouth, impeding the foreign sound.

"What was that?" I asked.

"He's acquired a number of stones that have given him different powers. That screech could kill any normal clan person."

"You're implying you're not normal?"

He shot me a look I didn't care to see. It was written all over his face. He had more secrets. Before I could react, he continued, "I promise, after all of this, no more secrets." He looked back over toward his brother. "I loved her, too, but this has gone too far. Too many people have died. Hell, I died. This isn't you, Brother. Don't you think that if I believed we could bring her back I would do anything to make that happen? But this? All the blood shed? Not one person's life is worth so many others."

"You lie, Brother. You know we can bring her back. She foretold this. All of this. And look how many lives have been lost because of the one life you protect now? Is she more important than your own mother's life?" He pointed, disgusted.

I couldn't contain my gasp. Their mother? This was all about bringing back their dead mother? Although I could relate to the pain of that loss, I would never sacrifice another person's life to bring her back. We were at a dangerous crossroads. "We need to get out of here," I whispered to Ashe, never taking my eyes off Pyrrhus.

"No," he said loudly. "We finish this now."

His eyes were glued to his brother, as well.

"Are you going to finish me, Big Brother? Send me to a grave like her mother sent ours?"

This was too much. I was learning too much at once, and it was all bad. My head was spinning, and I was starting to feel nauseous.

"Arie, you have to stay with me. Don't listen to what he is saying. I will tell you everything."

He was right. This wasn't the time to buckle. I couldn't show weakness. "If my mother killed yours, then she had good reason," I lashed out my verbal assault loud and strong.

The hiss that projected from Pyrrhus was venomous. I saw the shimmer of the dagger of life and death in his hand. He lunged at us, aiming directly for Ashe's chest. I couldn't lose him again. A life without him wasn't worth living. I knew that now more than ever after the connection was solidified when we arrived here. Without a second thought, I pushed Ashe out of the way, the shock of our touch launching him further than I had intended, but there was no time to react to anything.

Pyrrhus was on top of me in a flash, and when I looked down at my chest, the dagger was protruding from it, releasing blood and an illustrious light. I didn't feel any pain. I was numb as Pyrrhus' laugh faded, and Ashe's voice shrieked in agony. The light exploding from my chest became warm and blinding, but my mind was still strong. Was I in transition? Is that what happened when our essence released into the universe? It seemed odd that I would remain so aware during the process, but it was tranquil and painless, and that I was thankful for.

Chapter Twenty-One

The light was so radiant I couldn't see anything, but a tugging on my arm alerted me that I was alive.

"Arie, we have to go. Now!"

I winced at the urgency in Ashe's voice, but I was still trying to regain composure. He grabbed my cheeks and spoke very methodically.

"I need you to come back, Arie. It has begun. The balance is destroyed, and the veils lifted. We have to get to Amary."

Hearing Amary's name and the fear in Ashe's voice was enough. The light dissolved, and Ashe came into blurry focus.

"I have to pull out the dagger. You shouldn't feel any pain."

I nodded, but instinctively squeezed my eyes shut anyway. He was right. I didn't feel any pain as he pulled it out, but instead, I felt a squishy sensation as the muscles and blood vessels sped to repair themselves. It was a peculiar feeling, kind of like having my gums anesthetized while getting a cavity filled. I could feel everything the dentist was doing, but there was no pain.

"You can open your eyes now," Ashe instructed calmly.

He put one hand under the base of my head and helped me up to a sitting position. Everything was coming into focus slowly.

"How are you feeling?"

"Like I got daggered in the chest," I teased, trying to lighten the situation. I just realized he was touching me and not flying across the river. "How are you touching me?"

"The veils are dropped. The chaos has begun. Without balance, there's nothing regulating the energy."

I was horrified as my vision became clear to see that my mother's real life work of art had turned gray. It was as if a downpour had washed away the color. "What's happening? Why is all the color gone?"

"All the realties are sharing the same realm now. This is one of many side effects, I imagine," he replied.

"How do we fix this? This is all my fault."

An act of love will destroy the balance.

Saving Ashe did this.

"You shouldn't have saved me," he said sternly.

I put my hand on his cheek and forced him to look at me. "I would do it all over again." He pressed his lips to mine urgently, the power of it taking my breath away. I tried to keep him there forever, but he pulled away carefully.

"I love you, Arie."

"Forever," I responded.

He helped me up, but my strength was returning quickly.

"Pyrrhus will go searching for our mother. She was trapped in your old reality where River and Amary are. The only way we can be together is if all the realities merged into one."

"Are nature spirits the only ones who can reality jump?" I asked.

"Yes, and only a small handful of you."

I knew there weren't many who could do what Tivon and I could do, but I didn't realize other clans were excluded from the ability, but the shadow stalkers could jump. "What about the shadows?"

"They aren't anything more than shells. They can't emerge from the shadows there. They can be controlled and do bidding, but that's it. They can't communicate or fight."

It made so much sense. When they came for me, they never fought. Being around them paralyzed me, but that was it.

"That was then, Arie. They have free reign everywhere now. Everyone does."

The thought was terrifying, but a little part of me yearned for that freedom with my old life.

"The world can't sustain this kind of imbalance. It'll implode. The monsters made from the imagination of children will become real, love will be confused with hate, light will succumb to darkness, and color will fade. Eventually, the moon and sun will collide, leaving all that feed off their energy weak and defenseless. Pyrrhus thinks those stones will sustain him and his self-proclaimed clan, but they won't. The stones feed from the natural energy of the universe, and when that's gone, they will be just rocks."

The destruction he was talking about seemed unimaginable, but it was already happening. The color was gone, and a fuzziness hung in the air. "Everything looks like it's trapped within a cloud, like low-lying fog hanging on to the mountain peaks at dawn."

"And it'll get worse. Pyrrhus let his greed blind him from the reality of what he was doing."

My wings flew out from my sides, and I felt my anxiety build. "Let's find Amary and River."

"You're getting better at that," he said, referring to my wings. He wrapped his arms around my waist, tucking my messy tresses behind my ears. "One day I will have you to myself," he whispered.

His breath on my earlobe caused us to take flight. He gripped hard as my wings flapped rapidly, taking us high above Geyser Valley. It was depressing to see how quickly the landscape had changed and blended together. Even the dark beauty of The Dead Forest was somber and no longer stood out from the rest. The memories of all the people lost were unrecognizable now. The sky was grim and cold, the chill leaving a wet layer on my skin. We flew in silence and completely alone, our past escorts finding shelter from the bleak days to come.

The waterfall that served as my private sanctuary was my only indication we had made it back to the village. It looked like everything else, fuzzy and dreary. I landed in front of Tivon's house. Ashe detached as Starling ran out of the house.

"Arie, what's happening?"

The fear in the air reeked like rotting swamp life.

"It's happening, Star. We need to find River and Amary. They can be anywhere, and they're in danger. Did Tivon and the others make it back?"

"We're here."

I turned around to see the exhaustion and the battle wounds on the faces of Tivon, Heath, and Malin. Tivon was carrying Norinda's lifeless body. "Is she..." I couldn't bear to say it.

"No, but she's in bad shape, and with the veils destroyed, we have no way to heal her. The universe can't heal any of us anymore," Tivon informed us.

This was bad. Really bad. They all looked beat up and ready to fall to the ground. I could feel the familiar lump of panic rising in my chest, but I refused to break down in front of them. They were still relying on me to restore balance. I just didn't know how. "I need to go. Ashe and Starling, are you coming with me?" Ashe grabbed my hand in his. Seeing the look in Heath's eyes as he watched the simple gesture made me blush with guilt.

"Of course, I'm coming," Starling boasted, trying to hide how terrified she really was.

I walked to Norinda, still lying in Tivon's arms, touched her forehead, and whispered, "Thank you." When I locked eyes with Tivon, I could tell his pain for Norinda ran deeper than friendship. I couldn't believe I didn't see it sooner. He was in love with her. We shared my revelation silently. *I'm sorry.* He didn't respond, but he nodded. "I'll fix this. I'll fix her. I promise."

"Be careful," he said.

I turned away before the threatening tears flowed. My wings came to life, ready to fly.

"You don't need those," Malin spoke. "There's nothing veiling this reality from the others. You could walk three steps in that direction," she pointed to the right and finished, "and be at your old house."

"Really?" Starling exclaimed excitedly.

"Don't be so happy, child," she scolded Star. "Pyrrhus and his shadows can just as easily do the same."

Starling scrunched back.

"How does it work?" I asked.

"Just believe it. Nothing governs it now. Anyone can go back and forth anywhere and stay as long as they want," Malin said.

"How do you know so much about this?" I questioned. She seemed to know a lot about everything that was happening.

She sighed deeply. "Because this happened once before."

The revelation was mind-blowing for everyone. We all stared at her like a hungry pack of wolves ready to pounce. Tivon spoke up first.

"It is treason to keep secrets from the council regarding the history of our people." The anger flared in his voice.

"And what would you have had me do exactly? You see now how untrustworthy they can be. I knew back then they weren't to be trusted with this information. I have been around longer than anybody on this planet, but I was never asked to be an elder. I can see the future and the truth, yet I was shunned because you were afraid of me. Because I wasn't one of your kind. Don't threaten me with your treason crap. You talk of a time of balance and peace like it was yesterday. Ha! There hasn't been unadulterated balance since before the first coming. Since Vienna's greed consumed her heart and spread through her family." She bit through her words like a kid gnawing on a piece of licorice.

"Who is Vienna?" I asked.

"My mother," Ashe jumped in.

I understood now why Tivon wanted River for me and tried to keep me away from Ashe.

"No, my child." He was reading my thoughts. "It's so much more than that."

I shouted louder than I probably should have, but my frustration was boiling over. "This is ridiculous! Are there any more secrets anyone would like to share before we all knock on death's door?" Everyone remained quiet. "Fine, we don't have time for mistrust. I grabbed Ashe's and Star's hands, closed my eyes, and pictured River and Amary. An image of the two became clear as they sat in a wooden cabin next to a fire. It was cold again, which meant I had missed my birthday. Time was irrelevant here, but it was still nostalgic for me.

When I opened my eyes, we were standing in the snow outside of the cabin. My bare feet instantly froze. *Stupid*, I cursed myself for not being more prepared. I nudged Ashe and Starling. "They're here. My feet are about to fall off, so we need to get inside." We walked to the door, and I knocked quietly saying, "Hey, guys, it's me."

River opened the door and immediately looked defeated when he saw Ashe, but seeing Starling shattered that pretty quickly, especially because she jumped into his arms and started crying. I watched as he squeezed her tightly while keeping his eyes on mine. The tension was uncomfortable, something that was lost on Starling before, but now she joined in it, too.

"Huh, a love square," she pointed out. "This ought to be interesting."

I knew she was trying to lighten things, and I loved her for that, but I didn't think a machete could cut through this. My body started convulsing I was so cold, so Ashe put his arm around me to warm me up.

"Let's get you by the fire," he said as he pushed me inside quickly.

Amary was sleeping on the rug just in front of the fire, but now was awake from the disturbance and jumped up.

"Arie, you're back!"

She smashed into my stomach so hard she nearly knocked me over. I loved this kid with everything in me. I grabbed her firmly and relished in the moment. My shivering limbs forced me to shuffle toward the warmth of the fire with Amary still attached to my waist.

"She needs shoes," Ashe directed to River.

"There's a general store not too far from here. I'll get some supplies."

"I'll come," Star announced.

I watched Starling take her place beside River. In a way, it was hard to see, since in my imagination growing up, it was always me by River's side. Now, I had Ashe, and River had Star, and it just seemed to work. It *felt* right, although it was going to take time to get used to. River's stance was stiff, signaling he wasn't at ease with the current situation. Something it would take Star years to identify. River had many "tells" for his mood that I knew better than anyone, even River. There were times growing up that I would tease him about it. Wow, things were so different now.

"We'll be back," River said as they left.

Amary looked up at me. "What's happening? Everything feels different."

"Did River notice the shift?" I asked her.

"I don't think so. He didn't say anything to me. We've been here since you left."

"How long have you been here?"

"Almost a month."

In the other reality, it had only been a few hours. I knew time was slower there, but it almost seemed to slow down even more.

"I missed you. I wasn't sure if you were ever going to come back."

"I missed you too, buggie." The warmth of the fire pulled

me in. I sat as close as I could before getting burned and Amary snuggled up on my side. Ashe took a seat on the couch behind us. His usual casual demeanor was gone and replaced by anxious foot tapping. He sat up stiff, refusing to let his body sink into the comfort of the cushions.

"We can't stay here long," he announced. "When they get back, we need to go."

Amary tugged on my arm. "Are we going to be okay?"

She was instantly the innocent four-year-old I first met wanting solace from the closest thing to a mother she had. I wrapped my arms around her and pulled her onto my lap, kissing her head and petting her hair. "I hope so, buggie."

Chapter Twenty-Two

My airway was constricted, and I gagged uncontrollably to breathe. Pyrrhus' ice-cold fingers held firm as I ripped at them violently, leaving gashes on my neck in the process. The evil that penetrated the last moments of my life was terrifying. Tears blurred my vision as the world started to become dark. I could hear Amary screaming through tears in the background, but I couldn't offer her any comfort. Not anymore. I had made a choice, and it was one I would stand behind until my last breath.

I darted up, my heart racing and my face wet from crying. I looked around, trying to reorient myself with my surroundings, realizing I was lying on the ground. The fire was barely smoldering, and Amary was sleeping in Ashe's arms on the couch. He was sitting upright with his head resting on the back of the couch. I couldn't see his eyes, but I assumed he was asleep by the deep breathing sounds coming from him. The last thing I remembered was telling Amary about the dreams I used to have when I was her age. The fairytales I had created. *How long had passed since River left?*

I peeled off the blanket that Ashe must have placed over me and went to his side, shaking him gently. He threw his head up in high alert.

"It's okay," I whispered. I pointed with my eyes to Amary still sleeping in his lap. "How long was I asleep?"

He looked across the room to the clock ticking away on the wall by the kitchen table.

"A couple of hours. Are they not back yet?"

"No, and they should be, right?" I was worried. It wasn't snowing that bad outside for it to take them that long to go to the general store and back. Ashe carefully shifted Amary off him and walked to the table with me following.

"We should go. Look in the bedroom for something to put on your feet."

I pleaded, "We can't leave without them."

Ashe looked defeated. "We don't have a choice, Arie. This is about keeping you and Amary safe. Not them. If something happened to them, we couldn't help right now anyway. We only have the natural powers we were born with. No help from the gemstones. We have to keep running until we can meet up with Tivon and Malin again. They will know how to restore balance. They'll figure it out."

I studied him closely. Something wasn't right. His words were telling a different story than his eyes. "You had the dream, too. Didn't you?"

It was as if confronting it head-on had broken his heart.

"Yes," he mumbled as he rubbed his eyes warily.

We shared dreams now. It must have happened when the veil between realities dissipated. *Did that mean Amary was having the same dream, too?* I was sick to my stomach as I watched her sleep peacefully.

"Arie, look..." he trailed off. The tone behind his words choked me. "We both know this isn't going to end well, but I'm not giving up. I'm not going to sit back and let fate steal you from me, again." He grabbed my wrist as I turned away to hide my pain. "Don't hide. Don't ever hide from me. I want to feel you. Everything."

He stood up and turned me so I was facing him. He caught a tear and wiped it away thoughtfully with his thumb. I snuggled into his hand, enjoying the security it brought. "When will it get easier?" I asked him. The layers of complication kept building upon our relationship. I loved Ashe, and I trusted in the love he felt for me. I understood now that no one else could complete us like we did.

He raised my chin so our lips could meet. I pressed hard against his and let the tears flow freely, knowing we had an impossible love from the beginning. One that would never work, but would last forever. A vision of the future overwhelmed me.

Ashe and I were sitting by Deer Creek near the house I grew up in and where we shared some of our first moments together. Our bare feet rested in the slow moving water while we watched a little boy splash a few feet away. Amary, who was a beautiful teenager, stood closely by his side splashing him back. When the boy looked at us to make sure I was watching, we locked eyes, and I was immediately struck by my mother's eyes staring back at me.

The cabin door slammed open, pulling me from something I hadn't felt confident in for a long time... hope for a happily ever after. I studied Ashe's eyes for recognition before addressing River and Starling who staggered inside.

"I saw it, too." A new glimmer replaced the bleakness only moments ago.

He wrapped his hands around my cheeks and kissed me gently. It was the kiss every girl wanted. The kiss that said everything was going to be all right. Finally, the kiss I needed.

River coughed obtrusively.

After another quick reassuring peck, I acknowledged their presence again. Amary had woken up, too. "We were starting to get worried."

"Oh, really? You would never know," Star sassed back playfully.

It still made me blush when I was caught in an intimate moment. River nudged her.

"River, she's kidding," I defended her.

"Oh," he responded.

I shook my head. "Loosen up already," I teased him.

Starling raised a heavy plastic bag over her head. "We got you shoes." She smiled. "I mean, really? Who goes out in a winter storm barefoot?"

I stomped over to her and tried to grab the bag from her. She was a lot taller than me, which she thought was quite funny at the moment. She made me jump up for the bag. "Star, stop," I begged as she giggled. Before I knew it, everyone was laughing at my expense, so I did the only thing a vertically challenged girl could. I went for the 'jugular'. I tackled her to the ground, pinned her under me, and tickled her.

"Arie, stop!" she shouted between painful laughs.

"Say mercy."

"What? Are you kidding...." She couldn't finish due to the breathless laughs consuming her.

Ashe placed a bet. "Five on Arie," he said to River.

"I don't know. I think Blondie is going to make a comeback," River declared.

Meanwhile, I was still torturing Star. The boys got bored and walked to the couch with Amary who was laughing hysterically at the sight of two grown women wrestling.

"Mercy, mercy," Star spat out.

I grabbed the bag and rolled off her onto my back and lay next to her. We both stared at the ceiling while we regained a semblance of maturity. I missed moments like this so much. I missed being a kid. I missed a lot of things.

"That was nice," Star spoke first.

"Yeah, it was."

"Arie, are you really okay with River and me?"

I turned my head to face her. "I wouldn't want anyone else for either one of you."

A grateful smile lit up her face. "Thank you. That means a lot. I really love him."

"I know." I was genuinely happy that they had found each other to lean on amongst all the chaos. They were my best friends and knowing they had each other made the next steps of my life a little easier.

Amary suddenly jumped in-between us and mimicked

our position and stared up at the ceiling with us. Star and I burst out into laughter, quickly followed by Amary. I scooped her into my arms and hugged her tightly. "You're so silly, buggie." She giggled.

"We need to plan the next step," Ashe affirmed.

I rolled Amary off me and sat up. "Yes, we do."

River put more wood onto the fire as we all settled on the couch and floor around it. I sat on the couch next to Ashe with Amary squeezed tightly between us. River sat on the other side of me, and Starling inched between his legs and rested her head on his knee facing us.

"When do we meet back up with Tivon and Malin?" I asked Ashe.

"They gave us twenty-four hours based on the time here."

"So, we still have time to kill," Starling contributed.

"A lot of time," Ashe said nervously.

"It'll be okay," I said as I placed my hand on his knee. "They have been safe here for a month. It's just a few more hours."

"You're right."

The look Ashe gave me didn't match his words. He was worried and protecting Amary from it. All I could do was return it with a confident look. It was dark outside now, and the normal necessities of life in this reality were grumbling loudly in my tummy.

"Maybe we should make dinner," Starling said as she jumped up. "We bought groceries. I can make tacos."

"Ooooh, I love tacos," Amary said excitedly.

"You love everything," River teased her.

She giggled. "Can I help?" she asked Star.

"Of course!"

Both Star and Amary went into the little kitchen area and started to fill the cabin with sounds of pots clanking and bags crinkling. It was so normal and human and perfect. I wanted this life again. I liked my new life, but my heart was here.

River leaned in and whispered, "We bought Amary her favorite food and a cake to celebrate her sixth birthday."

That's what took them so long.

I couldn't believe two years had passed here since we left. No wonder she sounded so much more mature. Time was slower in the other reality, but her maturity seemed to flourish faster. It was like an optical illusion. "What's the date?"

"December fourteenth," he said reluctantly.

The next words got caught in my throat.

"I know," he said as he rubbed my leg.

"What?" Ashe asked as he witnessed the odd exchange.

River left us to help the girls in the kitchen.

"Today's my mom's birthday, too." I stared blankly as I digested the words. After my mom died, the only date I ever focused on was the one she died on. Today was the first time that her birthday affected me like this.

"Then it's really a day to be celebrated."

He always said the right things. "Yes." I squeezed his hand.

I snuggled onto his shoulder and closed my eyes, enjoying the simple sounds and smells of the house. *This would be my life again.* But that dream about Pyrrhus had me doubting my vision of Ashe and me in the future. Pyrrhus had killed me, or at least it seemed that way, but I woke up before I could find out for sure.

"Dinner's ready," Starling announced as she laid the taco bar out onto the only counter.

We filed through, building our tacos like a buffet bar and crowded around the table. There were only four chairs, so River leaned against the wall to eat. The food was delicious, and the banter was light and fun. It was the perfect birthday celebration.

After everyone was finished eating, I helped Star clear the dishes as River covertly prepared the cake with six candles. It was a generic store-bought cake with flowers covering the top. They looked just like amaryllis flowers. She was going to love it.

"Amaryllis, go sit at the table. We have a little surprise for you," River said.

Her eyes widened, and she bounced to the table. I stood by her side, and Ashe turned off the lights after River lit the final candle.

River counted, "One, two, three," and we all began to sing "Happy Birthday". Amary was thrilled. River put the cake down in front of her, and when the song was over, I leaned down and told her, "All my wishes came true, so wish for something that means the most to you."

She smiled back enthusiastically and then closed her eyes tightly for a long moment. When she was done, she blew out all the candles in one breath. We all clapped liked idiots, and then River slid the cake over to cut into pieces. I didn't know how the night could be any more magical for her. She deserved this. She deserved many days just like this one, and I planned on giving them to her.

The rest of the evening was much like dinner. We talked around the fire. Amary eventually wore out and fell asleep on the floor. River scooped her up and carried her to the only bedroom. They were close before I left her with him, but now I had a feeling he would be just as devastated as me if something were to happen to her. I was going to share the bed with Amary, Ashe was going to take the couch, and River and Star were going to sleep on the floor by the fire. It was a cozy cabin, but I wouldn't have it any other way. It felt safe.

As everyone was settling in for the night, I went and sat at the kitchen table. I was tired, but I wasn't ready to retreat to the bedroom yet. River sat with me while Ashe and Starling chatted comfortably from their sleeping spots.

"It's been a while," River said.

"Yeah, it has."

"How are you holding up?"

"Meh, but I'll be okay."

"So, what happened?"

We hadn't had time to talk, so I filled him in on my wings, the battle at Pyrrhus', and finally, about being daggered. I left out the parts about Ashe and me.

"And you lived?" he inquired.

"Yeah, instead of dying, it caused the veils between realities to fall. Then the three realities bled together, and everything went gray and dark. Shadow stalkers, Pyrrhus, us... we all have free reign. You can't even tell where one reality starts and another ends. There's no distinction. It's all just one reality now. I can transport anywhere at any time for as long as I want."

"You mentioned the gemstones."

"They have no power now, which doesn't have to be a bad thing. It puts us all back on a level playing field. We only have what we were naturally born with. Unfortunately, though, Pyrrhus has the numbers. Except..."

"What?"

"My ring still has power. It seems to be the only stone that does. I have a feeling Pyrrhus knows it, too, which is another reason why he wants it so badly. As long as the veils are down, which he wants permanently, this is the only source of outside power."

River sat silent as he processed and then spoke up, "But you have the power. Does Tivon or Malin have any idea what you have become?"

"Not really, but Pyrrhus alluded to me being the next thing in evolution. I am some sort of hybrid, an evolved species."

"The first, which makes you a target. Either way, people will want you and Amary dead..."

"Or they will want to control us so they can control the new species," I finished. "I know, River, which is why Pyrrhus needs to be killed."

He lowered his voice. "We need to find out how his mom plays into all of this."

"You don't have to whisper. Ashe doesn't agree with what his brother is doing."

"I understand that now, Arie, but there is no bond stronger than that between a mother and child. No matter what. You know this, and you need to remember it. Your blind faith can get you killed."

A small part of me knew he was right, but a bigger part of me believed that Ashe would choose truth above anything else. He would choose me. It was naïve thinking, but it was a trait that I cherished and was hoping to never lose.

It had been so long since River and I were able to talk so easily and freely. It felt good. We had both accepted that our fates were not aligned for us to be together, and it had made our interactions comfortable again. I needed him like this. He was always there for me. He was my first friend, my first boyfriend, my first love, and my first rock. He was my everything.

 # Chapter Twenty-Three

It was a typical warm evening in the meadow with clear skies and stars sparkling for miles. There always seemed to be a light breeze carrying sounds of the buzzing nightlife and the fragrances of dew on the horizon. My body sank into the lush grass that blanketed the butterfly circle. I wanted to stay here forever in this moment without a worry in the world. Just the universe and me like it used to be. I closed my eyes and freed my mind of idle chatter. I couldn't remember how I got here, but I didn't care. It was perfect and just where I wanted to be.

"Arie."

A gentle voice enticed my eyes to open. Malin stood above me. "Am I dreaming?"

"Yes," she replied.

I sat up and stared up at her. Her clothes were dirty, signifying the broken veil and her face looked worn, but her eyes still glowed a vibrant purple. "How did I get here?"

"You can go anywhere in your dreams, Arie. You have a control in which no one else does. You're evolved. You're new."

"Can I live in my dreams?"

"I don't doubt the limitations of your extraordinary nature, but those who aren't evolved wouldn't be able to."

That thought made me sad. "Amary is evolved."

"Yes."

But no one else was. It was just the two of us. I couldn't

leave Ashe, and I couldn't break up her and River. "I won't stay then. We would be lonely and miss everyone."

"Good girl," she said as she faded, the breeze swirling around her and taking her away into the night sky.

I accepted this as normal and lay back down, closing my eyes again.

"Arie."

This time it was a deep and strong voice. I looked up at Tivon who was leaning over me. It reminded me of the time I died, and he stole my light from the universe. His face hadn't aged a day, and his eyes weren't riddled with pain. "I'm dreaming," I informed him.

"Yes, I know."

"Do I need to wake up?"

"Not yet, but soon."

"I like it here." I smiled.

"It's pleasant," he responded as he looked over the meadow. "This place will always hold my heart."

"Do you miss her?"

"Every day," he replied as he too faded away.

I thought about what Malin said. I had control. I could do anything in my dreams.

Be anything.

See anyone.

I thought about my mom.

"Hello, my sweet baby."

My mom's voice carried on the breeze. I sat up and found her standing next to her gravestone, so I floated over to join her. My wings had opened and spread across the area.

"Your wings are beautiful, Arie. I'm so proud of what you've become."

I lifted my hand that adorned the ring. "I understand this now. The power it possesses. I'll never let anyone have it."

"And with that ring, I will always be with you, but you will need to make a choice. I want you to know that even without that ring, I will always be with you." She reached out her hand

and rested it over my heart. "Here."

She was giving me permission to destroy her essence. To destroy her. It broke me because I knew I would need it to beat Pyrrhus. I sullenly responded, "I know."

"Your compassion and strength will see you through this," she said as she leaned over and kissed my forehead. She faded as she released her embrace.

A loud rumbling in the sky startled me, and black clouds manifested out of nowhere, darkening the sky. The sounds increased in intensity, sending shivers through my bones. I looked around the meadow and considered running into my house, but it had disappeared. The grass had turned black to match the sky, and the flowers that were displaying their brilliant colors only seconds ago had wilted. Everything was dying. The first raindrop of the impending storm landed upon my cheek with a thud, jolting the pounding in my heart. I didn't know where to go. There was no shelter. The wind kicked up and brought with it the violent hissing of Pyrrhus' voice. I needed to run and hide, but there was nowhere. The dirt beneath my feet started to swallow me slowly. Within minutes I would be suffocating under the earth. I tried to pull up my feet, but they wouldn't budge. I was trapped. The panic rushed through my veins, causing every muscle to twitch.

But this was *my* dream.

I had control.

"Stop!" I yelled at the top of my lungs. Everything froze. The mud that had swallowed my legs turned to dried dirt and crumbled, giving me freedom again. I stepped away, observing the unmoving chaos. It was black as night, so I waved my hand to the sky like a paintbrush across canvas and erased the clouds, letting the natural light of day retrieve its spot. I spun around, surveying the colorless landscape. I summoned the breeze and blew out a kiss of life. Instantly, the black dripped off the grass blades, revealing a glossy dark green. The wilted flowers came alive, and new ones burst through the earth. A giggle overtook me as I watched in awe over the power I possessed. My house had reappeared, and the world had come alive again. Time in motion once again.

"Arie."

I turned to face Ashe. He was so enchanting. The green speckles that once floated amongst the amber in his eyes had become more prominent, the amber barely visible now. His toned muscles were visible through his fitted black shirt, and his short, thick, dark tresses were perfectly messy around his olive skin. "I love you," I said.

He stepped closer to me, leaving only centimeters of space between us. The heat from his body left me breathless. I was anticipating his lips on mine. My body willed him to touch me.

His lips wisped past mine, and he whispered into my ear, "I love you, too. Forever."

His hot breath sent goose bumps racing down my neck and bouncing over each vertebra on the way down my spine. His mouth glided over my skin in search for my lips. When they made contact, I lost myself within the confines of my sensations, forgetting everything around me. He grabbed the back of my neck and pushed his chest into mine. I was going deeper into a world of emotions undiscovered. I was falling fast, but from where, I didn't know. My wings made the descent graceful and the landing gentle. Before I could get a grip on what was happening, a light blinded me and a pain in my chest overcame me.

"Arie!"

I could hear Ashe, but I couldn't respond. I couldn't move. I couldn't feel.

"Arie!"

I felt my body convulse, and Ashe's voice said, "She's coming out of it."

A tingling sensation traveled under my skin and raced to my face. When it reached my eyes, they opened obediently. The first thing I focused on was Ashe's eyes. The green was just specks again, giving the rich golden color a chance to shine. He stroked my cheek meticulously.

"Welcome back," he said.

I was still in a daze. "Where did I go?"

"Somewhere wonderful." He smiled.

"Then why am I back?"

"Because I'm selfish," he replied.

He leaned down and kissed my lips gently. "Don't scare me like that again."

What had I done? I racked my mind for recognition. I started with my current state of awareness. I was lying in Ashe's lap on the bed. The light was bright from the windows, which meant it was daytime. Before my eyes opened, I heard him talking to someone.

Before my eyes opened.

I was sleeping. No, wait. I was dreaming, and I had control.

The fog started to lift. I sat up and spotted River standing in the doorway, his arms crossed uncomfortably across his chest. I heard Starling and Amary in the other room.

River looked at me for another second and then left the room without a word.

"What's wrong with him?" I asked Ashe.

"He's scared."

"Of what?"

"Of losing you."

I crawled off Ashe's lap and walked to the door. River was sitting at the kitchen table with his face hiding in his hands while the girls prepared food. *Was it breakfast?* I turned back to Ashe. "He's upset."

"Yes."

"What happened?" I inquired.

"You went to sleep with Amary. When we all woke up, you were still asleep, so we left you alone. But then you screamed, and when I found you in bed, you were barely breathing. A moment later, you were gone. Your breathing ceased, and your body became stiff." He shuddered from the memory. "You were gone, but you were happy."

"I was with you," I responded.

"I know."

I raised my eyebrow in question.

"I came to you to bring you back."

"You can do that?" I asked.

"Apparently. I wasn't sure, but I had to try, especially after seeing our connection yesterday with the vision."

"Maybe the veils being lifted isn't such a bad thing," I said.

"No, Arie, it is a bad thing, particularly for you. You're getting caught in-between the fabric of reality and dreams. We could have lost you today. This is real. What's happening right now is real. *That* was a dream. You're losing the distinction."

He was right. My mind was having a hard time deciphering what was real. "It seemed so real, Ashe. I felt real, and it was so peaceful. I had control over everything. Pyrrhus couldn't get to me."

He stood up and placed his hands on my shoulders as if to shake me out of my stupor. "Listen to me. Until you have restored the veils, we need to be careful. We'll sleep in shifts. I want someone awake while you sleep at all times."

His grip tightened on my shoulders with his anxiety. "Okay," was all I said. He needed to be reassured that I understood the situation was grave. *He needed me.* He pulled me in tight and held me close.

"Breakfast is ready!" Amary yelled from the kitchen.

"Have we heard from Tivon or Malin yet?" I asked Ashe.

"No." He was concerned.

We made our way to the kitchen. It was buffet style again, but only this time the counter was crowded with eggs, pancakes, bacon, and potatoes.

"Wow, buggie. This is quite the spread. Thank you." I patted her head.

"Um, hello? What about me?" Star asked.

"Good job, little buggie," I teased as I ruffled her hair.

She swatted my hand away. "Hey, don't mess with the hair."

We filled our plates and gathered at the kitchen table. Ashe and River took their plates to the couch to powwow privately. I wasn't sure if they were shielding Amary or me or maybe both of us.

"Are you okay?" Starling asked.

"Yeah, I'm fine." She gave me an unconvinced glare. "How did you sleep, buggie?"

"Great!" she shouted as she shoveled eggs into her mouth. "This is the best birthday ever!"

And it was. My mom would have loved us celebrating like this. Celebrating life. I watched as the guys whispered to each other. When Amary was finished, she put her plate into the sink and went into the bedroom.

"What's going on with them?" Star inquired.

"I'm not sure," I responded apprehensively. I deflected. "How are you and River?"

"Really good. Thank you."

"Thank you for what?" I was confused.

"Thank you for being okay with us."

"It was meant to be." I smiled supportively.

The time was ticking by so slowly. It made me antsy. Ashe played cards with Amary at the table, and Starling read a book she found in the cabin. River was on guard as usual. He was standing in front of the back window.

"It's still snowing." I stood next to him. "All the white is so pretty."

"Masks the colorless landscape," he responded.

"I guess it does."

More silence.

"It's almost time. Are you sure you can get us all to where we need to meet?"

"Yes, I can do pretty much anything with the veils down."

"Now there's a scary thought," he joked.

"Ha-ha." I nudged his side.

The smile disappeared from River's face, and his body stiffened. He was staring intensely out the window. "What's wrong?"

"There's something out there."

Ashe was by our side in a flash. "What is it?"

"I'm not sure yet."

The tension was building. I surveyed the forest, but didn't see anything.

"What's wrong?" Amary tugged on my arm.

I addressed Star,"Starling, can you..."

"Yes." She jumped up and collected Amary. "Let's go sit by the fire and let them talk."

Worried, Amary looked back at me. She could feel the shift in the air. Danger was near. "We need to get out of here," I proclaimed. The darkness was getting stronger. I ran over to Amary and took her hand. "Don't let go. No matter what." She nodded in mild horror. My ring came alive with energy as it pulsed quickly. "Everyone get over here and hold tight," I demanded.

Starling grabbed Amary's free hand. Just as the guys turned to join us, a loud boom resonated from outside that shook the cabin. In a flash the cabin was gone, and we were standing in the snow completely exposed.

Ashe yelled, "Go!"

My eyes filled with panic at the prospect of leaving them behind.

"Now!" River added.

Shadows ascended on us quickly from the forest. The guys tried to make it to me, but it was too late. My wings jetted out to the side, and we took flight. As we got higher, I watched in horror as shadow stalkers surrounded the guys.

"Arie, look out!" Ashe shouted.

We were pounded from the side and rapidly falling to the ground. The pain from the impact was intense, causing my strength to diminish. Amary and Starling gripped onto me tightly. Amary screamed as we got closer to the ground. *I can do this. I have control.* I took a deep breath and imagined the pain away. Just before we hit the ground, my wings lifted us again, but we were being hunted down for another attack. I caught a glimpse of River and Ashe fighting below.

"Another one is coming!" Star yelled.

I caught sight of it. The shadow was closing in quickly, but I was faster and stronger. "Hang on," I instructed them. It was my turn. I aimed straight for the shadow barreling down on us. I knew it wasn't going to budge, but I had something it didn't. I aimed the ring toward it, emitting a ray of light that encapsulated the shadow like the chocolate coating on an M & M. When it was completely consumed, it disappeared within the light, the ray retracted and then faded within the ring. *It worked!* I had trapped the shadow stalker's essence.

"How did you do that?" Star was shocked.

"We have to get out of here." The guys were still being surrounded. I flew down and landed in front of them in the center of the chaos. "Hold the girl," I demanded. Amary and Star fled by their side. I raised the ring and spun in the circle, the ray of light consuming all the shadows.

"That was cool," River boasted.

"We have Malin to thank for that one," I replied.

"Thank me for what?"

Malin, Tivon, and Heath emerged from the trees. Amary giggled.

As they approached, relief settled the air, but it wasn't lost on me that I was now in the company of all three men who at some point vied for my affection. My emotions were conflicted among guilt, shame, and love.

"Arie just swept the floor of shadow stalkers," Star offered.

"Oh, she did now?" Malin pressed.

"My ring. I figured if it could trap my mom's essence, why not others', too? I mean, you said this was the only thing that could."

"Yes, my dear, I did, but it can't hold it long-term. Only titanium possesses that power."

"Do you mind sharing with the rest of us?" River encouraged.

Tivon spoke up, "When I made Arie's ring, it was only intended for her mother, Ariana."

"I'm confused about something," I said. "If it can only trap, then this was never going to hold my mom's essence forever?"

"I'm afraid not, Arie," Tivon responded. "I only intended for it to be short-term. To help you through this."

I was shattered. "But I don't understand." I was instantly transported to my seven-year-old voice.

"Let me explain," Malin said. "Arie, your mom has to find peace. She deserves it. When it's her time, you need to let her go, and I know that's what you want. For your mom to find peace."

Of course, I did. I wanted my mom to fly free with all the others. It was just a hard pill to swallow. She told me I would need to make a choice, and now I understood why. Either way I was going to have to let her go, but it might be sooner than I wanted.

"It's still unclear what just transpired here." River sounded annoyed.

Heath stepped forward. "The opal and Herkimer diamonds act as conduit and trap lost essence, but only titanium can hold it long-term. The purpose is that whoever is in possession of these lost souls has power to control them."

Without skipping a beat, River asked, "And you are?"

Right. He hadn't met Heath yet, nor had I mentioned him. "This is Heath. He's been watching over me since you left Serendae."

Dead silence.

"Serendae?" It was like a unison of vocalists.

Amary giggled. "Serendae is what they call mine and Arie's new home."

Malin bent down to Amary's height. "Where did you hear that name, my child?"

"Iris. She said she and some other kids saw it written on a stone near the river, so that's what they call their world."

"Huh," was all Malin said.

"What?" Tivon inquired.

"It's just interesting. I haven't heard our reality called that in a long time, but yes, Amary, that is correct. Our world was once referred to as Serendae."

The revelation didn't seem like much, but I could tell there was a fascinating history behind it and why the name disappeared over time.

Chapter Twenty-Four

With the elders potentially after Amary and me, and Pyrrhus on the loose, we had to find another safe place to hide, so Malin brought us to where she had been living since the raid on her village. The lot of us stood in front of a large rock several stories tall and just about as wide.

"Arie, come here," Malin requested. I stood beside her. "This rock is no different than the façade Pyrrhus manufactured to hide his own home. However, without the power of the gems, I no longer have access." She pulled a malachite stone from her pocket. "Would you mind?" She gestured to the rock.

"I can try." It still made me uneasy to be so heavily relied upon. *Acceptance. Wait.* "No." Everyone froze, completely shocked by my response. "Buggie, want to give a try?"

She beamed from ear to ear while skipping to my side. Malin was pleased as well. I addressed the group. "She needs to build confidence in her ability." *Because I may not always be around.* They nodded in silent understanding. "Remember what I taught you at the waterfall?"

"Uh-huh. Just picture something, and it'll appear," she replied.

"Exactly. Just imagine a house is here instead of this rock, and it will break the concealment."

She squeezed her eyes closed, scrunching her face funny and causing all of us to laugh quietly while being careful not to disturb her concentration. A moment later, the rock was gone, and a simple quaint house stood in its place. It blended with the forest with its combination of neutral colors and materials. It was perfect for her. "It's lovely."

"Thank you. And thank you, Amary. You did great." She gave Amary a little squeeze.

"That was easy." She gleamed.

"Glad to hear it," I said.

"Please, everyone, let's get inside. Arie, would you mind?"

"Of course." I waited until everyone was inside, and then I concealed the house once again with the boulder. I stood just outside the front door to re-energize under the sun. I raised my face and arms to it, allowing all my bare skin full exposure.

"Are you okay?" Heath asked as he stepped back outside.

I put my arms down quickly. "Yes, I just needed a little fix."

"You did that back there. Didn't you?"

He caught me. "Yes, it's not that she needed to be able to do it. Not yet at least, but she needs to feel confident that she can do it one day."

"I get it, but I'm worried about you. You are draining faster."

I sighed. "You noticed that, huh? Please, don't tell anyone. I don't want anyone else worrying."

"Is there something else you aren't telling us?" He propped himself against the wall.

There was so much, but my visions were conflicting and causing me a lot of grief. One showed Pyrrhus killing me, and the other showed Ashe and me with a son. Neither of those things I felt comfortable sharing with Heath, so I just shrugged.

"Well, that makes me feel better," he said sarcastically.

"I know. I'm sorry. I only have pieces, and they don't really make sense. I just know that Amary and I are wanted dead, and I'm trying to keep that from happening." I sat in a little chair on the front porch in defeat.

"You're doing a great job, Arie. Don't ever question that. She loves you, and we all know that you will do whatever it takes to keep her safe. But you have to respect that we will do anything to keep *both* of you safe."

"I know, but sometimes I wonder if the cost is too high. If all the deaths will be forgiven once all is said and done."

Heath sat in the chair next to me, reaching his hand over and taking mine in his. His skin was soft and reassuring. "Listen to me. You can't live life worrying about the future, whether it's a few hours into the future or a day or a year. We can't predict what's going to happen, so there's no sense in stressing over it. Take this one moment at a time. One tick of the clock at a time. Make decisions based on now, not later. This is your destiny, and although I know you want to rebel against fate, it's real and it's happening. You can't stop it. So stop fighting it, and follow your heart. It will tell you what needs to be done to make all this right again. You are badass, Arie."

I looked at him, startled. He always seemed to pop in humor at the best times to lighten a heavy situation.

"What? You are. You have butterfly wings, a sacred marking of the nature spirits, and a ring that can evaporate shadow stalkers. Not to mention that you are the most powerful being that has ever existed. You. Are. Badass. And don't you forget it." He playfully knocked my shoulder with his.

I half-giggled half-whimpered. I was emotionally exhausted. "I love you, Heath. Thank you."

"You're welcome." He smiled. "Now, when you're fully juiced, come join us. We need to talk about our next move."

He got up, leaned over, and kissed my cheek. Then he disappeared inside, leaving me to soak up the sun's rays in silence again.

"You know you can stay here forever if you want."

I was staring at a woman I had never seen before. She

was mesmerizing with long, thick, jet-black hair, bright green eyes, olive skin, and full pink lips. Her frame was tall and frail, but her confidence was fierce. I must have fallen asleep. I was dreaming.

"Yes, Arie, you are dreaming," she said wickedly.

I was standing face-to-face with her, and the darkness oozed from her pores. "Who are you?" I dared her.

She laughed. "You know who I am. Look at me more closely, little girl."

The way she said 'little girl' sent a wave of ice over my skin. I studied her harder, but it wasn't until I locked my eyes on hers that it hit me. They were the same eyes as Ashe's, only the colors were reversed. Hers were prominently green with amber specks. "Vienna." The hatred spilled off my tongue.

She clapped just like Pyrrhus had done when he tied up Norinda in his courtyard. "Very good, but I thought you would have sensed it sooner, being who you are and all." Jealousy filled her words. "How is my son? Or should I say, my sons?"

"What do you want? Why are you here? You know I can control all of this, right? I could kill you right now if I wanted." I threatened her.

"Try it. See what happens."

She was bluffing.

"I'm not bluffing, little girl. You aren't the only special one. I have a few secrets of my own. So, go ahead. Try to kill me right now. I dare you," she seethed.

My confidence was fading, and she could see it.

"That's what I thought. Just a little girl. You aren't ready for all of this. You aren't ready to become one of me."

My heart stopped.

The noises silenced.

The world stood very still.

I froze and then started to spin. First slowly and then as her words repeated in my head, 'you aren't ready to become one of me', I spun faster. I was on the verge of a panic attack and losing consciousness when a pair of hands gripped my arms and stopped my body in motion. They stopped everything but the words that wouldn't quit repeating over and over again.

'You aren't ready to become one of me.'

"Snap out of it, Arie. Wake up."

I heard his voice and felt the invisible bruises forming on my arms, but I was having a hard time making my way back to him. Back to Ashe. Vienna was gone, but she had torched my entire existence with her revelation.

A little hand touched my cheek and calmed my soul. I opened my eyes and smiled back at Amary. She had brought me back all on her own. I placed my hand over hers. "You did good."

She giggled proudly.

Ashe lifted her off me and scooped me up into his arms. I had made my way to the ground during my encounter with Vienna. I felt so utterly drained that I could barely move. He brought me back into the sun and cradled me as the sun fed me life. I loved how it felt to be in his arms. I would miss his touch when the veils were back up. I wouldn't take his physical comfort for granted. "I love you."

"I love you, too."

I looked up at him and met his lips halfway. They were moist and soft and filled my heart with joy. Another thing I would miss.

He pulled away. "Are you better now?"

"I am." But I wasn't really. I had just found out that I was like his mother, and I *wasn't* the first of my kind. Would I turn to darkness as she had? And if I was like his mother, is that why we couldn't be together? Malin had mentioned this happening before. Something not even Tivon knew. I needed to talk to her alone somehow.

"Your color has returned." Ashe smiled. "Let's get you inside."

"I can walk." I didn't want anyone to think I was weak. Not now. My toes touched the ground as he slid me out of his arms. I interlaced my fingers with his, never wanting to let go and led him inside with me. Amary had been sitting on the front porch picking petals off a flower, so she bounced in ahead of us.

The interior of the house looked like a French-style cottage. It was so simple and pretty with the white lace ruffles around the pale pink window treatments against the crisp white walls. River and Starling sat on a couch facing the fireplace whispering and smiling. Their reunion had lightened their aura. Amary had skipped deeper into the house where the kitchen was located. There was a large, thick, beautifully carved honey-colored butcher-block picnic table in the center where Amary happily hopped on and started coloring. Malin was sitting on the back porch. *Perfect.* "I'm going to chat with Mali," I said to Ashe.

"I'll color with Amary."

We walked through the house together. As we passed Amary, Ashe sat with her, and I joined Mali. She had left open the back door, so I closed it. She was sitting on a white park bench sipping what smelled like raspberry tea. "May I?"

"Of course, my dear."

I slid next to her and immediately started twisting a finger in my hand.

"You're fidgeting, my child. What's on your mind?"

"I just had a vision." I paused. "Of Vienna." I studied her face for a reaction. It was blank.

"I'm surprised it took so long."

"Wait. You knew she would come to me?"

She sighed sadly. "Yes, Arie, it was only a matter of time."

"Why wouldn't you tell any of us? Why wouldn't you tell me?"

She stood up. "Let's go for a walk."

I didn't stand up.

"It's safe here," she added.

I pushed myself off the bench and walked alongside of her down the steps and across the clearing that signified a backyard. When we reached some trees, she followed a dirt trail and started to speak.

"Vienna was my best friend."

A revelation I wasn't expecting. I stayed quiet.

"She was actually more like a sister to me. She was younger, and her parents had joined the universe when she was still a child. My parents took her in and treated her like their own. She had an unparalleled spirit that glowed way beyond that of anyone else. Everyone loved her, and she loved in return, but losing her parents changed that. Her aura shifted, and the glow became dark in nature. It started with little things, like being mean to another friend or destroying flowers. I tried to intervene before it got out of hand. I covered for her on several occasions. Something I will never stop regretting. Had I told my parents, they might have been able to take her to the elders to save her. I thought I was doing right by her. Protecting her. I was wrong."

The shame covered Malin like a layer of fog. I felt bad for her. "I can tell you loved her."

"I did. I still do. When your mother, Genesis, killed her, I was the only one who cared that she was gone."

I blushed from remorse. My mother was responsible for Malin's pain. "Why would Genesis kill her?"

"Vienna was a hybrid just like you, Arie. When she turned eighteen and ascended like the rest of us, her butterfly wings manifested. She kept it a secret from everyone but me. She still trusted me. A mistake she would later realize. Her power scared me." She stopped walking and grabbed my arm.

I sat on a rock watching two girls my age fighting a few feet away.

"Vienna, you're scaring me."

"You better not tell anyone, Mali. You can't betray the sister pact," Vienna said viciously.

"You are out of control, Vienna. You need to stop," Malin demanded.

"You're just jealous. I'm younger, stronger, and the first

to be anointed with wings."

"Don't fool yourself. Don't mistake my concern for jealousy. I'm proud that my little sister has been bestowed with such a gift, but I'm worried you will abuse it."

Vienna scoffed, "How I use my gift is none of your business or anybody else's." She took to the sky, a trail of hatred left behind.

I stood up on the rock and took flight after her. I kept my distance, not sure how the vision jumping worked. She disappeared in the billows of white clouds expelled by Geyser Valley. I followed as she flew through the purple valley. I was stunned to see it, just as my mom had painted it, since she didn't exist at this point. Vienna landed inside the valley and disappeared behind a hanging wall of mossy vines. I landed just outside. The sounds of a baby crying caught my attention. I ran to the vines and peeked inside. Vienna was cradling a small infant in her arms while a toddler played on the ground in the corner.

She called for the toddler, "Ashe, come here, honey."

I was rendered speechless. That was Ashe, and the baby in her arms was Pyrrhus. And no one in the village knew. A familiar man's voice called from a corner I couldn't see.

"I'll take the baby. Ashe needs some time with his mother."

I couldn't breathe.

I couldn't think.

I was terrified.

Tivon walked to Vienna and took Pyrrhus out of her arms.

The rush of tears blurred my vision. My wings carried me high into the sky away from the scene. Away from the deceit. Away from the vision.

Malin tore her hand from my arm and watched me, carefully assessing my stability from the truth she had just divulged. I was frozen in time. The pain from Tivon's lies was disturbing, but what that truth meant for Ashe and me was unbearable.

"I'm sorry, my child. I didn't know. I never knew who their father was. I learned with you."

I shook my head of the vision. "No. No, it can't be. It can't be, Mali." I fell to my knees and crumbled for the first time since my mother's death.

I was lost.

I was alone. Again.

Malin held me as I purged the hell that had become me. She didn't say a word.

She just rocked me and let me fall. And I fell hard. My muscles tightened and loosened in accord with my cries, causing excruciating pain throughout. My heart split one small piece by one small piece slowly. I thought of the pain I felt when I stood over my mom's lifeless body. How useless I felt. I cried for her loss again. For the deceit of Tivon. Not only to me, but also to her. I cried knowing why Ashe and I could never be together. Knowing why the universe kept us apart, even though our magnetism flourished. I cried for what I was about to do.

Chapter Twenty-Five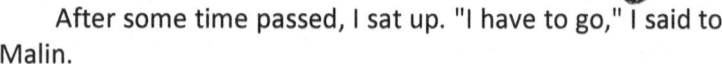

After some time passed, I sat up. "I have to go," I said to Malin.

"I know," she replied simply.

The revelation was a game changer. I couldn't go back to the house and pretend, but this was also not the time to make some big announcement that could jeopardize the safety of the group.

"She will be safe with me. No matter what Tivon did in the past or what he's hiding, there's no question that he loves you and Amary and would give his life for you two."

I felt that way, too, but I still couldn't go back. I was stripped raw, too exposed to conceal. "Thank you." I stood up and shot into the air without another word. I had no idea where I was going, but I didn't care. My anger had taken hold, and I had become a prisoner of the infectious venom produced by Tivon's secrets. I would do this on my own. I would uncover everything this reality was hiding. I would truly bring back the light that had been missing. Vienna was the beginning of the destruction here. She was the key, and she would be the end.

If I learned anything the past few weeks, it was that I had control. I had the power to resurrect the purity and close off the darkness where it belonged. But to do that, I had to let go. I had to let my instinct take over. More importantly, I had to trust it. Something that didn't come easy anymore. As I flew across the gray sky, I let the sun's rays continue to power me. My first trust test was to close my eyes and just feel. The wind whipped through my hair, and the heat prickled my skin. I heard the whiz of my wings as they fluttered ferociously. I was at peace in my angry state. I wondered if this was how Vienna felt. Free. No more guilt, no more pain, no more shame. Just free.

Time continued to pass, but I never opened my eyes. I would know when it was time. My instincts would tell me. Instead, I focused on the dream with Vienna. I felt so much aversion in her, but the way she cared for her sons was anything but. She loved them unconditionally. She would do whatever it took to protect them. Someone of pure evil wouldn't be capable of that kind of love. It made me believe there was a way to save Pyrrhus. Bring him back for Ashe. He would need his brother more than ever after he found out the true nature of our connection. One of familial bonds rather than true love. He would be as devastated as me. Maybe more.

A tingling in my shoulders alerted me that my wings were preparing to ground me. I opened my eyes and found the bookstore below. How odd they should bring me here. I landed gracefully in front of the *Closed* sign and my wings disappeared. It was hard to be angry here. It was hard to be happy, too. I shrugged as I tried the knob, but tt was locked. I raised myself on my tiptoes and reached above the wooden sign and retrieved the spare key. I unlocked it and went inside. Nothing had changed except the layer of dust collecting on everything. The store had been closed for almost two years now. It broke my heart. My mom and I loved this store. It was our home away from home. I brushed my hand along a spine of books on the first bookshelf. I always loved the way books felt in my hands. I added e-readers to keep up with the trends, but they just weren't the same as the real thing. The smell of vintage or freshly printed paper and the artistic creativity of the covers told the story without words. E-readers could never give that feeling to a reader. My fingers were caked with dust by the end of the aisle. I looked around the store in the dark trying to figure out why I was here. There had to be something I was missing.

"You aren't missing anything, Arie."

I spun around and let a hissing sound escape my lips. It was Vienna. "I'm not dreaming," I stated.

"No, you're not. You don't have the same kind of control here."

"But I have the power," I challenged her.

She let out an obnoxious cackle. "Let it go, child. You can keep fighting your fate if you want, but in the end you will lose. You and I are one in the same. Tivon tried so hard to keep it from you. From all of you. And then your wretched mother found out. She was jealous, so she killed me."

I was shaking my head in disbelief.

"Don't try to hide from what you feel is true. She killed me in front of my sons with no mercy. But like you, my essence came here. I was reborn, only I didn't know who I was. No one came to me to help me understand why animals approached me unnaturally or why butterflies clung to me whenever I was outside. I had no one when I turned eighteen here when the visions of my past life were slowly killing me. I had no one because your father kept it a secret. He never sent anyone to protect me. You got River and Starling and the others. I was alone." Her voiced cracked.

I felt sorry for her. I knew I should hate her, but she was a victim of circumstance. Something in which I was familiar. "Why are you here? What do you want with me?"

"I need you, Arie. Well, not you," she said as she waved her hand to define my physical body. "I need your essence to return to what I once was."

Before I knew what was happening, a piercing pain filled my head. I clawed at my scalp as I collapsed to my knees. All I could focus on was the deafening ringing in my ears. My ring began to glow brilliantly, and the pain subsided. I looked up and saw Pyrrhus by Vienna's side. I was weakened from the attack, so getting up was not an option yet.

"And you said you were strong." Pyrrhus laughed. "You are nothing without that ring." He stomped over and yanked the ring off my finger.

"Noooo!" I cried out.

"Your mom stole mine, so it's only fitting I should take yours." He glided back to Vienna.

"Have them bring her with us," Vienna ordered.

Shadows descended upon me. I wanted to fight, but I was weak and paralyzed. All there was to do was wait and see how my vision of the future played out.

I was starting to enjoy being stuck between dreams and reality. I didn't have to worry or feel. I could just be. I knew in reality I was in danger, but I didn't have the energy to care. I knew Amary was safe, and that was all that really mattered to me. I woke up in the room in which Pyrrhus had imprisoned Ashe. Without my ring, I wasn't sure what kind of power I had. I probably should have thought of testing it before, but I never imagined being separated from it. I could still smell Ashe's natural scent on the sheets. It was both comforting and pungent at the same time. I didn't know how to feel about him anymore.

"You know Ashe was always my favorite," Vienna said from the darkness in the corner of the room.

"Great, another person who can read my thoughts."

"Don't get me wrong. I love Pyrrhus. He's always been more loyal, but Ashe is such a momma's boy. He loves so passionately. He is my sweet, sweet boy."

"Can you not talk to me like we're friends?" I bit at her. "Why am I still alive?"

"In a rush to die, Arie?"

"If I have to listen to any more of your mommy stories,

maybe."

"Sass. I like it. We have to wait for the blood moon, so you will need to put on your patience hat, little one."

"Please, tell me it's soon."

"Oh, it is. Make yourself comfortable. You won't be getting out of here. None of your tricks work anymore."

She walked out the door, which wasn't concealed as a wall anymore. No veil, no magic. All we had was what we were naturally betrothed, but my ring still had its power and was now in the possession of Vienna and Pyrrhus. Who knew what they could do. If they had the ring when the veils were back up, all the magic would return, and they would be the most powerful of all the people here and quite possibly in all three realities. Once Vienna was reincarnated into her past life with my essence, she would be the leader of the new hybrid clan and be stronger than anyone. She would have the control. *Did that mean she would have Amary?* Panic set it. I could handle anything, but not if it involved Amary.

I slid off the bed, but I was so weak. I was able to feed off the sun and moon, but this room was closed tight without any source of energy. How long had Ashe been in here when I found him? He was barely alive. I stumbled along the wall, hoping for some place of escape, but there was nothing. My chest started to hurt as thoughts of Amary being raised by Vienna and Pyrrhus plagued me. I was stronger than this. I could find a way to save her. *My telepathy!* I knew I was weak, but it didn't take much to reach out to Amary.

I went back to the bed and lay down, my body relieved to rest. I closed my eyes and pictured Amary at Malin's house sitting at the table coloring. A moment later, the image went black and a new one materialized.

Whimpering, Amary was sitting on the couch at Malin's house between her and Starling. Malin was doing her best to ease her by rubbing her back. Starling's knees were tight to her chest, and her face was buried. What happened? Where were Ashe, Tivon, and River?

"Amary," I projected. Her whimpering stopped, giving me a signal she might have heard me. "Amary, can you hear me?"

"Uh-huh," she responded in her head. "Where are you? Why did you leave?"

"Listen, buggie. I'm in danger. I need you tell everyone Pyrrhus took me to his house. I can't get out. I'm too weak."

"It's only Star and Grandma Mali."

"Where are the guys?"

"They went looking for you."

I was afraid that would happen. "I can see you, buggie. I don't know how, but I can. Can you please tell Mali where I am?"

She looked at Malin. "Arie is in trouble."

"What?" Star popped her head up and wiped away the tears.

"Where is she, my child?" Malin asked.

"Pyrrhus took her to his house."

"Is she still with you, Amary?"

She nodded. "Uh-huh."

"Tell her we are on our way."

"No!" I yelled, making Amary jump. "Sorry, buggie, but I don't want you in danger. They have to find the guys. You need to stay as far away from here as possible. Do you hear me?" I said coldly, scaring her. I had never raised my voice to her.

"She doesn't want us to go. She says I need to stay away."

Malin looked to the sky as if talking to a spirit. "Okay, Arie, I won't let her go near there."

"Thank you," I whispered weakly.

The image was fading as my energy dispersed. I had lost them, but they knew where to find me. I wanted to try harder to get out of here on my own, but I knew I needed to save my energy for whatever was to come, so I just lay there in darkness without a clear picture of the future, just fear.

Chapter Twenty-Six

An arm yanked me off the bed, and my limp body fell to the ground.

"Get up," Vienna's voice demanded.

My eyes peeled open but refused to focus beyond blurry. I stumbled to my feet, but I had to use the bed for leverage.

"You're pathetic. This won't do." She interlaced her arm in mine and led me out of the room. The Herkimer diamonds in the hallway walls lost their ability to glow, so we walked in pitch-black darkness. I was better off with my eyes closed. Vienna dragged me mercilessly into one of the rooms I had ventured into when I was here before. *Or had I?* I flew through to the courtyard, but it was so fast I couldn't remember.

The grayish sun was starting its decent but sizzled on my skin through the skylight. I wondered if she knew it was energizing me. I played along. She dragged me to the courtyard and threw me into the center.

"Juice up. I need you at full capacity tonight."

Of course, she knew. How much time had passed? We weren't due for a full moon for several weeks. Had I really been out for that long? My strength was returning.

"Don't bother trying to fly away, little butterfly. I clipped your wings."

What? I couldn't get them to appear no matter how hard I concentrated. She took a part of me.

"Don't look so hurt. You'll be nothing in a few hours

anyway. Unless..."

I rolled to my knees. "Unless what?" I spat venomously.

"You can embrace all of this with us." She motioned to the world.

I couldn't stop the laugh that filled the air. "You're crazy!"

"Your point?"

"I would never join you."

"Even if it meant saving Amary? Saving everyone?" she challenged.

"I wouldn't be saving them. I would be selling them to darkness. I won't do that."

She approached me and squatted down inches from my face. "I can show you how much power you are capable of. No one else can do that. They will only try to hold you back. Hide you. I know the elders want you and Amary dead. You won't have to fear them anymore if you join us."

I hated admitting it, but she was right. "I don't get it. I thought you needed my essence to become a hybrid again?"

"I do, but with this ring I can take just enough and spare you. I will still be the leader, though, the stronger of us all." She clutched my chin tightly. "But you won't be dead." She dropped it and walked away. "Think about it."

She disappeared inside, leaving me alone. Or so I thought. I was being watched. I squinted and scanned the perimeter of the courtyard. It was dark due to the lack of light in the blended realities, but then I caught one of the shadows move. There was a wall of them hidden along the edge like an invisible fence.

Insurance.

I stroked the back of my shoulder, mourning the loss of my newborn wings. I knew it was only temporary either way, but they were a part of me just like my arms and legs. I felt so defeated. If I had been out for that long, then the likelihood of someone saving me was bleak. I took comfort in knowing they would be safer staying away, but I also wasn't ready to die, and I most certainly wasn't ready for Vienna to come into the kind of power I possessed. Maybe I should just relent. *If you can't beat them, join them.* Maybe I could still make a difference? My purpose was to restore balance, which I would be doing. No one ever said how. My confidence was rising. I was in control of my own destiny. If taking orders from Vienna meant I could keep the others safe, then I needed to consider it. I knew the only reason she wanted Amary and me was to continue the hybrid line. I could play along until the time was right to take her down, but would the darkness consume me in the process? Both of my choices sucked. Die or take my place beside Vienna and Pyrrhus. Which was the lesser of two evils? If I died, I would be sealing the fate of Amary and all the ones I loved without any protection from me. If I succumbed to the situation, they would be better off.

"It sounds like you have made a choice." Pyrrhus stepped into the dismal light.

"If you call that a choice," I retorted.

"We always have a choice, Arie, and you made the right one."

"What happened to you? You're from the Love clan. Shouldn't you, I don't know, love more?"

He circled slowly around me. "Oh, but I do, Arie. I have loved you since you were born."

I wanted to gag. "Pretty sick to be in love with your sister."

He bellowed loudly, "Is that what you think? That I am your brother? That Ashe is? This is too much."

My state of confusion was painted all over my face.

"Oh goodness. You do think that. No, no, no. We are not blood related, Arie. Whatever gave you that idea?"

"I had a vision of Tivon taking care of you two when you were babies. I just assumed."

The look on his face told me he had no idea about Tivon. "Tivon is *not* my father nor Ashe's. My father was a coward and left us right before I was born. I know nothing about him except hate," he hissed.

Relief settled into the crevices between my muscles and tendons.

Ashe wasn't my brother.

Nothing else Pyrrhus said mattered. Ashe and I were not related. That's what mattered.

"Haven't you figured it out yet? Ashe thinks we are from a love clan, but we aren't. We are hybrids as you are. Your attraction to us is because we are meant to continue the hybrid line."

"My attraction to Ashe," I corrected him. "I deflect from you." All along everyone thought I was special, but I wasn't. I wasn't the first of my kind or the second or third. Who knew how many more of us there were? But I wasn't bred from Vienna, so then how did I become a hybrid?

"Why don't you have wings then?"

"Because the male hybrids don't need them." He demonstrated by flying a circle around the courtyard.

I knew it. Well, I didn't actually know, but I had a feeling. When Ashe saved Amary and me from the room, we had crossed the threshold, but we also felt weightless. And then there were all the times he was there one second and then gone the next. It made sense, but I still didn't know how I came to be a hybrid.

When Pyrrhus finished showing off and landed in front of me."Tivon's not a hybrid, and I think he would have mentioned if my mom was."

He laughed again. Something that was worse than a dog whistle to a puppy. "Think, Arie. It's really quite simple. I'm really surprised you haven't figured it out yet, but then again, you have been pre-occupied."

"Enough!" Vienna shouted from behind him.

Pyrrhus cowered in response.

"Get her back in the room." Several shadows flashed to my side and carried me away. I looked back to catch Vienna slap Pyrrhus across the face. He deserved it for so many reasons, but something inside me still had hope for his light.

I was at full strength again, but the shadows still rendered me paralyzed, so all I could do was observe. I scanned every room for exits and possible weapons. I was also careful to map out the path they took to get me back to the room. It was different than the way Vienna had taken me out. As we passed through the grand room to the hallway that led to the room, I spied a pair of eyes glowing in the far dark corner where I had emerged several times from the basement. Being paralyzed, I couldn't sense who it was, but I knew from the purple eyes it was Heath. They had finally come. I had almost given up hope.

The shadows dropped me onto the bed, and I was once again barricaded, but Heath knew where. I had brought him here before. I wondered where the rest were. Where was Ashe?

"I'm here," Ashe said as he stepped out from a dark corner.

"Ashe." I launched into his arms. I thought his embrace would never feel the same after thinking he was my brother.

He pulled me back. "You thought I was your brother?" he questioned.

"It's a long story." I buried my head back in his chest.

As he rubbed the nape of my neck, he asked, "Are you okay? They didn't harm you. Did they?"

I tensed in his arms.

He squeezed me tighter. "I'll kill them," he declared without hesitation.

I peeled myself free a few moments later and sat back down onto the bed. "Vienna clipped my wings."

Silence.

"I'm sorry, Arie. I'm sorry my mother has done this to you."

"It's not your fault, and it's only temporary."

More silence.

"Ashe." I was searching for the right words. "Why didn't you tell me you could fly?"

He came and sat down next to me. "I didn't know until that day I got you and Amary out of that room. It happened on instinct. I knew I had the gift of speed that seemed almost like flying, but I wasn't sure what it all meant. I had been estranged from Pyrrhus for so long, and my mother never told us. After I died and Pyrrhus resurrected me with his gemstones, he told me what we were. I wanted to tell you, but there was never a good time. I just knew why we were instinctually connected. We were made to be together." His voice had lowered several octaves.

"You sound disappointed," I responded self-consciously.

"No. Not at all, but I was worried you would question our attraction. Whether you would think it was fabricated rather than natural."

For the first time, I saw Ashe's vulnerability. He hung his head low and was mindlessly moving one foot back and forth over the ground in a slow rhythmic motion. I placed my hand on his. "I can't tell you if this is real or not, but what we feel can't be fabricated, and I trust in that. I trust in us."

He turned his eyes to me and slipped his free hand behind my neck, sending the signature chills racing all over my body. My breath caught in my chest as he leaned in and kissed me deeply.

Heath staggered into the room loudly, startling both of us. He looked at us for a second, recognizing the moment he broke and then spat out, "We need to go. It has begun."

I looked at Ashe for an answer. "What?"

"The blood moon is almost at the top of the sky, so they are preparing for your sacrifice. Tivon, River, and Malin are getting ready to battle."

I jumped up. "What? No! I have to warn them. There are shadow stalkers everywhere." The panic was forthcoming.

"It's okay. They have backup this time. They knew we needed help, so Tivon went to the allegiance behind the elders' backs," Ashe responded.

"He'll be punished for that," I proclaimed.

Heath added, "We'll worry about the elders later. We need to finish this with Pyrrhus first."

"You're underestimating Vienna. She is strong and evil," I continued.

"I will take care of my mother. Don't worry, Arie. We have a solid plan in place."

"And what's your plan if it falls apart?"

"Run," Heath declared seriously.

I knew the decision I would have to make to complete my destiny would be difficult. I knew it would require courage I had never faced and a sacrifice I could never imagine. I knew it would change the lives of my loved ones and destroy a love I could never repair. My dreams had been preparing me for it, but no one could really be prepared for something like this. The unthinkable.

I felt doom looming as I walked with Ashe and Heath out of the room. I could hear loud blasts and voices barking orders echoing through the house. Chaos had erupted, and we had no idea who was winning. What was for certain was that people were dying.

"Are you all right?" Ashe asked as he grabbed my hand.

"I'm ready." I was saying it more for me than him, but I was.

We followed the chaos to the courtyard in silence. Before we joined the battle, Heath stopped us.

He addressed Ashe. "Can I have a second?"

Ashe bowed his head, kissed me on the cheek, and walked out of sight.

My heart started palpitating. Was it because of the madness only a few feet away, or was it the look in Heath's eyes, dark and determined?

"I get it now, Arie. I understand how you love Ashe. It's bigger than us, but I can't go out there without telling you that

I love you. I always have, and I will always be here for you no matter what." He planted a passionate and soft kiss onto my lips that left me breathless and my heart achy. I couldn't reciprocate the kiss or his love, but I could be a good friend, and I could give him this moment. I could say goodbye this way... for him.

He pulled away. "I should say I'm sorry for that, but I'm not."

"It's okay. It just can't happen again if we're going to remain friends."

"I know." His eyes penetrated my soul.

Ashe returned without a word. I wondered if he knew Heath was going to do that. I wondered if he saw.

"Arie, you go for Pyrrhus, and I will go for Vienna. Heath will follow you in case you need him."

"What if you need him?" I pleaded.

He kissed me on the lips quickly and sprinted deep into the house rather than out into the courtyard.

"Let's go," Heath said. He grabbed my hand, and we entered hopefully the last battle of our existence.

Chapter Twenty-Seven

I was completely unprepared for what I saw. The courtyard was barely recognizable. I knew most of the members of the allegiance from seeing them around the village, but there were other ones I had never seen. "Who are they?" I asked Heath as he watched diligently, ready to pounce when necessary.

"My people," he responded proudly.

"What? I thought..."

"Me too. Look." He pointed to the balcony on the far side. "He's up there."

We jogged around the perimeter underneath the balcony. Shadow stalkers and villagers were fighting to the death in every square inch. It was like watching a school of fish in a feeding frenzy. As we whizzed through, a shadow stalker hurled at me, only to be decimated before impact, spraying me with its essence. The one responsible for its death nodded. When I looked up, I saw purple eyes. I smiled in quiet recognition and continued to my prey with Heath still on my heels. The noise reverberated off the collapsing walls, and a light fog of essence accumulated with each death. I spotted Tivon in the center, but I hadn't located River or Malin yet. *Wait!* I stopped so quickly that Heath ran into me, knocking us both down.

"Arie, what's wrong?"

"Who's with Amary?" I snapped.

"She's in good hands."

"Who?" I demanded.

"With the girls. Starling, Sage, and Norinda."

My stomach tightened. None of them were strong enough to fight off any would-be attackers. Norinda was the strongest, and she was on her deathbed the last time I saw her.

"Arie, you have to trust that she's okay. We need to get to Pyrrhus."

I didn't feel good about it, but this was my opportunity to take him out. I jumped up and tried to mask my worry as I scaled the staircase. "I need the dagger."

Heath pulled it out from behind his back and handed it to me. It was no longer hot or cold to the touch. "What if it doesn't work like it did when the veils were up?"

"Well, we're about to find out. Twelve o'clock!" he shouted.

A shadow stalker was barreling toward me from the front. I challenged it, and when it was upon me, I impaled the dagger into its heart. It immediately exploded into a cloud of black glitter like dust. *It worked.* I had destroyed its essence permanently, boosting my confidence. Pyrrhus was going to die today. I took a second to look up in the sky. The blood moon was a river of red and at the highest point in the sky.

As we ran around the balcony, closer to Pyrrhus, Heath fought off shadows giving me free reign on Pyrrhus. I slowed down when I reached him, not hiding the dagger. He knew why I was here. I searched his fingers for my mom's ring, but came up empty.

"Looks like your mom either had all the confidence in the world in you or she didn't care if you died."

He scowled in reply and poised to fight.

I pressed further to agitate him, hopefully enough to throw him off. "You know Ashe is your mom's favorite, right?"

He laughed loudly.

"She told me so when she visited me just before she

juiced me up."

His face scrunched into hatred of the likes in which I had never seen before. "Lies."

I kept agitating him as I inched forward. "Oh, really? She said that while you were always loyal, Ashe was her sweet boy."

I struck a nerve because Pyrrhus fumed and leaped at me. He lifted his hand and forced me backward. I didn't know his power without the gemstones, but apparently, it was more than I had previously thought. I jumped up quickly. "That all you got?" I taunted.

As he ran at me again, I swung the dagger, getting a slice across his arm. He looked at his arm in shock as it bled. None of us understood what it meant with the veils down. No healing. The horror disappeared from his eyes, and he launched again. This time he latched onto my hand holding the dagger. He grabbed my neck with his other hand and squeezed tightly as he lifted me off the ground. I saw Heath being pummeled by several shadows while Pyrrhus' stupid laugh echoed in my ears. This was my vision. Almost. But then I heard it. Amary screaming through broken tears. She was in trouble. I closed my eyes and summoned all the strength I had left. I regained the strength to overcome Pyrrhus' grip on my hand and twisted the dagger to his side. He was still restricting my airflow, but his eyes glared with frightening intensity as he yielded that he was going to die. I thrust the dagger into his side, causing him to drop me. I clutched my neck and gasped for breath. Pyrrhus was bowled over, but he was not dead.

Heath rushed to my side. "What's happening? Why isn't he dead?"

"I don't know," I said as my thoughts raced for an answer. "His heart. It needs to be in his heart." I sprang to my feet and jumped on top of him. He was trying to pull out the dagger, but his strength was depleted, and the skin around the wound had hardened. I grabbed the ornate metal and gripped it hard.

Pyrrhus clutched my hand. "Please, I beg you."

He was looking for mercy. For a second chance.

I heard Ashe's voice from below. "Do it, Arie."

I made eye contact with Ashe for final approval. He nodded, and I mouthed to Ashe *I'm sorry*. I pulled hard, and the dagger gave way. Without flinching, I plunged it into Pyrrhus' heart. The horror in his eyes would stay with me forever. I jumped off him just as his body exploded into the black glittery dust. *Amary*. "We have to find Amary." I ran past Heath across the balcony to the stairs. The shadow stalkers retreated as soon as Pyrrhus died, and the allegiance was recuperating. I flew down the stairs blindly, the only thing occupying my thoughts was Amary. I slammed into something hard, and when I focused, I realized it was Ashe's chest. He stepped in front of me and was gripping my arms tightly. I fought against him. "Let go. I have to get to Amary."

"I know, but you need to calm down. You can't help her like this."

I must have looked like an insane person. The tears filled my eyes. "I have to help her. She's in trouble."

Heath caught up. "What's going on?"

"I couldn't find Vienna. Arie just had a vision that Amary was in trouble."

He heard it, too. The villagers surrounded us. One of Heath's clan spoke up.

"We are ready," he said to me.

I nodded quietly, not trusting my voice.

Heath asked, "Are the veils restored?"

"No," Ashe replied.

"It's Vienna. She's keeping them down with my ring. We have to go," I announced.

Ashe made me focus on him. "Arie, we don't know where they are. You need to find her."

I nodded, closed my eyes, and thought about Amary. I couldn't see her, but I could feel her. She was scared and mourning, which meant someone had died.

"Amary." I didn't hear a response. This time I

commanded. "Amary."

"Arie," she replied. "Help."

"I'm coming, buggie. Where are you?"

Silence.

"Amary?"

More silence.

My heart started to race, and my words became more erratic. "Amary!" I screamed, but she was gone.

I had to focus on how her surroundings felt. I could locate her that way. I just needed to force away my fear and concentrate. Amary felt protected, but scared. What did I hear in the background? I dove deeper into the connection. Water. I could hear water. A lot of it. *The waterfall!* I snapped out of it and shouted, "They're at the waterfall!"

Tivon pushed through the crowd, carrying Malin.

"Is she...?" I couldn't finish.

He responded, "Yes."

I would deal with that later. I would mourn the loss of her and everyone else, but I couldn't let it defeat me. Not now. Not until Amary was safe. Tivon handed her to one of the protector clansman. I watched as they all gathered around her, hiding her body from view.

"That's how they mourn. They will perform the ritual," Heath informed us.

"You should be with them," I said.

"I will join them when this is over," he replied stubbornly.

Tivon commanded loudly to the crowd, "Follow me."

We all obeyed and quickly fell in step behind him as we sped out of the courtyard, through the house, and into the forest. We all flew as if floating just above the ground. The universe gave us all the gift of speed. Amary's suffering filled my soul as we got closer to her.

Norinda's body was the first one we stumbled upon. Tivon collapsed to her side. His distress consumed my heart. We were connected through our essence line, so anything he felt I felt. I put my hand on his shoulder in comfort, but the air rushed from me.

Tivon and Norinda were sitting on his back porch talking and laughing. They were sitting comfortably close to each other, and I could feel the love they had for one another. They were so content, without a worry in the world. The feeling of innocent love.

I removed my hand from his shoulder. "I'm sorry," was all I could manage to say.

With his head still down, he replied, "Go. I will follow in a moment."

His grief had taken him. I led the group to the waterfall.

Sage was the next body we encountered. Her brother pushed through the sea of people and fell to the ground. "No, no, no. Sage. Wake up, Sage."

My heart hurt. I had lost my best friend, and her family had lost a piece of them. Another broken family.

I had to stay strong. I kept walking, dreading what was inevitably coming next. Starling. River took my hand in his hand. We would face this together. His palm was sweaty, and I could feel his pulse throbbing.

At the entrance to the waterfall is where we found Starling. I shook off the despair. I had to. I couldn't feel this. Amary needed me. I whispered to River, "Go." He released my hand and lifted her body, hugging her close to his heart.

Don't feel.

"She's alive. I can still feel her essence, but it's fading quickly."

"Then we need to get the veils up quickly so she can heal," I said flatly, but with hope.

Don't think. React.

I had the dagger. I had swiped it as soon as Pyrrhus disappeared. Vienna was the key. I turned to the village of people here to assist. "This *has* to be done right. I have to be the one to do this. Take out any shadow stalkers you see, but don't interfere. No matter what." I looked over the Ashe. "You ready?"

He took his place beside me, grabbed my hand, and we walked up to the threshold of the waterfall together. As planned, shadow stalkers emerged on us, only this time they emerged from their shells and took their human forms. I knew Vienna was trying to play on the villagers' emotions since they were family and friends, so I yelled amidst the fighting.

"Don't look at them! Your loved ones aren't there anymore. Vienna is controlling them. They won't hesitate to kill you, so don't hesitate to kill them." That was all I could do for them. Ashe and I crossed the threshold. Ashe took possession of the dagger momentarily and took out shadows as we carefully navigated the wet rocks. At first I didn't see Amary and Vienna, but then Vienna stepped out from behind the waterfall. I had never been behind it because I just assumed it was a drop-off. Amary wasn't with her.

"Where is she?" I demanded.

"Tsk... tsk... tsk. You shouldn't yell at your elders so," she mocked.

Ashe came into view.

"Aw, my only living son. Or do you deserve that title anymore after sealing your brother's death?"

Her voice was even, so I couldn't tell how she felt about Pyrrhus being gone.

"I don't want that title. I'm ashamed to be of the same essence line as you."

"Oh, my child, you say that, but you would be nothing had you not come from me. You wouldn't be a hybrid, and you wouldn't have been pulled to Arie."

I interrupted, "I want to see Amary. Now!"

"She's safe. For now. You should be more concerned about yourself. You are the hunted."

She was implying the elders. I hadn't seen any of them in the fight, which meant they had retreated somewhere together.

"Not just somewhere. Here."

The elders showed themselves one by one. All of them

had stood in Tivon's gathering room not that long ago swearing to protect me, and now they were here. They had betrayed all of us. And they were strong. Together with Vienna, they were catastrophic.

"You look stunned, child. How about this? I give you one more chance to join us and avoid all this unnecessary drama."

Ashe secretly slid the dagger into the back of my jeans. I caught sight of my ring on Vienna's finger. It had a faint glow. I had one chance to use it. If I destroyed it while she was in possession of it, then it would kill her and raise the veils again. The dagger would do the same, but it was good to have an insurance policy. "You say if I join you, Amary and I will be safe, but how can you claim that when all of them want us dead?"

"We have come to an understanding."

The way she said that was not the least bit comforting.

Ashe whispered, "Don't make a deal, Arie. We can still do this."

His confidence was uplifting, but she had the numbers and the power right now.

"Your time is up," she said hastily, and with a wave of her hand, Ashe was thrown away from me and restrained by two shadow stalkers.

That was it. She was in control of them now that Pyrrhus was dead, which meant the source of that control had to be with her. That's when I spotted a shiny piece of metal dangling from her neck. It was hidden underneath her clothes. If we took hold of the shadow stalkers, we would have the numbers, but how?

Vienna approached me aggressively and grabbed my neck as Pyrrhus had done.

"Why are you so damn stubborn?"

Her hand burned my skin as it drained me of power. I knew I only had a matter of seconds before I was gone. I reached out and jerked hard on the necklace. At the same time, Amary appeared with her hand outstretched as she approached us slowly. Vienna's grip on my neck was loosening. Amary was fighting her.

"Stupid little girl," Vienna cursed.

I took the opportunity she had given me and broke free of her grip. I was weak, but I had the source of the shadow stalkers power. I enclosed the titanium amulet in my hands and concentrated on them releasing Ashe. I looked over to confirm that it had worked. Amary was leading Vienna back to the drop-off at the waterfall. "Tap into my energy, Amary."

I couldn't help her until I fed, which the plants on the ground were slowly doing. Ashe snatched the dagger from my jeans and sprinted toward Vienna. "No, Ashe!" It was my destiny to restore balance, not his. It wouldn't work unless I plunged the dagger into her heart, but it was too late, and Ashe was too angry. He daggered her, but nothing happened. Instead, she took him and Amary hostage as she stood on the cliff.

"What will it be, Arie? Will you join me or lose them?" Wings sprouted from her shoulders, boasting dark colors of gray and black. My essence had restored her hybrid nature. The elders surrounded me ready for the kill, but I had control of the shadow stalkers, so I summoned them to fight. Immediately, droves of them engaged in battle with the elders. I crawled toward Vienna away from the mess. "Let them go, please."

"Now you beg. I can't let you have them both. I need at least one to continue our line. Pick."

"What? I can't..."

"I can take them both if you'd like, but I think it's kind of fun to see whom you would choose."

She was playing with me. We all knew whom I would pick. It would always be Amary. My energy wasn't restoring quickly enough for me to fight her. And then out of nowhere, Tivon raced through the fighting past me and jumped on Vienna, causing her to drop Amary and Ashe off the cliff. My shoulders tingled to life, and my wings burst to the side.

Without hesitation, I flew off the cliff after them. Only I didn't need to. Ashe was flying up with Amary wrapped around his body. "You're okay?" I cried happily. I hugged them both tightly in midair. "Tivon needs me."

"Go. I'm going to take her home."

I kissed Amary on the head quickly and shout back up the cliff. Tivon and Vienna were rolling around the cave. I looked around for the dagger. I needed it, but it was gone. I didn't have any other choice but to destroy the ring. It pained me to do it, but it was the only way. I gripped the titanium amulet in my hand and stomped over to them. I waved my hand, forcing Tivon off her. Without a word, I raised the amulet and smashed it down hard on the ring that still adorned Vienna's finger.

She released a loud screeching sound as the light encapsulated her. Both of my mothers appeared in the light. This was the first time I saw Genesis. She was beautiful with thick sandy blonde hair and chocolate eyes, a color not seen here yet. My mother, Ariana, stood next to her. They acknowledged each other with a smile and then disappeared in the whirlwind of light. The wind became stronger as it took away Vienna's essence. The light exploded for miles. After several minutes passed, it burned out, and in its place, the color of the world returned. The shadows that served as a shell for the ones trapped crumbled, and the people's essence restored as they came back to life, something none of us had predicted. Tivon lay in a corner of the cave unmoving. I ran to his side and turned him over. I gasped when I saw that the dagger was deep in his side. "Dad? Wake up," I cried.

His eyes opened slightly, and he managed to say four words, "You called me Dad," before he went completely limp.

I had lost him. The first time I let him in and accepted him as my dad, and he was gone. Another parent lost. The ache started in my throat and then slowly invaded my chest, trickling its way to my heart. It was a familiar and haunting ache that I would never forget. I screamed in anger and pulled out the dagger and forced it into the ground. I had accumulated a crowd. River and Starling had pushed through and stood just above me, holding hands. Star's eyes were threatening tears for me, and River's skin tone had turned ashen. As I looked at the different clans, I recognized the remorse in all of them. This was their leader. He had been around long before any of them and had always protected them. The elders had retreated when Vienna died, but I imagined it wouldn't be the last time we saw them.

Chapter Twenty-Eight

It was hard to describe numbness. Maybe it was like the shadow stalkers. You were just a shell of yourself...

Not feeling.

Not seeing.

Not hearing.

Your body was working on instinctive impulses. Put one foot in front of the other. That was how you walked. Wrap your arms around someone. That was how you hugged. Move your lips. That was how you talked. My chest moved up and down, and my heart pumped blood throughout my body, but wasn't its other job to love?

I felt a hand rest upon my shoulder, but it didn't awaken the part of me that mattered.

"Come with me and let the villagers take him," Ashe said remorsefully.

I didn't want to leave him. I didn't want to say goodbye. Amary and I had lost so much, and this just didn't seem fair. "No." My voice was even.

He bent down and put his arms around me, but my body remained stiff and unresponsive. "He's gone, Arie."

He was trying to help, to comfort me, but I didn't want it. Not now. "No," I said again, not raising an octave in my voice. He was questioning my stability. "I am a hybrid. Evolved. The most ascended you all have ever seen. How can I have so much power and not be able to save the ones I love. How?" I demanded an answer without moving. My eyes were locked on my dad. A gasp came from the crowd. Ashe stood up and moved away from me. I was intrigued enough to investigate. I followed their stares to the cascading water. An image of Malin was there. She smiled sweetly, and then she spoke, something I had never experienced through the waterfall visions.

"My sweet child. Look within yourself and believe. It's not too late."

And then she was gone.

What was she talking about? Believe what?

Amary rushed in and yelled excitedly, "That he's alive!"

She threw herself down next to Tivon's body and placed her hands onto his chest. I followed suit.

Nothing happened.

Amary pleaded, "You have to really believe."

It was hard to believe since I felt numb, but I wanted to, so I sucked in a deep breath, closed my eyes, and imagined Tivon and his giant chuckle, his smile crossing his face from ear to ear.

A thump hit the palm of my hand. And then another one. Slowly at first, coming in long intervals and then it quickened. I opened my eyes and asked Amary, "Do you feel that?"

She giggled. "Yes."

The numbness melted away and was replaced by a grateful smile and tears. No one else knew what was happening. They just watched and hoped. And believed.

"Maybe we need to tickle him," Amary teased.

"Hmmm maybe," I agreed.

She jumped on her feet and plucked a deep purple amaryllis flower from the side of the cave and ran back. She bent over Tivon and tickled his nose and lips with the flower. It was so quiet. It would seem as though not one person was breathing, but I could feel their energy. Excitement rose in the air.

Tivon's nose twitched, causing Amary to giggle again. Finally, Tivon's eyes opened. He locked with mine first and then Amary's. Whispers from the crowd started as they spread the word.

Tivon opened his mouth and said, "Now that is a nifty trick, girls."

We laughed in unison, the voices in the cave amplified, and the claps bounced off the walls. It was celebration time.

"To think, only hours ago we thought we would be planning his last ritual?" River teased beside me.

This was truly a massive celebration. Clans had been reunited with the lost souls that were trapped as shadow stalkers, the veils had been returned, and all darkness had been vanquished out of Serendae. No darkness remained, which meant the elders were forced into the realm of darkness where they belonged. While I was grateful to have evaded a death ritual for Tivon, we still had one to perform for Sage and Norinda. I barely got the veils back up in time to save Starling, but I felt the loss of my lost friends. The Protector clan would be performing the ritual for Malin, so I would be attending our ritual in the morning and theirs in the evening. I wanted to say goodbye, but I knew it wasn't going to be easy. I never did well with death, and no matter how much of it surrounded me, it never got easier.

River and I watched as Tivon danced with Amary and hundreds of other people. He was silly and awkward, and it made it that much more entertaining to watch.

"I wonder who taught him how to dance." River laughed.

"Not me, that's for sure."

We watched comfortably for a few more moments. There was something I had wanted to tell River that made me nervously fidget.

"What's on your mind, Arie?" He gave me the all-knowing look.

"I shouldn't have kissed you when I visited after Starling

died. It wasn't right. I'm sorry."

He looked at me thoughtfully. "The kiss wasn't one-sided, and I think we both needed it for closure."

I realized he was right. We loved each other, but not the way he loved Starling, and not the way I loved Ashe. We were both lonely and seeking solace in each other. "Thank you, River."

"For what?"

"For being my everything." I leaned over and kissed him on the cheek.

"You too," he replied.

Ashe and Starling walked up to the steps together where we were sitting. Star pulled at River's hand to stand him up. "Come on, bad boy. Let's see your moves," she taunted.

I burst out laughing because I knew what River's dancing skills involved, and they were comical to say the least. River glared at me playfully as he followed Star to the dancing area. Ashe nudged next to me and put his arm around my shoulders, pulling me in close.

"How are your dancing skills, my love?" he asked seductively.

"Better than River's." We watched as River tried to mask his offbeat moves by mimicking silly dance moves from home.

"You know I was afraid that when the veils went back up we wouldn't be able to touch again," I said shyly.

"Me too, but I guess we have evolved to the next level."

"Do you miss them?" I asked.

"Vienna and Pyrrhus? I miss who they used to be before the hate consumed them. I loved my mom, and she was always so caring and loving with us when we were little. She had this uncanny ability to love us unconditionally. I don't know what happened. I think Tivon hoped her having kids and with his help, her light would return. But as we got older, it continued to fade until it was just gone."

"Do you know why Genesis killed her?" I inquired.

"No, but that's the moment I lost my brother to the

darkness. I tried to take her place, but Tivon had abandoned us, too, and the hate grew. He became lost, and no matter what path I laid out for him, it kept leading him back to darkness. You should ask your dad about Genesis."

A smile crept up on my face. I liked the way that sounded. It took me two years, but it finally felt right. *My dad.* I hadn't really thought about it until now, but I was twenty and officially out of my teens, which meant I was an adult. So many things had changed.

Ashe stood up and reached out his hand. "I want to take you somewhere."

"Ooookay." I took his hand.

"It's your turn to hold on," he whispered into my ear. "And no peeking," he added.

I clutched my arms around him securely in excited anticipation. He was being very secretive. The feeling of weightlessness tickled my stomach, so I stole a quick look and watched as the crowd became smaller and the music distant. It was fun flying this way, letting someone take charge.

"You can open your eyes now."

We were flying above the enchanted purple ravine, hidden deep within Geyser Valley. The colorful blooms had returned and covered most of the white-faced cliffs. Mystical insects buzzed around, and the gemstones that layered the bottom of the river glowed brilliantly, a sign their power had returned. The only thing missing was my mom. I rubbed my empty finger, devoid of her ring now.

We landed softy inside the valley in front of the cave opening shielded by mossy vines that had been his hidden home for many years.

"Let's go inside," he said as he took my hand. It was just as I had seen it in my vision, only I hadn't seen the caverns that led to different rooms all ornately decorated.

"Wow. Did she do all of this?" I asked as we walked through.

"Yes, she hated how plain Serendae was, so this was her

rebellion. Well, one of many. At least this one didn't harm anyone."

"Which room is yours?"

He took me into a brightly orange and red room. The colors came from the multitude of gemstones embedded in the rock walls. *Of course!* It finally dawned on me.

"What's with the surprised look?" he asked.

"Your butterfly essence. It's orange and red. I mean, I suspected, but now I know." I was grinning stupidly. "You were always with me even when you couldn't be."

"I would never leave your side, Arie."

He pulled me in and kissed me passionately and more deeply than he ever had, showing me the last of what I needed to know.

Vienna was pacing back and forth in their home. Her mind was in a frenzy, and her sanity was in question. Tivon was trying to calm her. I could sense his worry for the kids. The madness blazed in her eyes. She raced to a corner of the space and pulled the dagger of life and death out of the wall where it was ingrained. A bright glow filled the corner, revealing a large Herkimer diamond. She launched at Pyrrhus, who looked to only be about four years old. She pointed the dagger at his chest, but Tivon smacked her away. Vienna tried for Ashe, who was a few years older and able to outsmart her by putting out his foot and causing her to stumble. She grazed him with the dagger, and he fell quietly. Tivon knocked into her and tried to retrieve the dagger. As they struggled, it fell from her hand several feet away. They both tried to reach it, but a hand picked it up first. It was Genesis. Without hesitation, she took the dagger and plunged it into Vienna's stomach. She didn't explode into black glittery dust. Instead, her body was whizzed away by a swirl of brilliance out of the cave into the universe.

Ashe released me from his embrace and held my face close to his. "I didn't remember," he said.

"Now we both know," I replied supportively.

When we returned to my dad's house the party had

fizzled out. The music had stopped and there were only a few kids left running around the back yard. One of them was Amary. My dad was sitting on the back porch enjoying the view. I wished that I could bring back Norinda, but I knew that wasn't how things worked. He had lost three loves in his lifetime. It was cruel.

"But, my child, I was fortunate enough to love three times, as well," he said loudly.

I sat next to him and smiled. No matter what, he always found the positive light in everything. He even saw it in Vienna until the darkness won her heart over completely.

"Where did Ashe go?" he asked.

"To say some goodbyes."

"Oh?" Tivon pressed.

This was going to be difficult. "This isn't our world," I said as I stared at Amary. "My heart will always be where I grew up with my mom. I wish I remembered more of my past life. I wish I remembered Genesis, but I don't. What I remember is the love and safety of the meadow and the butterfly circle. My mom's spirit resides within the walls of that house and without her ring that's the only place I will still feel her presence."

"Have you told Amary?"

"No, but I will give her a choice. I would never force her to do something she doesn't want to do."

"That will be hard on you if she decided to stay," he added.

"I know, but just as I have to let her do right by herself I have to do right by myself. I need to listen to my heart."

"You have grown so much since your ascension. I'm so proud of you, and your mother would be, too."

He put his arm around me and squeezed. He was getting better at the normal fatherly shows of affection.

"It's good that you're able to go back. That you have a choice. I can't wait to see where this hybrid evolution takes you. You've broken all the boundaries that have separated us from the different realities. I know your kind will do great things."

That reminded me. "Can I ask you a question?"

"Of course."

"I understand why Ashe is a hybrid because his mother was, but you're not a hybrid, so does that mean Genesis was?"

"Genesis was more than just a hybrid. She was the purest entity that has ever existed. She didn't have powers like you, but her light was brighter than anyone else's. She was referred to as the messenger of the universe. Much like you she felt everything more deeply and intensely than anyone, but she wasn't able to control dreams and manifest visions or raise the dead." He nudged me. "However, she did have the most magnificent iridescent wings, and the way she flew around the waterfall captivated me every time, but we kept that our little secret."

He glowed as he spoke of her. "She sounds wonderful."

"She was and so many other things. I never imagined her essence combined with mine would create a hybrid. I was the only one who knew about Vienna, and I assumed she was the only one. I thought she was chosen by the universe to lead us, which is why I was trying to mentor her, but it didn't work out that way."

"No, it didn't."

We sat for a little while soaking in the last night together. Listening to the stories about both of my mothers and feeling the love in his heart connected me to him even more. He was my dad. I wasn't parentless. When it was time for me to collect Amary, I gave him a hug that I had always dreamed about giving my dad. It was bittersweet leaving, but I had the control to come back and visit any time, and I planned on doing so frequently.

I flew around the meadow showing off my purple wings to the creatures of the forest that I grew up with. As I flew over the butterfly circle, a large grouping of butterflies fell in line behind me and trailed like a shooting star across the night sky. Our wings fluttered in unison. The pain of the last four years was fading as we spun around the house and jetted in-between the trees. The head wind was inviting and the air clear as I took in gulps.

I was finally free.

The butterflies broke away, and I landed by my mother's gravestone. The butterfly flowers were growing thick and tall, but now there was a variety of colors intermixed with the purple. A beautiful dark-red bloom caught my eye, and at a closer look, it felt familiar. I touched it, and a butterfly came alive and landed on my hand. That's when I knew. It was Sage.

"Thank you for being there for me and for never forgetting me. I will always remember you."

The butterfly took flight, grazing my cheek and leaving behind a buzz of life. I watched as it joined others in the sky in a swirl of splendor. I saw another oddity in the flower patch. I didn't see it at first because the stem was shorter than the rest, hiding below a sea of yellow and pink. It was a single black flower with brown stripes. Norinda. I bent down, leaving it undisturbed and whispered, "Thank you for loving my dad." It came alive and circled my head several times, releasing a dusting of essence. The passion with which she lived and breathed covered my skin. She flew off and joined the others.

I watched the butterflies dance for a while until the sky began to darken for the night and they retreated to their resting spots. When I closed my eyes to sleep after the celebration, I knew I wanted to see them again. I wanted to thank them and say goodbye and dreams were the key.

"You're back."

I looked behind me to see Malin standing next to the butterfly circle with the orange and red sky behind her. I jumped up and ran to her, not stopping as I embraced her with a tight hug.

"You're here. I was scared I wasn't strong enough to bring

all three of you here."

She caressed my cheeks. "Oh, child, don't ever question your strength, especially in your dreams. This is where your mind is fully ascended, and anything is possible. Remember that, even if you feel doubt."

"I'm sorry I couldn't save you."

"It was my time, Arie. I've been alive too long. I outlived many generations of friends and family. I was ready to go."

"There are so many things I wanted to ask you and learn from you."

"Good thing you know where to find me." She kissed my forehead and disappeared.

It was strange that a butterfly didn't appear or I didn't see her essence taken away. She was just gone. What did that mean?

A rubbing on my leg stole my attention. It was the fox, only now it was full-grown from pink skin, white fur, bushy tail, and large pointy ears to a large stature with dusty blonde fur. Its tail was still bushy and the ears still pointy, but they fit the body better and stood out less. It was undeniably Heath when its amethyst eyes glowed up at me. I scratched behind his ear, but he kept nudging my leg insistently.

"What's wrong, Heath?"

He rubbed more urgently, causing a rash burn to start.

"Well, if you would stop rubbing me and just tell me..."

I woke up to Amary nuzzled against me. Her leg was kicking me as she struggled to get comfortable.

"Hey, buggie. Are you okay?" I petted the back of her head.

"Uh-huh. I just couldn't sleep. Is it okay if I sleep with you?"

"Of course. Any time." I kissed her on the forehead and continued to stroke her hair to lull her to sleep.

"Arie?"

"Yeah, buggie?"

"Are we leaving?" She looked up at me.

"I was thinking about it."

"Back home?"

"Yeah. Back home."

"Do you think my mom will still be there?"

I tried to maintain eye contact, but to lie to her like that was impossible. I needed to tell her the truth, but with us mourning the loss of several close to us, I just couldn't add this to her little plate. "I don't know, but we'll look for her, okay?"

"Okay." She smiled faintly.

"Does that mean you want to come with me?"

She had already become very still. I used to fall asleep like that. I covered her with the blankets and fell asleep quickly after.

Chapter Twenty-Nine

I sneaked out of bed as soon as the sun woke me. Amary was still sleeping soundly. I tiptoed into the bathroom, somewhere I rarely went since we didn't require it. Tivon did whatever he could to replicate a normal life for us. A life like at home. I stood in my usual sleep attire, a tank top and boy shorts, wondering what was appropriate to wear to the rituals. I looked in the mirror as if my reflection would have an answer. That's when I remembered that my eyes had turned blue again. My heart smiled. They were beautiful, and Ashe was right. They did glow more brightly than before. This was another sign that I was meant to go back home. My mood lifted slightly, something I needed to get me through the long day of mourning.

I picked out a simple black cotton sundress. Because of how I grew up, the tradition seemed to be to wear black to funerals. We still had some time before Sage and Norinda's ceremony, so I let Amary sleep. I didn't want her to come today, but she insisted. I was trying to shield her, but she had a right to say goodbye, too, and she was old enough to somewhat understand. She was more intelligent than an average six-year-old.

I was hesitant to go back to the waterfall, feeling it was defiled by Vienna, but it was important that this place, including my sanctuary, felt the same for me to come back to. I enjoyed the morning buzz from the energy of nature more than usual as I walked. Everything felt so different here, more intense, and I was going to miss it, so I started to imprint little pictures of everything in my mind, so I could recreate them in my dreams.

I hopped over the pebbled creek through the sunlit cave, past the waterfall, and onto my ledge. It was still magical to see the birds cliff dive and swoop down into the water. Actually, it looked like fun, so I stood up, reached my hands to the side, let my wings stretch as they appeared, closed my eyes, and fell forward. I opened my eyes and watched as several birds took the plunge with me. The wind whipped my hair violently, and I giggled as I got closer to the water. I reached my hands forward and glided them across the water as my wings jolted me up before I crashed into it. I flew across the water swiftly for miles, making a trail with my hand along the way. The birds kept me company, flapping their wings feverishly in an attempt to keep up with me. I was impossibly fast. With the veils up and the darkness gone, it felt truly magnificent here now, and I had done it. I had accepted my destiny and restored balance for the nature spirits and all the other people of this place. I had also saved my home from the realities of fairy-tale monsters, something I didn't wish upon anyone. My home wasn't perfect. It carried both the light and the dark, but nothing was perfect, no matter how it seemed on the surface. As of now, Serendae seemed perfect, and I would make my home as perfect as I could for Amary.

The ceremony for Norinda and Sage was the same as for my mother and all the others that had sacrificed themselves in my ascension battle. Everyone gathered at the river that was layered in a variety of flowers in every hue. The only difference was there were only two butterflies that adorned the flowers. They rested in the center of the unmoving current. One butterfly was black with tan stripes like in my dream, and the other was deep red. After a moment of silence, a swirl of hundreds of butterflies circled Norinda's and Sage's essence and carried them away. The river began to flow again, and people slowly started to break away.

None of The Protector clan had been present because they were busily preparing for the honor of the truest elder of Serendae, Malin. Everyone had been invited, and I imagined everyone would be there. I was curious what their ritual would be like.

I wasn't prepared when I walked with Tivon, Ashe, and Amary to Malin's send- off. They had it in the center of the village, but rather than a quiet and solemn remembrance, there were laughter, music, and...

"Are those streamers?" I pointed to them draped in all the trees surrounding the village.

"I believe they are," River answered. Tivon and Starling joined us.

I was in mild disbelief.

Tivon chuckled next to me. "Quite different from ours, but no less meaningful."

"Is someone having a birthday party?" Amary's voiced raised excitedly.

"No, buggie. I believe this is how they celebrate the life of someone they lose. This is for Malin."

"Oh, cool." She ran into the center where Iris and some other nature spirit children were playing.

Heath made his way over to us. "Thank you for coming. It's nice to see all the villages together again, even if it's under these circumstances."

"Malin would be honored." I reached out and squeezed his arm.

"I believe you're right."

A sudden silence washed over the crowd. We all froze in place to see what the cause was. From the furthest edge of the village, a crowd of people emerged. Some were old, and some were carrying babies.

Two words fell from Heath's lips. "Mena, Hazel." He walked toward the crowd without another word.

"Dad, what's happening?"

"It's their women and children. The ones they thought they had lost."

I clasped my hand over my mouth. I wasn't the only one in shock. When Heath approached an older woman with a young girl attached to her leg that looked to be about ten or so, I knew they were his mother and baby sister. Heath picked up the little girl and pulled his mom into his arms. The rest of the women and children unleashed themselves on the village, scurrying to find their loved ones. The moment was perfect, and I had no doubt that Malin had something to do with it somehow.

I wanted to say goodbye to Heath, but I didn't want to interrupt his reunion. I knew I would be back, and I was just happy that he had his family back, a luxury we didn't all get.

Amary had chosen to come live with Ashe and me in my childhood house. She was six now and needed to be enrolled in school, and I had to file for legal custody. There were all these ordinary human things I had to adhere to, and I loved it. I was elated to get back to my home.

The three of us stood in front of the waterfall. I had realized that it was an easier portal to home than the rushing river. All I needed was a good energy source, and this certainly had it. I was worried about River and Starling. I wasn't sure if they would be able to live in the same place, but when the veils went back up, it caused a ripple effect of glitches, and Starling was one of them. She had become human again. I tried not to worry about the other ripples. At least not until I needed to, which I was hoping was never. I sent them back right after I talked to Amary about going home. She still didn't know the truth about her mom, so that was something Ashe and I were going to have to discuss with her. After everything we had been through, I was hoping it would go over more smoothly, but I knew it would still crush her.

"Everyone ready?" I asked cheerfully.

"Yep," answered Amary first.

"Never been more ready in my life," Ashe said as he leaned over and kissed me.

"Ewwwww," interrupted Amary.

So human, I thought with a smile.

Epilogue

I moved Amary into my room, and I took my mother's. There was a small office downstairs that we converted into a bedroom for Ashe. We were trying to maintain a casual and stable atmosphere for Amary, and living together in the same room just didn't feel right. We hadn't formally talked about getting married because it wasn't the same here as it was in Serendae. It was all about paper pushing here, whereas in Serendae when two hearts connected, they were just forever tied. Ashe thought the custom here was barbaric and missed the mark. I kind of agreed with him, but if we were going to live in this world, there were probably some things we were just going to have to go along with, and really the act of getting married wasn't harming anyone.

Today was the first day of a new beginning, and I wanted to do it right. "Amary!" I shouted up the stairs. She came bouncing out of her room, beaming from ear to ear.

"I love my new room, and I don't want to change a thing."

I giggled. "Are you sure?"

"Yes, I love purple," she said as she hopped down the stairs.

"Let's go out back for a little bit." I held out my hand for hers. She latched on and skipped her way outside with me in tow. I led her to the butterfly circle. "Sit across from me," I instructed. We both sat facing each other with our legs crossed. "My mom and I used to do this every day. We would come out here and sit just like this and meditate."

"What is 'meditate'?"

"It's when you close your eyes, breathe in and out slowly and deeply, and try to clear your mind of all the silly chatter." She immediately closed her eyes, and I laughed as she squinted hard. "Buggie, you're going to hurt yourself." She laughed as she opened her eyes. "Watch me." I closed my eyes and counted to ten to myself as I inhaled deeply and then again as I exhaled slowly. I repeated that several times and then opened my eyes.

"That's it?"

"Yep, and once you've done it many times, then your mind will clear itself without you even trying. Now, why don't you close your eyes? I'll count to ten while you inhale slowly, and then I'll count down from ten as you exhale."

"Okay." She smiled and then closed her eyes.

I kept my eyes open for the first round to make sure she was relaxing her face. I joined her for the second round, but kept counting aloud for her. "...five, four, three, two, one. And again. One, two, three, four, five, six, seven..."

My voice trailed off into my head as my mind started to clear. Amary's presence was stronger than even my mother's was when we meditated together. It was comforting. The blank canvas of meditation started to take shape and form. It was reminiscent of the days I would watch the brush strokes race across a painting my mom was working on. It was similar to reading a book as I waited in anticipation to see what she would create. As the image pieced together, I recognized the space first. We were in the forest just on the outskirts of the meadow. I had a secret spot in a small clearing that I would sometimes carry dolls to and play. The space was no bigger than a walk-in closet and was defined by a circle of large gray boulders. Bushes filled in the spaces between, and a tree served as a low-lying canopy. The last time I came here was the day after my mother's death. I sat in the center and mourned her loss for hours. River had found me that night and carried me home. Being here again was not easy, but when I looked more closely, Amary was standing with me. She wasn't there a moment ago. She surveyed the surroundings until she saw me.

"Where are we?"

"I used to come here when I was little." I was in a stupor, but I tried to focus.

"This is cool."

My excitement was equal, but hesitant. My mother and I had never shared meditative states, something I didn't tell Amary. It was probably just our hybrid connection.

"I wish I had something like this. So, what do we do now?"

I didn't have an answer. Normally, I just relented to my dream states without reason, but this was certainly not the same. "I don't really know."

"Well, what do you usually do?"

"I mostly just wait and see what happens." I half-leaned and half-sat on one of the boulders, not ready to be one hundred percent comfortable with the situation.

"What's that?" Amary pointed excitedly to the ground beneath a rock.

It was sparkling brightly. She ran over and started to dig. She pulled out a large magnificent Herkimer diamond, holding it by the two points. I ran over to inspect it closer.

"It's amazing. Can I keep it?"

"Would you mind?" I asked as I held out my hand. She handed it over carefully. It was heavy and was larger than both of Amary's hands and filled mine. It was flawless beauty, a rarity in any world. I turned it over and over, not convinced what I was actually holding.

"What is it, Arie?"

"It's the diamond of essence." I was still shaking my head in disbelief. How did it get here?

"What do you mean?"

"It's the gemstone that makes transitioning from our physical forms into our essence forms possible." She still looked confused. "When we die, it makes us into a butterfly."

"Ooooh," she said loudly. "That's so awesome."

It was, but finding it hidden in our reality instead of deep in Geyser Valley in Serendae was unsettling. The only time I saw it was in the vision of Genesis killing my mother in Ashe's home behind the draping vines. It was embedded in the wall next to the dagger of life and death.

"Too bad this is only a dream." Arie sighed.

She was right. This was only a dream, and when we woke up, we would be back in the butterfly circle and the diamond would be gone, but I wondered...

Suddenly, everything erased, and Amary and I were back in the circle, completely awake. Ashe was standing outside of it.

"Are you girls ever coming to eat?"

How long had it been?

Amary jumped up. "I'm starving." She ran up to the house.

"Everything okay?"

I looked up at Ashe. "Yeah. Just a weird experience. Can I have a second? I'll meet you guys up there."

"Sure." He jogged after Amary.

When he was out of sight, I covered the distance between my forgotten hiding place and me quickly. I pushed down the overgrown bushes and climbed in. I didn't see anything sparkling, but I dug under the boulder it had been under in our dream any way. I almost gave up when my finger cut on something sharp and started to bleed. My heart stopped.

It couldn't be.

I dug carefully but ferociously, revealing the Herkimer diamond. Once it was all dug out, I was scared to touch it.

"This can't be real." I sat back and stared at it as it effervesced perfection.

I heard Ashe's voice in the distance. "Arie, where did you go?"

I couldn't leave it here for Amary to find, but I didn't know what to do with it. I didn't have time to move it, so I reburied it quickly, ran by Deer Creek to rinse the dirt off my hands and face, and headed back up to the house. I would have to go back when everyone was asleep.

My biggest mission today was reopening the bookstore. It was going to be an uphill battle getting business going again, especially with Barnes & Noble only a few streets away. It moved in soon after I closed. Not that mine closing was the catalyst. We were a small, used, boutique bookstore. No giant conglomerate would bat an eyelash at our little establishment. I was determined, though. This store was my life.

I stood in front of the *Closed* sign staring up at the wooden sign, *Books and Butterflies.* Just being here filled me with pure joy. I had dug up the diamond and was concealing it in the large tote bag façade over my shoulder. It would be safe here. I knew just where to hide it.

"Daydreaming, princess?" Starling stood next to me. "Are we ready to do this?" she asked with a nervous giggle.

"For sure," I replied. "Is your mom doing better?"

"She's okay, but not strong enough to run things anymore."

"I'm sorry, Star." I looked over at her flawless skin with lightly painted red cheeks and admired her strength. It had to be hard to watch her mom die slowly and painfully. At least I could take comfort in knowing my mother didn't suffer. Human diseases were unrelenting. We didn't have to worry about them in Serendae, where only light existed. Here, we had both light and darkness.

"I wish I could take her to Serendae. I know I would still be losing her, but at least she would be alive and not suffering."

I took her hand to show my support. "I wish that were possible, too. You don't have to do this with me. You could wait to reopen until..." I bit my lip. I couldn't believe what I was about to say.

"It's okay, Arie. She's going to die. The doctors gave her maybe six months. The cancer is spreading quickly, and there's nothing they can do. They can slow it down with radiation and medication, but my mom doesn't want to live like that for the last moments of her life."

"That's why I'm saying you could wait on this. Spend time with her," I suggested.

"It's hard, Arie. It's hard to watch her suffer. Sometimes she wakes up and doesn't even know who I am. I need this. I need to be able to escape from it for a little bit, you know?"

I wasn't sure how to respond. I just knew how to be a good friend. "Then let's do this." I forced a smile for her.

"Thank you," she replied.

We were going to start over together. No, we were going to thrive together.

We both placed our keys into the door, and at the same time, we said the countdown.

"Three, two, one." We swung open the doors together and stepped inside our shops.

Acknowledgements

I'm still in utter shock that I get to publish books. Book One in this series, *Reality*, was my debut novel on September 23, 2013, and so much has happened in the past year. So many bumps and bruises, but so much strength gained from it. If anything, those kinks solidified that I write because I love it, and I love sharing my creations with others and not for any other reason. It also shows my kids that life inspires greatness if you believe and not to let fear tarnish that.

As always, it takes a strong intimate team to get to a final product, so a few words are in order. Paige Maroney Smith, you are always amazing. I am so honored that we found each other and that you dedicate so much time to my edits. Your humor has me laughing in the most stressful times! Thank you to my betas, Nichole Aten, Tasha Burkowski, and Shasta Mosley. I love the different points of view you offer when reading my work and appreciate the time you take out of your own lives to help me enrich it.

My beautiful original covers I have Jennifer Renee Brenneman of Nosim Art to thank and these new covers by Desiree DeOrto of Desi's Art Designs.

My husband and kids get it all when I'm finalizing a project, so I will always be grateful for their understanding, patience, and support. And of course, the readers who keep me pumped up to continue publishing my stories. You are the foundation of my writing strength.

About the Author

DANI HART graduated from the University of Southern California with a degree in Theatre and a concentration in Screenwriting. Dani also writes under the penname D. Hart. To find other books by this author, please visit her website.

Website: http://www.danihartbooks.com/

Facebook: https://www.facebook.com/authordanihart

Twitter: https://twitter.com/authordanihart

www.ingramcontent.com/pod-product-compliance
Lightning Source LLC
Chambersburg PA
CBHW031710170626
46808CB00005B/1689